THE MYSTICAL ADVENTURES OF
STAVROS PAPADAKIS

THE MYSTICAL ADVENTURES OF STAVROS PAPADAKIS

MICHAEL LACOY

Monteverdi Press

Grateful acknowledgment is made to Faber and Faber Ltd. for permission to quote previously published material: "The Love Song of J. Alfred Prufrock," from *Prufrock and Other Observations* by T.S. Eliot.

ISBN: 9780960068913 (hardcover)
ISBN: 9780960068906 (paperback)
ISBN: 9780960068920 (ebook)
LCCN: 2019900079

Monteverdi Press
Concord, New Hampshire
www.monteverdipress.com

Cover design by Dissect Designs

Typesetting services by BOOKOW.COM

I will see you again and your heart will rejoice ...
John 16:22

ONE

"Are you busy?" said Stavros Papadakis. He was in his car, talking on the phone while speeding west on Storrow Drive in Boston. Traffic was unusually light.

"Sort of. I was sleeping," said Ida, his secretary. It was Christmas morning, eight a.m.

"Hey, any chance you could come into the office today? At some point?"

"Unfortunately, I kind of have plans. Also, I'm in Hartford."

"Hartford? Who's there, your sister?"

"My mother. I don't have a sister."

"Oh."

"We talked about this yesterday."

"OK, right. I remember … And when are you coming back?"

"Monday morning. I'll be in at nine."

Frowning at this, irritated, Stavros said nothing. He let the silence grow.

Finally Ida said, "I could come back early."

"You don't mind?"

"Uh, no. I could be in on Sunday."

"Good. I'll see you then—"

To his left, there was a sudden flash of movement. Racing alongside Stavros, a silver SUV was drifting dangerously into his lane, threatening him and his hundred-thousand-dollar Imperator sport sedan. Stavros blared the horn, let loose a barrage of profanity at the careless driver, then made an obscene hand gesture. The SUV promptly swerved away.

"What was that?" said Ida.

"This woman on her phone. Nearly crashed into me."

"A femme fatale?"

"Not quite."

Stavros heard what sounded like a yawn, then Ida saying, "So you're really working today? The merriest day of the year?"

"I have to. But I'm going to Cambridge first. I'm heading there now."

"OK. Well I'm going back to bed. Have fun today, and be nice to Brendan. I'll see you on Sunday."

* * *

By the time Stavros pulled into the driveway of his former home, his body was in a state: stomach cramped and gassy, neck muscles clenched tight, a sharp, pre-migraine pressure in his skull. It was, he knew, that old holiday stress—Santa's special gift—making its annual appearance. Not that it had always been this way, Stavros reflected. At one time he had actually *liked* Christmas. But how long ago was that—ten years? *Fifteen?* Now bothered, annoyed, he killed the ignition and reached for his flask. He took a good belt, then he took another. The singeing down his throat, the relaxing warmth spreading through his chest and limbs— it helped.

To lose the booze-breath he chomped on several sticks of cinnamon gum, his old standby. He kept a box of the stuff in his desk at the office, along with economy-size bottles of ibuprofen and liquid antacid. Bracing himself for the cold, Stavros stepped out of the car, retrieved a bag of gift-wrapped presents from the trunk, and turned to the house. It was an old Colonial Revival, big and stately, nestled on a snow-covered plot. He and Allegra had bought the place around Brendan's third year, when the money had started to roll in. What a feeling it had given Stavros, to own a classy home in a choice section of Cambridge, Massachusetts—a huge step up for him! He'd been raised in a rough town in Maine, the son of immigrants. As a child he had lived first in an apartment above his family's pizza shop, and by high school, in a small house near a dairy farm that cast a stench of manure over the neighborhood. There was no cow shit in Cambridge. No stink of pizza grease on Champney Street.

Walking up the shoveled path to the front porch, his thoughts shifted to Allegra. To be honest, he was looking forward to seeing her. Stavros could admit it. They had divorced several years back and it wasn't pleasant. Yet surprisingly, amazingly, things between them had been fairly civil this year. They could be in the same room without the situation erupting into yelling and screaming. The usual digs, insults, and accusations had all but ceased. It was a good sign, right? Then why this anxiety, Stavros wondered? Why this gut-gurgling unease?

He spit out the pink wad of gum and told himself to stop whining. With a determined step he mounted the porch and rapped his knuckles on the door. Whether it be Allegra or Brendan who answered, he would greet them with a peace-on-earth-and-good-will-to-all smile and say, "Merry Christmas!"

* * *

When the door opened Stavros was stunned, stupefied. His fake-merry smile vanished.

Standing before him wasn't his son or his ex, but a man. Or rather, a boyish man. A mannish boy. Stavros put him at thirty. The guy—the *kid!* —had thick blond hair, a dimpled chin, and translucent blue eyes. He was alarmingly good-looking. Like a young Paul Newman. *The Long, Hot Summer* Paul Newman. Even worse, he had a slender but athletic build. A build that made Stavros think, with great horror, of rabbit-like sexual potency. He wore a sweater with Christmas-tree patterns, khaki pants, and ... slippers? *Slippers?* As in, "spent-the-night" slippers? "I'm-here-on-a-regular-basis" slippers? They were tan leather jobs with plush white wool showing at the ankles. Very comfy, very domestic. Baffled, vexed, dismayed, Stavros could not take his eyes off the damn slippers!

"Hey Stavros," the man-boy said, his tone cool and chummy, as if they were old pals.

"*Who the hell are you?*" Stavros snapped.

Young Paul Newman recoiled. "I'm … Dylan … Allegra's friend."

A cosmic kick to the groin: *Allegra's friend!* Stavros's face contorted, and for several crazed seconds he contemplated throwing a punch at this intruder, this dimple-chinned invader. But thinking of the consequences of such a punch—the police, the press, a lawsuit—Stavros controlled himself. Raising a hand in a conciliatory gesture he said, "I'm sorry. I wasn't expecting any … guests."

A pouty, injured expression came over Young Paul Newman's face. "It's OK," he said in a superior tone. "I understand."

He *understands*, Stavros thought, his anger rising anew. Preposterously, or so it felt to him, he said, "Is Allegra here?"

"She's getting dressed … Do you want to come in?"

Stavros looked at the kid: *She's getting dressed?* Was this Dylan *trying* to piss him off? Standing on the porch, his breath steaming whitely in the frigid December air, Stavros said, "Yeah, I'd like to come in, Dylan. Thank you. I appreciate it."

The man-boy led the way through the foyer and into Stavros's former living room. In one corner was a decorated Christmas tree and a pile of wrapped gifts. On the mantelpiece, formerly crowded with family photos, was a row of Christmas cards. Stavros himself hadn't sent one. Should he have? No one from this house had sent *him* one! Of course Allegra was more than happy to cash his child-support checks each month and live in the house he paid for. But to send a holiday greeting to the man who made possible her pampered life was clearly asking for too much!

Fuming, Stavros turned on Dylan. The kid was already seated in one of the armchairs, which Stavros himself had purchased some years back from a showroom near Harvard Square. Setting the bag of presents on the coffee table, Stavros removed his coat and sat on the sofa. In a relaxed, proprietorial manner, he extended an arm along the top of the sofa and rested an ankle on his opposite knee. For some moments he stared at

Dylan, making a slight, menacing smile. Dylan's Hollywood face grew uneasy. Finally Stavros said, "Nice slippers."

"Excuse me?"

"The slippers," Stavros said, pointing. "They're nice."

A blank look. "Thanks."

"Yeah, I like them," Stavros said, nodding with something like admiration. "So … did you just get here? Your mother drop you off?"

"My mother?" Dylan said, baffled.

"I didn't see a car in the driveway."

"Oh, I'm … parked in the garage."

Again Stavros stared at Dylan, though this time he wasn't smiling. Dylan averted his gaze, then scratched the back of his neck.

Calmly, Stavros said, "How do you know Allegra?"

"Sorry?"

"*How-do-you-know-Allegra?*" Stavros repeated, distinctly enunciating each word.

"I work at the hospital."

"You're a doctor?"

Dylan nodded. "Anesthesiology."

Allegra was a cardiologist at Mt. Adams Hospital. Evidently, she and Young Paul Newman were colleagues. "And how long have you been seeing her?"

"I don't know … About a year?"

Stavros shuddered. *A year?* Yes, he and Allegra had gotten along reasonably well these past several months. The two or three times they had seen each other over the summer and fall there had been no drama, no heated outbursts. Gone were the tension and spite of the last, oh, ten years. Instead there had been something very different about her: a composed, knowing look; a look that hinted at satisfaction, or maybe triumph. The look had vaguely unsettled Stavros, but he'd chosen not to give it too much thought. Now, the truth was clear, and it hit him hard. He felt short of breath.

* * *

Stavros was still reeling when Allegra entered the room. He heard her descending the stairs from the second floor and turned in his seat, feeling a mix of excitement and dread. She could still provoke a reaction in him, an electric bodily sensation. Immediately his eyes locked on hers; but she, proudly defiant, would not look at him. Her bearing was haughty and resolute, and her hair, the hair he had always loved—an abundant mass of wavy red locks—flounced impressively as she moved. Normally a casual dresser, she now wore a stylish sweater that did not hide her curves, slim-fitting wool trousers, and high-heel shoes that clacked with great authority as she crossed the hardwood floor. She had never worn high-heel shoes with Stavros! She claimed they were too girly, and that they hurt her feet!

Without thinking Stavros had stood and stepped toward her, as though he were expecting to … *what?* What was he doing, the damn fool! Was he going to give her a hug? A holiday kiss? As if she wanted a peck on the cheek!

Regardless, she ignored him. Without a word or even a glance she strode past him, scenting the air with a perfume he did not recognize, and went straight to golden-haired Dylan, still seated in the armchair. She stood beside the man-boy, turned to face Stavros, and, with an air of great bravado, folded her arms across her bosom. At last she said, "Hello Stavros … Merry Christmas."

Dumbfounded, Stavros could only gape. He hadn't expected any of this: the boyfriend, the high-heel shoes, the vengeful gloating.

Allegra had recently turned forty-one. She was tall, nearly six feet, and sturdily built. She had grown up in Yonkers, New York, and was herself a child of immigrants. Her Italian father was an oncologist and her Irish mother a nurse. After excelling in public schools, she had gone on to Cornell—where she played volleyball and graduated summa cum laude —and then Harvard Medical. She was brilliant and accomplished and, to Stavros, a great beauty. Her unruly red hair, her strong body, her petite

Irish nose and long slender hands—they all did it for him. But more than any of these, what had truly entranced Stavros all those years ago were her eyes. Lively and expressive, and a warm shade of green, Allegra's eyes radiated emotion—be it love or hate, joy or rage. She had a volatile temperament, and her animated eyes let you know exactly how she felt. And right now Stavros could see she was pulsating with a ruthless mirth, reveling in the flawless execution of her little stratagem. For clearly, this was a setup: her grand entrance, this holiday threesome, had all been worked out in advance. Stavros had walked into a trap, an ambush. A Christmas Day Massacre.

And so what was there to say? She had wanted to crush him, and she'd done it. He had been routed, and he knew it. Feebly he said, "Merry Christmas to you too."

"You're here to see Brendan, I take it," she said, relishing the moment.

"You know I am."

"I'll get him," she said, and with her head held high she started back to the staircase.

Still standing, Stavros stepped toward her—surprising both her and himself. He raised a hand, saying, "Just a second." It was, he realized, time to fight back. She had delivered a blow, a good one, but he wasn't finished. Not even close. If she wanted fireworks on Christmas, it could be arranged.

Allegra stopped short, her face startled, and it emboldened Stavros. Turning to the man-boy he said, "Dylan, would you mind? I'd like to talk to Allegra."

"No!" she said.

"Just for a minute," he said to her.

"*No!*"

"It's about *Brendan*. Our *son*." To Dylan he said: "This is a family matter, you understand?"

In his slippers and ridiculous Christmas-tree sweater, Young Paul Newman seemed to go mute, staring at Stavros with a helpless, impotent expression. Then, to Allegra he said, "I'll go get Brendan." The kid shot up from the chair, scurried across the room, and ascended the stairs.

Stavros was pumped. He had taken control of the situation and made his rival look weak, a beta to his alpha, and it felt good. Oh yes, it felt *damn* good!

Allegra was less pleased. Eyes bulging, nostrils flaring, she was livid, apoplectic. Yet despite the homicidal rage on his ex-wife's face, Stavros paused. Allegra's nearness, her actual, physical presence, reminded him of how connected they had once been, and it pained him. It tore at his heart. At one time he had loved her, deeply. So why had it all gone south? Why was Stavros alone and miserable and separated from this woman? And just then he heard himself saying, *yelling,* "What the hell is going on here? Who *is* this kid? Is he even legal?"

"Do not start!"

"Allegra, who *is* this guy? What's he doing here?"

"*Are you kidding me?*" she bellowed. "He's my boyfriend you idiot!"

"Does he sleep here?"

"*That's none of your business!*"

"Of course it's my damn business, this is *my* house! That's *my* son up there!"

"This is *not* your house, Stavros, this is *not your house!* This is *my* house! It's in my name!"

"*Then why the hell am I still making payments?*"

She inched closer, burning with hatred. "*Don't you dare yell at me, do you understand? Don't you dare yell at me! This is my house, and you are a guest here! A guest!*"

When Allegra went off like this her head would shake and throb. Veins bulged on her forehead, red splotches appeared on her neck.

"Oh great," Stavros said, riled but also strangely exhilarated. His eyes shone with a mix of irritation and pleasure. "Here we go!"

But Allegra surprised him. The expected explosion did not occur. There was no venomous fit. Instead, she caught herself, throwing on the brakes in a way Stavros had never seen. Though her face was flushed she calmly gave him a bitter smile, saying, "No. No 'here we go.' I'm not going to do this with you, Stavros—ever again. You're here to see your son. I'll give you fifteen minutes to exchange gifts, and if you stay one minute longer, one fricking minute, I'll call the police. And I'm not kidding. We're done, Stavros. It's been over for a long time. I've moved on, and you need to do the same. Good-bye."

She walked away, clacking her heels on the wood floor. Stavros didn't speak or turn to watch her go. His breathing was labored and he felt lightheaded, uneasy on his feet. He rubbed his forehead.

What just happened?

* * *

Too weak to stand, Stavros was sitting on the sofa when he heard, "Hi Dad." It was Brendan. His son. Stavros rose to his feet and gazed at the boy, wondering at his reaction to the shouting of his parents. Brendan had seen and heard too much parental fighting, years of it, and it shamed Stavros. Subjecting the boy to these vicious displays was wrong, and possibly damaging too. Certainly he and Allegra weren't projecting a model of healthy adult behavior. Yet rather than apologize Stavros beamed and said, "Hey! There he is!"

In ripped jeans and an untucked flannel shirt, Brendan tried to smile. He was fourteen, a skinny kid, and a little on the passive side. Kind of soft, Stavros felt. Unlike his father, who had been a basketball star in high school and college, Brendan wasn't particularly athletic, though he had made second-string JV soccer that year, if Stavros remembered correctly. Also unlike his father, who stood six-feet-two, Brendan was short, maybe five-four. Though of course a good growth spurt would take care of that. With two tall parents, it was inevitable. No midget son for Stavros! The boy was a freshman at Thoreau Academy, a private day school in Cambridge with an annual tuition greater than the yearly income of the average American—millions and millions of Americans. Not that Brendan was even aware of that fact. But he was a good student, supposedly very bright.

"Safe to come in here?" the boy said. He was holding a gift-wrapped box.

"Hey, come on," Stavros said, forcing a laugh. "Give me a hug, huh?"

They embraced, then sat on the sofa. Brendan gave Stavros his present.

"Oh, thank you! This is great! ... So hey, uh, what's up with this Dylan guy?"

"What?"

"Has your mother really been seeing him for a *year?*"

"I don't know. Maybe."

"*Maybe?* Why didn't you tell me?"

"*Tell you?* When do I ever see you?"

"What do you mean? I see you ... quite a bit. At your games."

"That's bullshit."

"*What?*"

"You didn't go to any of my games this year. You said you would, but you didn't."

"That's not true."

"Yes it is. You went to one game last year. But none this year."

"Really? I could have sworn ..."

Brendan shook his head.

"But we've had meals," Stavros said. "We went for lobsters, remember?"

"In July."

"When was the last time I saw you?"

"Right before school started. We went for Thai food. You were on the phone the whole time."

Stavros had grown very hot, feverish, and maybe a little woozy. "Has it been that long?"

"Yep."

Stavros felt ... what? Guilt? Is that what this was? Yes, guilt. Three months was too long; he should have made some time for the boy. He should have gone to a few games, or at least called. But what could he do? Work was so damn busy. Case after case, they just keep coming. And then, of course, there was time—it just goes, sprinting past you, one day blurring into the next. Surely *that* wasn't his fault, right? *Right.*

His conscience cleared, Stavros said, "So is your mother serious about this guy?"

"How would I know?"

"What do you mean, how would you know? You've got eyes, don't you?"

Incredulity came over the boy's face, then disgust.

"OK, forget it," Stavros said. "But what's he like? This *Dylan*. Is he a jerk, or what? He kind of looks like a sissy."

"I like him. We talk about stuff. He played soccer at Yale. He was really good. Plus, he and Mom don't fight."

Stavros gawped at his son. "They don't fight?"

"No."

Stavros rubbed his forehead. He felt unwell. Dizzy. Slightly nauseated ... Brendan had said something. "What?"

"I *said*, are you OK?"

"I'm fine," Stavros said. But then came a massive pain in his chest, as if Mike Tyson had just slugged him, hard. Cringing, curling forward, Stavros groaned.

"*Dad?*"

"I'm fine," Stavros repeated, smarting from the pain and also a sharp tightness down his left arm. "Why don't you get me some water."

Brendan left the room. Stavros was queasy, and hurting, and short of breath. Obviously something was happening. But it was best not to think about it, he thought. Not right now. If he continued to feel like this, then he would drive himself over to the hospital afterward. But it was probably just nerves. He'd be home soon and there was a bottle waiting for him. Keller's Christmas gift. Thinking it a good idea to start winding this up—hadn't Allegra threatened to call the cops?—he reached for his money clip and peeled off three hundreds.

Brendan returned with the water and Stavros drank it down.

"Do you feel better?"

"Yeah ... much better," Stavros said, now holding out the cash. "I was going to get you some clothes but ... you grow so ... I thought it better

…" Stavros couldn't get the right words out. The dizziness was extreme. His vision was blurry.

"Oh, cool," Brendan said, taking the money. "Thanks!"

"And don't forget … your …" Stavros motioned to the boy's gifts. He just wanted to leave, get the hell out of here.

"Dad, are you sure you're OK?"

"Yeah … Open …"

Brendan tore the paper from his first gift. It was a boxed set of CDs: *The Miles Davis Collection*. The boy's face went glum.

"What? … You don't …" Stavros struggled to finish the sentence, but he couldn't do it. The words wouldn't come. His brain and body were failing, malfunctioning, and it hit him with instant panic that he might be dying.

Gazing dejectedly at his gift Brendan said, "You gave me this like two years ago."

There was a ferocious blast in Stavros's chest. The pain was excruciating, like taking a bullet. All at once his arms, neck, and jaw seized up and his eyes shut tight. With his heart stopped and his blood gone still, Stavros slumped over and fell to the floor.

TWO

Slowly he came to, waking to the world.

Stavros was on his back in a raised bed. There were people nearby, seated and talking—Allegra and Brendan. Stavros made no attempt to speak or move, no effort to attract them. He felt cold and weak, heavy-limbed, as though his flesh had turned to stone. He became aware of his heart beating and his lungs filling with breath. There were wires and tubes attached to his body, and the sounds of machines humming and beeping. Emotions surged in him and his eyes watered.

"He's awake!" said Brendan, springing to the bed. *"Dad, Dad ..."* The boy was ecstatic, his face joyous, shining with a strange innocence, and to Stavros it felt as though he were seeing his son for the first time.

"Stavros, how do you feel? Can you hear me?" This was Allegra, hovering over him.

Gazing into his ex-wife's eyes, tears spilling down his cheeks, Stavros felt his heart ache.

"Dad, you died. And Mom saved you."

A nurse rushed into the room, and then a doctor. Allegra and Brendan moved back and the doctor, placing a hand on Stavros's shoulder, said, "Sir, hello, I'm Dr. Martinez. You're at Mt. Adams Hospital, in Cambridge, Massachusetts, and you've been in a coma for three days."

Stavros said nothing.

"Sir, I have to ask you a few questions. What is your name?"

Stavros winced, and more tears fell.

"Sir? ... Sir, what is your name?"

"Stavros Papadakis."

"Ah, very good. And how old are you, Mr. Papadakis?"

"Forty-four."

"Excellent." The doctor checked his pulse, peered into his eyes, and asked him to squeeze his fingers, which Stavros did.

"And how do you feel right now, Mr. Papadakis?"

"Tired … Very tired … I want to sleep."

* * *

Ten hours later Stavros woke, groggy and discombobulated. His mouth was dry and he still felt very weak. He was alone now, alone in a small, windowless room. The overhead lights were off but the door was propped open, letting in a bright glow from the adjacent corridor. No people were visible but he could hear faint voices. The clock on the wall read 5:25— though was it a.m. or p.m.? For some time he lay still, feeling dazed, feeling numb.

Then he began to remember. One after the other the memories came —and they were incredible. Something amazing had happened to him; something horrific, something divine … But *had* it happened? Had it *really* happened? How could it be? Stavros became panicky, frightened, and his eyes burned with tears.

* * *

"You're very lucky to be alive, Mr. Papadakis. You should play the lottery!" This was Dr. Martìnez, marveling at his patient's progress. Stronger than he'd been the day before, Stavros could now turn on his side and raise a glass to his lips. Emotionally, though, he was off. He had no desire, no will. The doctor said he was lucky to be alive; Stavros wasn't so sure.

"Now, Mr. Papadakis, you've had a great shock," the doctor said, his demeanor growing serious, as if to mirror Stavros's grim expression. "Four days ago you went into cardiac arrest and lost consciousness. Your, uh … former wife, Dr. Barzetti, reported no pulse and performed CPR.

Eventually, after as much as fifteen minutes, the heart regained function. However, due to a lack of oxygen your brain suffered an injury, what we call a hypoxic-anoxic injury, and this is what led to the coma. Upon arrival here at the hospital, a CT scan revealed two blocked arteries, and with Dr. Barzetti's approval, a double angioplasty was performed—"

"Did Allegra do it?" Stavros said.

"No. Dr. Trang did the angioplasty. But Dr. Barzetti was present. She's been present all throughout, making regular check-ins. Now Mr. Papadakis, generally in cases of coma following cardiac arrest, there's expectation of lasting damage to the brain. But in your case—and this really is inexplicable to me—there's no indication of permanent injury of any sort: to the brain, the spinal cord, or any other of the organs. We still need to run some tests, but on the whole I'm feeling very optimistic about your prognosis. You really are a lucky man."

The doctor went over other matters, and when the update was finished he said, "OK, Mr. Papadakis. Your son and Dr. Barzetti are waiting outside. The boy is very excited to see you. I'll send them in."

"*No*, don't," Stavros said. The doctor looked at him, and Stavros felt his eyes becoming wet. "I'm very tired."

"But it might help your mood, Mr. Papadakis. And the boy ... He's come every day since you were admitted. He's been very worried."

"No. Not today. I want to be alone."

* * *

All that day and the next Stavros brooded, his spirits low, his emotions unstable. Several times he had broken down and wept, crying from confusion, and terror, and awe. He had experienced the implausible, the unthinkable. "But how could it be?" he kept asking himself. He wanted to tell someone, share his story, but who would believe him? Who would believe that he left his body? That he went to the afterlife? That he went to other worlds, other realms? It was crazy; it was insane! They would lock him up!

* * *

That afternoon, Brendan returned for a visit. The boy knocked on the propped-open door, and Stavros winced, thinking, No, *no!*

The problem was this: seeing the boy forced Stavros to remember a painful part of his afterlife journey. In heaven—yes, *heaven!*—Stavros had revisited the main events of his earthly life, from his mother's womb to his death on Christmas morning. It was like being inside a 3D movie, a cinematic retrospective staring Stavros Papadakis. And all the while Stavros was made to feel how he had made other people feel—the effects of his words and his deeds on Allegra, Brendan, and everyone else. And how agonizing it was! How excruciating! Stavros had no idea how awful he had been; how angry and callous, how selfish and uncaring, how dishonest and corrupt. In heaven he had sobbed and wailed, crying out again and again that he was sorry for his sins.

"Hi Dad," the boy said, entering the room with a timid but hopeful air, his eyes hungry for paternal connection.

Stavros tried to oblige his son, give him a warm, fatherly welcome, but he couldn't do it. He was suffering, tormented by a flurry of memories from heaven. Mercifully, they weren't all bad. When Brendan was little, the two of them had shared happy times: playing with blocks in the house; kicking a ball in the yard; exploring the tide pools at the summer rental in Mattapoisett, hunting for minnows and crabs. What pure joy Brendan had felt, interacting with his father! Ecstatic bliss! Stavros had no idea how much his attention had meant to his son, how essential it was, how much it was craved and needed. But the good times lessened as Brendan aged. There were missed birthdays, missed holidays, missed school events. Brendan on the soccer field, looking to the sideline for his father: he said he would come, but where was he? Same with playing in the school band: the child looking from the stage into the audience for the father who wasn't there. And then, on those rare occasions when they were together, just the two of them, how Dad still ignored him: "I've got to take this call." How many times had Brendan heard that, while he and

Stavros were eating a hamburger at some restaurant or watching a game at Fenway? Stavros would leave the child alone for twenty, thirty minutes at a time, fielding calls from Keller or some client. How crushing it was to the boy! Day after day, year after year, feeling diminished by his father, feeling unwanted, unimportant, unloved.

And then there was the domestic strife. Brendan listening in fear as his parents screamed at each other, yelling insults and obscenities, making threats. And worse: the times Stavros had turned his rage on the boy himself. Frustrated by his problems, aggravated by his imploding marriage and the stresses of work, Stavros might holler at Brendan to pick up his toys or eat his food or stop whining! Glaring at the child, eyes filled with rage, Stavros would let him have it, belittling and humiliating him. "For Chrissake stop picking your nose! What are you a monkey? You think this is the zoo?"

Now, his eyes prickling from shame, Stavros could hardly look at his son.

Brendan's hopeful expression had already faded. "How do you feel?" he said gloomily.

"Not too good," Stavros mumbled.

The boy was holding a gift-wrapped box: Stavros's Christmas present. And seeing it, Stavros cringed, feeling unworthy, feeling the burn of self-hate.

Brendan said, "I was just talking to Dr. Martinez. He says you're lucky to be alive."

"Yeah."

"He said it's practically a miracle."

"You could say that."

Silence.

Brendan tried again: "How's the food?"

"Terrible."

More silence.

"Do you want me to leave?" the boy said, looking hurt.

Stavros was mortified. *"No!* Of course not! I'm happy to see you. Always."

"Then why didn't you want to see us yesterday, me and Mom? Dr. Martinez said you could have visitors, but then after he saw you he said you wanted to be alone."

"No, I *did* want to see you. I just … I've been very weak, and very tired. That's all."

The boy scrutinized his father, mulling his words, and slowly the hurt left his face.

Relieved, and wanting desperately to turn this around, to show the boy that he cared, Stavros forced a smile and said, "So … are you skipping school today?"

"It's Christmas break."

"Oh. Right."

Silence.

Stavros wondered what else he could ask … *His friends,* said the inner voice. Yes, his friends! But Stavros didn't know any of the boy's friends. Frantically he tried to remember a name … just one damn name! And then it came: "So how's Freddie Durbin doing?"

"Who?"

"Freddie Durbin?"

"You mean Teddy Doobin?"

"Right, right," Stavros said, casually waving his hand as though he'd made a fluke mistake.

"He moved to Texas. Like eight years ago."

"Oh … Didn't he have a stutter?"

"No. That was Trey Gooch."

"OK. And how's old Trey doing?"

"He died when I was like ten. He got hit by a car."

Oh boy, Stavros thought.

More silence.

"Anyway, this is for you," Brendan said, handing his father the gift-wrapped box.

"Hey, my Christmas present," Stavros said, feigning a jolly tone. "I didn't get to it last time, did I?"

Brendan smiled, and it seemed genuine.

Stavros tore away the paper and opened the box. It was an MP3 player with headphones. "Oh, look at that—wow!"

"I put a bunch of CDs on it. AC/DC, ZZ Top."

"Really?"

"Yeah. You told me one time they were your favorite bands when you were in high school."

"I did?"

"Yep. And I also put some stuff on there that I like. You might like it too."

Stavros was touched. "Brendan, thank you. This is really great." He examined the MP3 player, which to him was like some alien artifact. "It's little, huh? When I was a kid I had a Walkman. You put a cassette in it. It was very trendy." Stavros donned the headphones and began pushing the tiny buttons, but nothing happened. "How do you turn it on?"

Brendan worked the gadget. "What do you want to hear?"

"You pick it."

The boy scrolled through the menu, and soon Stavros heard a frenetic jazz combo. It made him think of the Roaring Twenties, or rather, of films and TV shows set in the Roaring Twenties: *The Cotton Club, Boardwalk Empire*. He removed the headphones. "What's this?"

"Louis Armstrong. 'St. Louis Blues.'"

"You *like* this stuff?" Stavros said, surprised.

"*Yes*," the boy said defensively.

"It's kind of old, isn't it?"

"I guess. But so what? Mozart is even older, but people still listen to him."

"I just meant, compared to what kids are listening to today. You know … What's-his-name—Trevor Beaver?"

Brendan was outraged. "I don't listen to that crap!"

"I'm sorry," Stavros said, taken aback. "I didn't know you liked jazz, that's all."

"*What?*"

"I didn't know you liked jazz."

"What are you talking about?" The boy's angry eyes were eerily like his mother's.

"What do you mean what am I talking about?" Stavros said.

"I've been in the school jazz band for like four years."

"Yes—of course," Stavros said uneasily. He'd known that Brendan had played trumpet in the elementary school orchestra, but he'd known nothing about a jazz band.

"And if you didn't know that I like jazz, then why did you get me the Miles box set? *Twice.*"

Stavros pondered this: the Miles box set? *Twice?*

"*Miles Davis? The box set?*" Brendan said in a huff.

"Oh, right—the Miles box set," Stavros said, recalling the boy's Christmas present. The present that Ida, his secretary, had bought. Twice, evidently.

"And what about the other box set?" Brendan said. "The Maurice Andre? Why did you get me that?"

Stavros had no idea who Maurice Andre was, but he assumed the boy was talking about his other present. "It was a suggestion. Someone at the office. A big jazz guy."

"A 'big jazz guy'? Maurice Andre is a classical trumpeter—Bach and Haydn."

An ominous feeling passed over Stavros, and he became very alert. Cautiously, warily, he said, "Yeah, but … you were in the orchestra when you were little, remember?"

Brendan's eyes narrowed with suspicion. "Did you even buy my presents?"

"What?" Stavros said, laughing nervously. "Of course I did. I just … asked different people for ideas, that's all."

"OK … Then what was the other present?"

"The other present?"

"Yeah. The third one."

Stavros froze, staring at his son ... And there it was, he thought—checkmate. His cheeks flushed, and he said, "I don't know."

"You *don't know?*"

Feeling like a complete shit, Stavros said, "No. I don't know what it was."

"So you didn't buy them."

Stavros shook his head. "No."

Revulsion came over the boy's face, and the intensity of it alarmed Stavros. He said, "Brendan, look—I'm sorry. It was my secretary, she bought the gifts. I've been very busy, and she helped out ... It's what secretaries do. But you like them, right? The CDs? ... That's the important thing."

"Why did you lie? I hate liars."

"I didn't mean to ... I just ..." Stavros shrugged.

The boy's eyes flashed fire. "You know what? I always thought you were just a jerk, but you're really an asshole." He took off for the door.

Stavros called out to him, but Brendan didn't stop. He was gone.

* * *

That evening Allegra came to Stavros's room. Stern-faced and tight-lipped, she made no effort to greet him. There was no hello or even a curt nod. Instead she remained by the door, arms folded across her chest, glaring at him with cold condemning eyes.

Stavros likewise said nothing; he wasn't able to. Shame had paralyzed his tongue. The issue wasn't Allegra's hostile gaze, though that wasn't helping, but rather that seeing her had forced him to recall more memories from heaven, to revisit more scenes from his regrettable past.

Like Brendan, Allegra too had experienced happy times with Stavros. In their early days there had been numerous nights out across Boston and Cambridge, at parties and restaurants and bars. Walks along the Charles, fall hikes in New Hampshire, summer days in Mattapoisett. Their trip to Europe and their wedding in New York. The rapturous love-making, the birth of Brendan. Yes, they'd had many happy times! Many joyful times!

But life got difficult. It made demands on Stavros, and he handled things poorly. There was only so much time in a day, a week, a life, and when push came to shove he put his own needs above his family's.

In his afterlife review Stavros saw and felt how his words and deeds, his actions and non-actions, had affected Allegra: His devoting more and more of himself to his work. His arrogant presumption that she would manage most home and parenting duties even though she was pursuing her own career. His drinking and late nights, all of which he claimed were necessary because they were work-related. His emotional withdrawal and his labeling her a bitch or worse whenever she called him out on his bad behavior. And of course, the fights. The bickering, the quarrels, the verbal bloodbaths that grew more and more destructive over time. All of this, these scenes from a failed marriage, Stavros had experienced from her perspective. And how devastating it was! How crushing to see and feel what he had done to her, how he had suffocated her spirit, how he had strangled her love for him.

Filled with self-loathing, Stavros could barely look at his ex-wife.

"How are you feeling?" she finally said.

"I've been better."

"You're lucky to be alive."

"That's what I keep hearing."

She sneered, as though she thought he were being sarcastic. But he hadn't meant it that way! The last thing Stavros wanted was to offend her. But that's how things were with them. Their many battles had left her expecting the worst, sensitive to the least hint of insult. To allay her suspicions he said, "Allegra, I want to thank you. You saved my life. I'm very—"

But she didn't want to hear it. She held up a hand to make him stop, and he did. "It's OK," she said. "I just wanted to check in. That's all

... Dr. Martìnez says you're doing well, much better than expected. I've seen all your tests, and I've talked to some colleagues, and the consensus is you should be fine ... Anyway, I'm sorry but I have to go." She regarded him with some finality, then said, "Take care Stavros."

"Allegra, please." He knew she didn't want to be here, that she had come out of a sense of obligation. But he didn't want her to go. He wanted her to stay. He wanted to talk to her, connect with her. But most of all, he wanted to apologize. For everything. Every hurt he had caused her, every failure, every offense. But he wasn't quite sure how to do it. When was the last time he had apologized to someone—for anything?

He saw she was waiting, frowning with impatience. Flustered, he said, "Look, I know I've made some mistakes—"

"*Mistakes?*" she said, becoming inflamed. "Is that what you call them? Is that what you call what happened today with your son—a mistake? I know what happened, Stavros. I know all about it!"

"I didn't handle that well."

She scoffed. "Good-bye Stavros."

"Allegra, I'm sorry! For everything! Please let me explain—"

"No," she said, cutting him off. "I don't want to hear it. I don't. Good-bye." She started for the door.

"Allegra, wait—*please!*"

She did so, but grudgingly.

"There's something else," he said.

She looked at him.

In a faltering voice he said, "Something happened to me ... after my heart attack."

A trace of curiosity came into her eyes.

Stavros hesitated. He knew she would never believe his story. Not one bit of it. Allegra was, after all, a declared atheist, which she attributed to her scientific training. God, heaven, hell—where was the proof? Those things were relics from the past, primitive beliefs that led to wars, bigotry, guilt, and all the rest of it. She was on the side of reason, and believed in human progress: the idea that, over time, scientific thought leads inexorably to the improvement of the human condition. Science would save man, not superstitious mumbo-jumbo. Knowing she felt this way, he decided to just come out with it.

"I left my body," he mumbled.

Her brow contracted. "Excuse me?"

"After my heart attack, I left my body."

Watching him, her eyes growing doubtful, even perturbed, Allegra made no reply.

"I'm telling you, I left my body ... and I went ... to other places. Other worlds."

There was silence, and with one hand Allegra began rubbing her eyes, as though a headache were coming on. "OK ... so you're saying you saw a tunnel and a white light—is that what this is?"

"Yes! Exactly. But it's more than that. Allegra, I saw my mother! ... She's still alive! There is no death!" Stavros said, his eyes stinging and becoming wet.

Allegra's expression softened. Stavros's mother had died when he was thirteen, of pancreatic cancer. One day she went into the hospital, and within two weeks she was gone. Allegra said, "Stavros, this isn't an uncommon experience. Many heart attack survivors report seeing a white light or even seeing family members. Some of my own patients have reported this. When the heart stops functioning, the brain becomes deprived of oxygen and begins to shut down. And once this happens, we can begin to hallucinate. We can relive memories and these memories can seem very real."

"It wasn't a memory!" he said. "I talked to my mother like I'm talking to you now! It happened in the present, not the past. And she was much younger than when she died. She was young and I still knew it was her, even though I didn't remember her that way!"

"Stavros—"

"Allegra, it happened! And I saw you too."

"What do you mean?"

"You gave me CPR."

"That's true. I told Dr. Martìnez I gave you CPR, and I'm sure he told you."

"Yes, he did. But I knew before that. I knew because I watched you do it. After my heart attack I left my body. I just floated up, and I didn't even know that I'd done it. One minute I was on the sofa, talking to Brendan, and the next I'm looking down on the scene from above. And at first I was very calm, just observing everything, like it was a play. Brendan was frantic, saying 'Dad! Dad!' And then you and Dylan rushed into the room. And there was a body on the floor, and I thought—Wait, is that *me*? How could that be me? I'm *here*! And the body—I didn't really recognize it. It looked old, and heavy. Bloated. But then it hit me —Damn, that *is* me! But I didn't panic; I was just like, Oh well, bye-bye body—thanks for the ride! Then you started giving me CPR, and you kept saying, 'Don't let go, Stavros! Don't let go!' And Brendan was hysterical. He was crying, and Dylan tried to take him into the next room but he wouldn't go. It was heartbreaking to see him like that, so I started calling out, 'I'm OK, Brendan! I'm OK! Look at me, I'm OK!' But he couldn't hear me; none of you could. And finally you said, 'I have a pulse! There's a pulse!' Isn't that what happened?"

By now Allegra also had become emotional, trembling slightly, her eyes watery and red. But she replied, "No, it's impossible. You can't know this. You must have still been conscious."

"Even though my heart had stopped?"

She was shaking her head. "No. Stavros, we shouldn't be doing this. You're still in a weak state."

"Allegra, I'm telling you—it happened! I left my body!"

More head shaking.

"And there's more," he said. "Much more!"

She looked at him, waiting.

"I met Jesus."

Allegra brought a hand up to cover her eyes, grimacing as though the headache were coming on with full force.

"I swear to God, Allegra!"

She looked at him, and he could see she was struggling. Struggling with her thoughts, struggling with her response. At last she said, "OK, Stavros—you met Jesus. Fine. That's very interesting, and maybe we can talk about it another time. But right now the best thing for you is to not get excited. I'm going to talk to Dr. Martìnez and have him give you something to help you rest. I'll … I'll stop back in a few days."

She did not seem happy to say this. In fact, she did not seem happy at all.

THREE

Days later a large bulky man, holding a teddy bear over his face, walked into Stavros's room. A mock-dramatic voice boomed out: "I am Lazarus, come from the dead, come back to tell you all, I shall tell you all …"

Stavros broke into a grin, his spirits soaring. The teddy bear was lowered and there appeared the merry face of Wyatt Keller, Stavros's mentor, partner, friend.

"Hello old buddy," Keller said. "Back for round two, huh?"

A larger-than-life character, Keller was a celebrity lawyer. "The most prominent criminal-defense attorney in the country," according to the *Wall Street Gazette*. Keller defended the notorious—mobsters, murderers, terrorists—and the public loved him. He was a winner, a courtroom superstar. A showman and a charmer. With his custom-made suits, quick wit, and droll manner, he was a favorite of the press. Sophisticated and culturally astute, he was also a man of the people, someone who shook hands and remembered names. Now in his early sixties, Keller appeared much younger—mid-fifties, people said. He was brilliant and cagey and always in control: of himself, of others, of situations. At six-foot-one and a good two-fifty, he was nonetheless graceful on his feet, elegant in his bearing. All of which was unexpected given his background. Keller's people were farmers, sturdy Wisconsin Lutherans. Young Wyatt had grown up milking cows and running for touchdowns. He won a scholarship to Evanston University and was a gridiron star. They loved him in Chicago. But a back injury junior year ended his playing days and forced him to think about his future. Returning to the farm was out of the question. Keller wasn't meant to drive a tractor. He was meant for something better, something finer. An admired professor suggested the law, and after graduation Keller packed a bag and headed east, where he enrolled at Boston Law School.

He set the teddy bear down on the bed, saying, "Something to cheer you up."

Stavros smiled and the two men greeted each other, shaking hands.

"You really scared me, you know that?" Keller said. "Allegra called the day after Christmas. She said your heart stopped for fifteen minutes. I couldn't believe it. This isn't supposed to happen, Stavros. You're still a young man ... Anyway, I would've flown back sooner but Maggie's parents had just gotten in. She's still down there but I came as soon as I could."

Keller and his wife Maggie had gone down to their place on Marco Island for the long weekend. They'd flown out on Thursday night, Christmas Eve, and Keller had been expected back in the office on Monday morning. Today was Wednesday. Pondering this, Stavros wondered about the exact meaning of "came as soon as I could." But rather than pursue it he said, "I hope I didn't ruin your holiday."

"Come on," Keller said, grinning mischievously. "I was happy to get out of there ... So how are you? What are the quacks saying?"

Stavros gave him the latest: there was no permanent damage, he was recovering faster than expected, and he could leave the hospital once he could walk on his own. "I'm on crutches now," he said.

"That's great ... So what happened, exactly? Allegra said you were opening presents with Brendan?"

"Yeah. It was an interesting morning," Stavros said, and he told Keller all about it: meeting Dylan, arguing with Allegra, croaking in front of Brendan.

"A Christmas to remember," Keller chuckled. "And how's Brendan doing? That must have been tough on him."

"Yeah, it was. He's ... he's hanging in there."

Keller nodded, and for a moment there was silence. Then he said, "So who's been by? Have you seen anyone from the office?"

"Uh, no. I haven't. Ida called a couple days back, and we talked for a bit. She said she'd be coming to visit soon. But other than that, no one."

"Well, you know … people are busy."

Stavros shrugged. "It's not a big deal."

"Now what about work? Have they said anything about when you might be able to come back?"

"The doctor says I should take at least a month. Maybe two."

"Two months?" Keller said, surprised. "Well … we'll be fine. You take as long as you need. I've already pulled Sal on board with Bellingham, and I've given Ben and Inés some of your other cases; I'll handle the rest. Maybe in a couple days the four of you could do a conference call, in case they have any questions."

"Sure," Stavros said, fidgeting. "Whatever you need."

"That doesn't bother you, does it?"

"Not at all."

"Buddy, there's nothing to worry about. Before you know it, you'll be back at it. Maybe sooner than you think."

But Keller had misread Stavros. Over the past few days, the first idle days he'd had in many years, Stavros had thought about his life. He'd contemplated the choices he had made, the man he'd become. His goals, his achievements, his failures. And the more he thought about these things, the worse he felt. Year after year, all of which had raced by, Stavros had worked hard, regularly putting in sixty-, seventy-hour weeks, and had made many sacrifices—his marriage, his family, his health. And for what? For money? For success? If so, he had made it. He was wealthy and professionally esteemed. Co-partner in one of the top criminal-defense firms in the country. Stavros had made it, and he'd made it big. And so how was it that he now found himself in a hospital bed, feeling miserable, empty, and deeply alone?

Yet to discuss any of this with Keller was impossible. For it was through Keller that Stavros had achieved his success. Years ago, while working in Cambridge as an Assistant District Attorney, he had faced off against Keller in a high-profile murder case involving a Brattle Street heiress and her famous playwright lover. The case drew national attention and the verdict, a first-degree murder conviction, made Stavros a star. He was written up in the papers, interviewed on TV. He was spoken of as someone to watch, a comer, a man with a future. Certain pundits even deemed him a potential political candidate. Impressed by his opponent, Keller reached out to Stavros. They met for drinks. They met for dinner. They took in a game at the Garden. Ideas were floated, possibilities discussed. And soon afterward came the surprising news that Keller & Associates was now Keller, Papadakis & Associates.

"Hey, I'm sorry," Keller said, as though responding to Stavros's silence. "I should've waited to talk about work. You just got out of a coma and here I am telling you I gave your cases to the associates."

"It's not a problem, Wyatt. And to be honest, I think I could use a break."

"Like I said, take as long as you need."

With the work question settled, Stavros's thoughts turned to another matter. Without question he had to say *something* about his otherworldly experience. Keller was his closest friend, after all. But how would he take it? The fact was, Keller rarely spoke about personal things, and certainly not about mystical things. Still, Stavros felt it had to be done. He said, "Wyatt, there's something I want to tell you ... It's kind of out there."

"All right," Keller said, becoming attentive.

"You've heard about people dying and seeing a white light?"

"Sure."

"Well, that happened to me."

"Really," Keller said, evenly, but with a hint of amusement.

"Yes. But it was more than that. More than just a light."

"OK."

"First I ... went to hell."

"*Hell?*" Keller said, now perplexed.

"Yes."

"As in ... *devil hell?*"

"That's right. And then I went to heaven. And I met ... Jesus."

Keller laughed. "You're screwing with me, right?"

"No. I'm not."

"Come on."

"Wyatt, I'm serious."

Flummoxed, Keller lowered his gaze. With one hand he began rubbing both cheeks, mulling the situation. Finally he said, "I'm gonna sit down." He lowered his heavy frame onto a chair. "OK—so first you went to hell."

"Yes. After my heart attack I left my body. My consciousness, my soul —whatever you want to call it—just rose up. And for a while I watched as Allegra gave me CPR. But at some point something pulled on me; and I mean, *literally* pulled on me. I went from being in the living room in Cambridge to a place that was complete darkness. There was no light at all. No shadows, no nothing."

"No fire and brimstone? No pitchforks?"

Stavros ignored the sarcasm. "No, everything was black, and it was perfectly quiet, and cold. And there was a stench, a foul, sewer stench. And for a while nothing happened, there was just stillness, complete stillness, and I wasn't afraid. I was mostly just curious, wondering what was happening. But then I started to hear sounds off in the distance, and everything changed." Stavros paused, and he began to tremble, his eyes prickling. "There were voices, and laughter, and howls. But they weren't human voices. They were ... half-human, half-animal. And gradually the howls and the voices got louder, and I realized that the creatures were coming closer. That they were coming ... *for me.* They were demons, Wyatt. Actual demons."

Keller was frowning, but Stavros couldn't stop. He had to tell his story.

"They said they'd been expecting me. They *knew* me, Wyatt! The demons knew who I was! And I couldn't escape. I couldn't even move; it was like I was paralyzed, and it was terrifying. I felt completely helpless, and vulnerable ... And then it started."

"What?"

"The attacks, the torture."

Keller's frown deepened.

"At first they covered me with filth—"

"Filth?"

"Shit. Actual shit. They threw it at me, then they started rubbing it on me. Then they made me eat it—"

Keller laughed. It was too much.

"Wyatt, I'm telling you, it happened! And then they began to hit me. Harder than I've ever been hit before. It was like getting hit in the face with a baseball bat, again and again."

"But you said you left your body! If you left your body, then what were they hitting?"

"When you die you have a light body, not a physical one. You don't have flesh but you can still feel things."

"Right … A light body," Keller muttered.

"Yes. And the pain was excruciating. Beyond words. I was screaming and begging them to stop. But they just laughed. Then they did other things to me. Sexual things."

At this, Keller broke into a wide grin. "OK … you *are* screwing with me, right?" he said expectantly, as though he were getting ready to laugh when Stavros confirmed that this indeed was all a joke.

"*No.* I'm not," Stavros said, fighting back tears. "And after that they started tearing at my body, ripping away whole pieces, including my—"

"OK, OK," Keller said, holding up a hand for Stavros to stop. He'd heard enough. "Stavros, look … maybe we should get a doctor in here." Stavros's eyes were wet and his nose was running. Keller stood, snatched a tissue from the box by the bed, and handed it to him, saying, "Buddy, this isn't you. What do you say? I'll call a nurse."

"No. They'll just want me to take a pill."

"Maybe that's not a bad idea."

"Wyatt, I know how this sounds. I know it sounds crazy. It sounds crazy even to me. But it happened. It really happened!"

"All right … But let's just take a step back for a second, OK? Let's just think about this. Sometimes dreams can be very real—"

"Wyatt—"

"Just hear me out, Stavros. The other night I had one. It was very vivid. This brunette, a Latin girl, absolutely gorgeous. She's naked, and she gets into bed with me, and I'm thinking, *Wow*. I mean, she's hot, right? And then she drapes a leg over mine, and I can *feel* it—I can feel the weight of the leg on mine, the softness of her skin, the texture. It's as real as can be. And I get so excited that I wake up. *Boom!* I'm up and ready to go, looking around in the dark. But she wasn't there."

"Wyatt, this wasn't a damn dream, OK? I've had dreams before too, believe it or not, and this wasn't one of them!"

"All right, all right," Keller said. "So this really happened. Well, then let me ask you this. How many people have you told?"

"Just you and Allegra."

"Good," Keller said, relieved. "Because what I'm thinking is, maybe we should sit on this for a bit. You've been through a lot. A heart attack and a coma. Traumatic stuff. So let's just sit on this, keep it quiet, and with a little time, you might have a different perspective."

"That's not going to happen. Everything I experienced was real. It was realer than this place," Stavros said, waving his hand at the room. "This world is just a dream."

Keller's face darkened. "Stavros, my point is this: how do you think this story will go down on the street? That Stavros Papadakis claims he died, went to hell, and was attacked by demons? Demons that rubbed shit on him and did sexual things? You think maybe the press wouldn't like a little taste of this? The *Bugle*? The *Telegraph*? The smartasses on talk radio? And what about our clients? Would you trust your life to some guy who said he left his body and spent some time in hell? You think that might inspire confidence in a guy looking at twenty-to-life? What do you think?"

"Wyatt, I get it. But it was never my intention to go to the press."

"Fine. But you tell one person, someone you don't know, and suddenly it's on the internet. And then it's on the news and in the papers. Stavros, as I always say, we're public figures. We have to be careful. At all times."

"I know, Wyatt."

"Buddy, I'm not trying to tell you what to do. But this *is* a sensitive situation, and it involves both of us. It involves the firm. We've worked hard to get where we are, but it can all go in the shitter just like that. And there are plenty of jerkoffs out there who'd love to see it happen, and you know it."

"You're right. You're absolutely right."

"Yeah?"

"Yeah … I just needed to hear it."

"So we understand each other?"

"I won't say a thing."

Keller nodded, and his expression changed. His face became somber, morose, as though he'd just gotten some bad news. With a weary sigh he stood, then said he had to get back to the office.

FOUR

On New Year's Eve, Allegra swept into Stavros's room. It was about five o'clock, and she was dressed in a white lab coat, which meant she was still working. Stopping at the foot of the bed, she gave him a hard, flinty look and folded her arms across her chest like some female mafioso.

Oddly roused by this, Stavros removed the headphones he'd been wearing.

"How's the music?" she said curtly.

"Good. I was listening to my new favorite. Louis Armstrong."

Allegra snickered, making it clear she wasn't impressed.

"Did you know about this?" Stavros said, holding up the MP3 player.

"Of course."

"It was a nice gift. Very thoughtful."

"He's a thoughtful kid. Not that you would know."

The comment stung, but Stavros didn't want to argue. He said, "Do you have plans for tonight?"

"Stavros, I didn't come here to chat. There are two things I want to discuss. The first is I don't want you to tell Brendan about the dream you had."

"*Dream?* Allegra, I'm telling you, it really happened. I left my body and I went to heaven. I also went to hell."

"You went to hell?"

"Yes. And it was ... you wouldn't believe it."

"Well, good. I'm glad to hear it."

"What? How can you say that?"

"Stavros, it was your *conscience*, OK? Which means you actually have one. It was telling you what a shit you've been."

"My *conscience?* Then why did I see Jesus?"

"For the same reason you didn't see the Buddha."

"What does that mean?"

"You saw Jesus because you were raised Christian. It's part of your deep psyche; it's ingrained there. Had you seen Krishna or Mohammed, it might seem a little more plausible."

"That's ridiculous! A Christian sees Christ, ergo Christ doesn't exist. Yeah, very logical."

Fire came into her eyes. "Stavros, everything you saw, everything you describe—Jesus, heaven, hell—took place in your *brain*. It happened here!" she said, jabbing an index finger into the side of her head. "And all it means is that you're dealing with some heavy guilt, and you desire absolution. That's it. That's all this is."

And just like that, Stavros understood: no one in his world was ever going to believe his afterlife story. He was on his own with this. And Keller was right. If news of Stavros's heavenly sojourn were to leak, it would be disastrous. His many rivals and enemies would pounce on the story and use it against him with great glee, in the press and on the street. They would eat Stavros alive, mock him for the rest of his days, and worst of all, steal his clients.

"Stavros, I mean it. I don't want you to say anything to him."

"Fine."

"If things were different, maybe it wouldn't be a problem. But he's in a vulnerable place right now and—"

"What does that mean: a 'vulnerable place'?"

She shook her head. "I don't have time for this, Stavros. I don't have time to bring you up to speed on the last, oh, ten years of your son's life, OK? So don't start acting like the concerned parent all of a sudden."

"That's not fair."

"*Fair?*"

Stavros readied for an explosion ... But it didn't come. As she'd done on Christmas day, Allegra caught herself; she hit pause, controlled her tongue. It was very strange. Then, calmly, she said, "Stavros, Brendan's opinion of you right now is very low, which is why on top of everything else I don't want him to think his father is crazy. That's all I'm going to say. So again, keep the story to yourself."

He sighed. "All right. I won't say a word."

"Good ... Thank you."

"How's he doing?"

"He's furious at you, and I don't blame him."

"Neither do I."

Allegra flinched, and she looked at Stavros with puzzled eyes.

"I feel terrible about what happened," he added.

"You should."

"Do you know if he's coming back? To visit?"

"Don't hold your breath. You lied to him, Stavros. You ignored him and you lied about his Christmas presents."

"I didn't mean to ignore him. I just ..." Stavros shrugged. "It's hard to explain."

"Good answer. And what about the lies?"

"I know. I should be taken out and flogged."

"*You think this is funny?*" she snapped.

"*No.* I mean it. I should be taken out and flogged. I feel awful about this, Allegra. About everything."

Again her eyes were puzzled. Allegra had come expecting to do battle, but Stavros seemed more interested in ... contrition. It confused her. Finally she said, "The other thing I wanted to say is, I've spoken to someone in the psychiatry department, Dr. Edelman, and she's agreed to meet with you."

Over the years Allegra had often pushed for therapy—for Stavros on his own, for the two of them as a couple, and once for the three of them as a family. But in each instance Stavros had resisted, citing all sorts of reasons: He was too busy. There really wasn't a problem. Therapy is a racket. Etcetera.

Now, though, he was ready to concede. He was ready to concede to anything. Were she to demand that he give up drinking and begin training for the Boston Marathon, he would say, "I'll start tomorrow." Were she to hand him a contract transferring all of his worldly assets to the charity of her choice, he would say, "Where do I sign?" Yes, she was right. About everything. He would do as she wished … But then he heard himself say, "I don't know."

"Why not?" she said, re-folding her arms.

"Look, I know I need to fix some things. That's becoming very clear."

"Well, listen to this—maybe you really did meet Jesus."

"Why do you have to be so sarcastic?"

She looked away, shaking her head in frustration. Then, after a calming breath she said, "Stavros, you're going to be out of work for at least a month. Why not take advantage of that and use the time to talk to someone? Seriously, do you want to be lonely and depressed for the rest of your life?"

"I'm not depressed," he said defensively.

"*Oh my God*," she said, rolling her eyes.

"And I'm not lonely!"

"Oh really, is that right? OK. Name five friends. And that doesn't include bartenders or people from college you haven't talked to in twenty years."

"Always mocking. You can't resist, can you?"

"Go on! Five friends."

He gave it some thought. Then he gave it some more thought.

"OK, make it three," she said with a smirk.

Apart from Keller, Stavros had nothing, and it was humiliating. Angered, ashamed, he fired back, "Look, I don't need a shrink, OK? I can fix this on my own."

"Fine. You do that. Enjoy the rest of your life." She turned and marched out of the room.

* * *

Five days later Stavros learned that he was being released from the hospital. It was exciting news, but also somewhat distressing. Hospital policy required that he be accompanied by an adult at checkout, but whom could he ask? Certainly not Allegra. She would say, "Why not ask one of your friends?" As for Keller, it was a workday, and thus out of the question. Unthinkable. So Stavros called his secretary.

When she arrived, he was sitting in a chair by the window, half asleep, enjoying the late-morning sun on his back.

"Wow, look at you—are you meditating?"

Stavros opened his eyes. Ida, entering the room, was holding a stuffed duffel bag. She had come to visit him several days earlier, on New Year's Day, and had even brought two gifts: a box of chocolates and a book on meditation and stress reduction. Stavros had eaten the chocolates, but the book remained unopened.

"Hello Ida. No, not meditating; just resting."

She came closer, gazing at him. "You know, you really look different. I noticed it last time too. Your face is thinner, less bloated. And your eyes seem clearer somehow. Brighter. I have to say, sobriety suits you."

Stavros just smiled. Late twenties, brunette, and bespectacled—her glasses frames were shaped like cat's eyes—Ida Findelton was something of an enigma to him. She was sharp-witted and well-paid, but had a peculiar taste in clothes. Today she wore oversize pink earmuffs and a hip-length coat made of whitish fur, now yellowed and matted, that could only have come from a secondhand store. At the office she wore strange shoes and outfits that looked like something out of *Mad Men*, 1960s prints and cuts, half stylish, half nerdy, and on her bicep she sported a tattoo of Popeye the Sailor. Her boyfriend was the bass player of a punk-funk-country band called the Stinkpots, and she herself was a poet. She had a master's degree from a famous school in Iowa or Idaho —Stavros could never remember which—and had already published one book, which Keller said showed lots of promise, and which Stavros had yet to finish, though he had told her that he "really loved it."

Regardless, Stavros liked Ida, and of course it didn't hurt that she seemed to like him back. They'd been together for three years now, which for Stavros was a personal best. Prior to Ida, he had gone through an average of two secretaries per year. Unlike the others, Ida could handle his mood swings and gruff manner, and had no problem, professionally speaking, ordering his home groceries, keeping his office stocked with scotch and chewing gum, and buying birthday and Christmas presents for his son, all in addition to performing her actual job duties, which she did very well.

"Here you go," she said, holding out the duffel bag. "Though I think I prefer the johnny."

Stavros was still in his hospital getup, with his arms and calves—flabby, hairy, and very white—on full display. He had decided not to wear the clothes from Christmas day—the death clothes—and had asked Ida to get some things from his apartment.

"Thanks for doing this," he said.

"No problem."

She left the room and Stavros changed. It felt good to lose the johnny and put on his own clothes, made him feel like this hospital nightmare was finally over. He stuffed the shirt, khakis, and everything else from Christmas day into the trash, then gave the room a final look-over. In truth, part of him had been dreading going home, going back to that empty apartment. But no more. Stavros was ready to leave. He was ready to get back to it.

FIVE

They were in Ida's car, racing into Boston. She drove an old Chipmunk hatchback, with dents and body rust that reminded Stavros of the shitbox he'd owned back in law school. In the cup-holder was a coffee mug filled with lipstick-stained cigarette butts, and hanging from the rearview mirror was a foot-long hula girl figurine, complete with grass skirt and naked breasts, the tips of which were covered by a red lei. Ida didn't explain, and Stavros didn't ask.

Instead he took in the scenery along Soldiers Field Road: the river, the boat houses, the brick dormitories. It was great to be outside, away from the hospital. Stavros felt liberated, energized, joyful even. But immersed in the heavy traffic, connected once again to the bustle of city life, he was soon reminded of his pre-Christmas worries.

"How are things at the office?" he said.

"Busy," Ida said. "Newt Bellingham was in this morning."

Newt Bellingham was the son of Republican senator Claiborne "Clay" Bellingham of Pennsylvania. A twenty-three-year-old Thaxter College graduate, he was accused of date-raping a then seventeen-year-old girl in JFK Park, outside of Harvard Square, following a house party the previous May. Bellingham had been in Cambridge to visit a friend, and had already returned to the Thaxter campus in Vermont when he was picked up by police several days after the incident. The accuser, known in the press as the "unnamed victim" due to her having been a minor at the time of the alleged crime, was a local high school student named Aimee Gibblin. She was also, as it turned out, the daughter of five-term Cambridge city councillor Colin Gibblin. The young woman had gone to the party with two friends but had returned home alone several hours later, disheveled and disoriented. Her mother questioned her (the parents were divorced), then took her to Mt. Adams Hospital. An initial exam revealed light bruising on both wrists and semen stains on her underwear. A rape kit was collected, and blood tests came back positive for alcohol and cocaine. Questioned by police, Gibblin said she'd been forced into sex, but when asked as to where and by whom, she told a number of conflicting stories. At first she claimed the rape occurred at a party at a friend's house, but that she didn't know the boy's name— he was "just some guy." But when asked for the name of the friend who had hosted the party, Gibblin said the party actually took place at a different house, and that she wasn't sure where this other house was, only that it was "near the high school." The more police questioned her, the less credible her story became. Days later the girl finally admitted all the facts as she knew them, including the identity of her assailant: Newt Bellingham. She hadn't told the truth at first, Gibblin claimed, because her mother had forbidden her from going to college parties.

For his part, Bellingham denied any knowledge of the accuser. But when presented with video evidence that proved otherwise, he admitted to having met the young woman at the party and also to having had sex with her in JFK Park. But the sex, he maintained, was consensual. He was then extradited to Massachusetts and charged in Cambridge District Court with several offenses: rape, rape of a minor, battery of a minor, administration of illegal drugs to a minor. Bail was set at one million dollars, and Bellingham was back on the street the same day. He completed his final exams and graduated that June. In August, at his arraignment in Cambridge, Bellingham pleaded not guilty to all charges. In November, a grand jury determined that the Middlesex County District Attorney had sufficient evidence to indict Newt Bellingham on all counts. The trial was set for February.

"What do you think of Bellingham?" Stavros said.

Ida gave him a startled, questioning look. At the office it was no secret that many of their clients were guilty as charged. But this was never discussed. Ever.

"It's just between us," Stavros said.

Ida hesitated, and Stavros reassured her it was OK.

With a sigh she said, "*Allll right,*" drawling her words in a tone that seemed to say, "You asked for it": "I think he's a smug, arrogant shit, and he obviously raped that girl. He got her drunk, gave her drugs, then raped her. He did it, and everybody knows he did it. He should be castrated."

Now Stavros sighed. When he'd first met Bellingham, back in May, Stavros himself had been repelled by the kid; he presented as affable and courteous, but it was the sham courtesy of the prep-school prima donna, phony and superior. To young Bellingham, Stavros and Keller were the hired help and the charges against him an inconvenient matter that had to be dealt with, like having a tooth drilled. Stavros had known guys like this in college, and he didn't like them. In fact, they kind of pissed him off. But as Keller always said, they weren't paid to like their clients; they were paid to keep them out of jail. And for fifteen-hundred an hour, the fee for Bellingham's defense, it was easy to put aside any personal feelings.

* * *

On Tremont Street, busy with the usual crush of traffic and pedestrians—taxis, buses, students, tourists, professionals, the homeless—Ida pulled up to the front of Stavros's building. In her pink earmuffs and cat's-eyes glasses she turned to him and said, "It just occurred to me that you probably don't have any food. Should I order some things?"

Looking at her, Stavros felt a pang, a sudden weakness in his chest. Ida could be cheeky and irreverent, and certainly Stavros found her entertaining. But she was also a kind and generous soul. A thoughtful, considerate soul. And it struck him, as if for the first time, that over the past three years Ida had served him, literally served him, day after day. Whatever Stavros asked of her—work the weekend, stay late, come in early, do this, do that—she always did it, willingly and without complaint. Yet had he ever acknowledged this, or shown his appreciation? Had he ever offered to do anything for *her?*

"Are you OK?" she said. "You look … sad."

"No, I'm fine. I'm just tired."

"Do you want me to go up with you? I could take your bag."

"No, no."

"What about the groceries?"

Stavros refused, then became flustered. Should he thank Ida for her three years of service? Apologize for his three years of ingratitude? No, it would be … awkward. Awkward and embarrassing. Instead he reached for his money clip, peeled off a fifty, and held it out to her.

"What are you doing?" she said.

"For the ride, and getting my clothes."

"Put that away."

But Stavros insisted, and finally she accepted.

"So when are you coming back to work?" she said.

"In about a month."

Ida smiled, skeptically. But she only said, "OK. Well let me know if you need anything. And take care of yourself, all right?"

* * *

Stavros's apartment—two-thousand-square-feet of luxury living space, twenty-seven floors high in the sky—overlooked Boston and beyond. From the windows you could see the Common, the State House, and across the river clear into Cambridge. Inside, the place was filled with expensive stuff. Furniture from trendy South End showrooms, art from a Newbury Street gallery, top-of-the-line entertainment equipment. The apartment was meant to dazzle, to make people say "Wow!" And on those rare occasions when Stavros did have a guest, the place never failed to impress.

Yet as he walked into the living room, tossing duffel bag and coat onto the sofa, Stavros became aware of a peculiar feeling. Taking everything in—the sexy view, the expensive stuff—he felt … bothered somehow. Vaguely unsettled. What was this, he wondered? He didn't know.

He went down to his bedroom. When he'd last been here, Christmas morning, the place was a disaster. Cast-off clothes on the floor, dirty dishes and empty bottles on the nightstand, DVD cases strewn on the bureau. Now the room was immaculate. The cleaning lady had seen to that. Satisfied everything was in order, he headed to the kitchen.

Opening the fridge, Stavros saw that Ida had spoken correctly: he was out of food. There was some milk and a carton of eggs, both past their expiration date; a half-empty jar of pickles; and some leftover takeout pad thai, which he'd bought on Christmas Eve. Then his eye alit on a salami, tucked into one of the shelves in the refrigerator door. His mood perked up, and the saliva kicked in, moistening his mouth. But Stavros held back. During his hospital stay a dietitian had lectured him on the life-threatening qualities of red meat, processed foods, and saturated fats —essentially, all the stuff that Stavros liked to eat. The dietitian wanted him to switch to a plant-based diet of fruits, nuts, vegetables, and whole grains, with occasional servings of fish and poultry. The bacon, sausage, steak, and ice cream—the four pillars of the Stavros diet—had to go. Stavros had said he would do his best.

But not today, he thought. Maybe tomorrow. He reached for the salami, cut off a hunk, and started chomping. It was delicious. Reveling in the salty-fatty goodness, he spotted the McLagan 25 on the breakfast bar—Keller's Christmas present. Instantly, Stavros was hit by desire, his knees going weak. He looked at the clock on the stove: 2:06. A little early for a pop. Normally, unless there was some stressful event to deal with, like a holiday visit to his family, he held off till seven, eight p.m., depending on the day. Yet today *wasn't* a normal day, was it? He had just been released from the hospital, having survived a major heart attack, a coma, and countless disgusting "heart-healthy" meals. Surely he had earned the right to a quick snifter, no? A tiny tipple? But then Stavros recalled his final meeting with Dr. Martìnez. In plain English the doctor had warned Stavros: either cut back on the alcohol or risk another heart attack and an early death. A glass of red wine at night was fine, but continued abuse of the hard stuff would be fatal. It was that simple.

Fine, Stavros thought. He could wait. Till six. Or five. He took another bite of salami, and as he chewed, the thought hit him: what was he going to do for the rest of the day? And what was he going to do tomorrow? And the day after that?

All his life Stavros had been a worker. His father had seen to that, forcing the boy to put in regular hours at the pizza shop from age eight. In those days Stavros stocked the soda cooler, cleaned the toilets, swept the floor. He was always moving, doing something useful; and if he wasn't, his father would chastise him for being lazy. "There are no free rides in this family," the old man would growl in his thick accent. And so Stavros worked. And thanks to his mother, who'd always insisted that her boy would go to college, he worked even harder at school. He might not have been as cultured or as learned as his peers, but no one worked harder than Stavros. He was no slacker. And if he wasn't working, there could be problems. With his law practice he liked nothing more than a challenging case, one that consumed him, kept him going sixteen, eighteen hours a day. Such cases exhilarated him, gave him focus. But once the case ended, once the adrenaline-rush had passed, the blues weren't far behind.

Again he checked the clock: 2:11. Anxiety swept over him. Maybe he should call Keller. Just to check in. Just to see what's going on. But part of Stavros recoiled at the idea. Part of him wasn't ready to deal with the firm. Not yet.

So what to do?

He honed in on the McLagan. *Yes.* Yes indeed. He got a tumbler and poured out a good splash. This was prime whiskey, some of Scotland's finest. The *good* good stuff, aged twenty-five years. He stuck his nose in the glass and inhaled: the aroma was magical, a potent promise of full-body bliss. The fact was, Stavros loved scotch. If it were a woman, he would propose to her. If it were a man, he would ask him to be his best buddy. Though come to think of it, scotch pretty much was Stavros's best buddy. After Keller. Though sometimes Stavros felt closer to the booze.

He tipped the glass back and luxuriated in that lovely, lovely burn—wow, amazing! He'd tried the 25 before, but this batch seemed extra special. Perhaps it was because Stavros hadn't had a drink in almost two weeks. Immediately he could feel the narcotic calm, the alcohol's tingly comfort, spreading through his body. *Oh yeah!* Another taste. Even better. Fantastic!

Spirits rising, Stavros thought everything was going to be OK. His problems, his worries—everything was going to be fine. Though the 25 was meant for savoring, for bringing out on special occasions—it went for a grand a bottle—Stavros couldn't resist a little more. Just a touch.

Nights after work he would come into the living room with his drink and stand before the windows, gazing across the Charles in the direction of his old home in Cambridge. It was a sort of habit. But now, looking in the vicinity of Champney Street, Stavros thought not about Allegra and the failure of their love, but about the failure of his body on Christmas day and the improbable journey that followed. Allegra thought the experience had taken place in his head; and Keller seemed to think Stavros was *out* of his head … Were they right? *Had* Stavros suffered a hallucination? Or worse—was he bonkers? It was possible. People hallucinate and go crazy all time. What makes him so special? But no, Stavros thought; the experience had been too real. In heaven he had experienced an unfathomable love. A boundless love. Never before had he felt so accepted, so contented, so fulfilled. How could *that* be imagined? Or invented? And more than this, Stavros had learned that he'd not been a good man; that he'd been a *bad* man. It was undeniable, irrefutable, for he had *seen* it, in his life review. He had seen what a selfish, pushy, greedy, uncaring bastard he had been. And so the question wasn't just, Did the experience really happen? It was also, How was he going to make up for all the wrong he had done? All the hurts and sorrows he had inflicted on Allegra, his son, and countless other people. *Atonement.* Was such a thing even possible for someone like him?

Sure, Jesus forgave Stavros—but what about everyone else?

Regardless, he knew that his life had been fundamentally altered, and it scared him, vexed him. "Love everyone and forgive everything," Jesus had told him. That was the takeaway. And yes, it sounds good. But what does it mean, really? It's an abstraction. A cliché. Something for books and Sunday sermons. But what about the rest of the week, Monday through Saturday? Because real life was different. On the street, abstractions were for suckers. Life is hard, Stavros knew, and the only way you get ahead is by beating the next guy. That's just how it goes.

He knocked back the rest of his drink and decided another wouldn't kill him. He poured out a double. The fact was, he didn't want to think about God anymore. It was too confusing, too stressful. To be honest, he didn't want to think about anything.

He settled into his stylish-but-uncomfortable sofa and put his feet up on the designer coffee table that you weren't supposed to put your feet on because it might break. With the remote control Stavros clicked on the TV, seeking distraction. He went through the channels, but it was just garbage, all of it—the idiotic commercials, the dimwit talking heads, the insipid dramas. He scrolled through the on-demand movie selections, but nothing interested. Maybe a little porn?

And all the while he sipped from his glass. Sip, sip, sip. Yet still there was that nagging thought. It was like a continuous whisper in his head, a haunting refrain: he had experienced the divine, and from now on nothing would be the same. It was confounding, disturbing, even terrifying. So Stavros drank, putting away one glass after another until, at last, everything went black.

* * *

The next morning he woke in pain. Head pain, body pain, everything pain. He called his go-to breakfast delivery place then staggered into the kitchen to make coffee. Soon the guy arrived with the bulging plastic bag. At the breakfast bar Stavros opened the styrofoam container and released a glorious aroma. Fried eggs, home fries, white toast, and yes, bacon and sausage. A man had to live, he thought. He would start the healthy diet … soon. Right now, he needed some pleasure, some palate euphorics. He covered the eggs and home fries with a good amount of salt and went in for his first taste. Amazing! He hadn't had food like this since before his heart attack. Relishing each greasy bite, he wolfed it all down and wiped up the last bits of yolk with his butter-drenched toast. Perfect, just what he needed. Already he felt better.

But then came the dreaded question: what was he going to do all day? Certainly not hang around here. He'd be tanked by noon!

* * *

With a brisk, springy gait, a happy-to-be-back gait, Stavros entered the Pell Building on Arlington Street, one block from the Public Garden. He passed through the lobby, exchanged a cheery greeting with the guy at the security desk, and stepped into one of the elevators. For Stavros, this felt like home. When he'd first joined up with Keller thirteen years earlier, Keller already had offices in the building. But as the firm continued to expand they acquired additional space and knocked down a few walls. Keller, Papadakis & Associates now employed fifteen people total. Officially Keller was managing partner, though Stavros did most of the actual managing. He hired and fired the associates and kept tabs on all current cases. The two partners each had their own clients and caseloads, but for the blockbuster trials—the ones that drew the national media—they teamed up. Of course Stavros always took second chair, but he was fine with it. Keller loved the limelight, whereas Stavros preferred grinding it out behind the scenes. Keller's charisma and brilliance drew the big names, and Stavros's tenacity and hard work ensured they won in court.

Exiting the elevator on the seventh floor, Stavros strode buoyantly toward the Keller, Papadakis reception area, visible behind a glass wall with two glass doors. The startled receptionist stood as he entered, her face creasing with surprise. "Mr. Papadakis … how are you?"

"Never better, Michelle," he said with a smile as he swept past her. "And how are you?"

"I'm OK," she called out, watching him go. "Welcome back!"

As Stavros approached his office, Ida looked up from her computer.

"Has it been a month already?" she said.

"Well … I just thought I'd check in."

"Actually, you won me lunch."

"Lunch?"

"Katie and I had a bet." Katie was Keller's secretary. "She said you'd be in next week; I said this week."

"Congratulations," Stavros said. He asked for his messages, and Ida held out a stack of paper notes. There were at least a hundred. Maybe more. Stavros quaked, looking at the notes as though Ida were offering him a scorpion, its tail raised for a strike. "Forget I asked," he said, now in a panic as he turned for his office.

"Oh, and Marty Dolloff just called," Ida said.

Stavros froze. "When?"

"About five minutes ago. You just missed him."

"What did you say?"

"I said you'd been in a coma for a week—what's a few extra days?— and that you'd be out for at least two months, maybe three, and that he could call back then." Ida grinned, looking both amused and pleased at how artful she was at protecting her boss's backside.

Without a word Stavros went into his office and shut the door.

* * *

The place was just as he'd left it on Christmas Eve: The desk cluttered with notes and documents and food-stained takeout menus. The numerous archive boxes stacked willy-nilly on the floor and against the walls. The shelves of rarely consulted law books that were there mostly for display. And the handful of mementos from grateful clients, including a stuffed parrot and a football signed by a famous linebacker whom

Stavros had successfully defended against an attempted murder charge. Here, in this familiar space, surrounded by familiar things, Stavros had been hoping to find some solace, to find some peace. But it wasn't to be. Standing in the center of the room, still in his overcoat, he was gripped by growing anxiety, his stomach writhing, his hands sweating.

* * *

Marty Dolloff, who headed up the Massachusetts Legal and Judicial Ethics Board, had spent ten years as an ADA in the Suffolk County District Attorney's office prosecuting white collar crimes. Now he was going after corrupt lawyers and judges. A month earlier he had sent Stavros an "informal request" that he appear before the Ethics Board to provide closed-door testimony regarding a Judge Arthur Zanger. Because the Ethics Board was solely an administrative body, lacking prosecutorial powers, it was easy to disregard such "informal" requests. However, many of the cases investigated by the Ethics Board were later taken up by the DA's office. Dolloff himself had opened files that had led to the eventual prosecutions of a number of high-ranking persons, including corporate attorneys, state prosecutors, and even an appellate justice of the Massachusetts Appeals Court. Regardless, Stavros wanted nothing to do with the Ethics Board. Why? Because several years earlier Stavros had blackmailed Judge Zanger.

At the time, Zanger was presiding over a case that Stavros was likely going to lose, and because Stavros did not want to lose he'd decided to go after the judge. It wasn't difficult to do. For years there'd been rumors that Zanger was a drunk with a gambling problem and that one time he had even "sold a verdict." Stavros, through various channels available to him, and for a certain fee, obtained material proof of the judge's malfeasance. At the outset of the trial Stavros met with Zanger in his chambers, presented the incriminating evidence, and told the judge what he wanted. Stavros won the case.

What Stavros feared now was that Zanger possibly had named names, or that someone close to Zanger had named names, and that Dolloff's real motive in asking Stavros to appear before the Ethics Board was not merely to investigate Zanger but to investigate Stavros as well. In fact, that was precisely what Stavros suspected. Dolloff was onto him, and this was his first move.

Now, as he stood in his office, Stavros shuddered, cringing as an inner voice whispered, Shyster … *shyster!*

Yes, it was true—Stavros couldn't deny it. In addition to the blackmail, he had bribed a juror and paid off a cop. He had illegally obtained evidence, more than once, and had regularly accepted off-the-books payments from clients. Stavros had safety deposit boxes at a number of Boston banks filled with diamonds and cash, gold and silver ingots, jewelry and antique watches. He even had a hand-written letter by Abraham Lincoln.

Oddly, or so it seemed to him now, Stavros had never thought of himself as a crooked lawyer. He had considered himself a guy who did what had to be done. A guy who knew that life wasn't black and white, but was gray. Moral absolutes? Those were for kids. Kids and taxpayers. In Stavros's world, the *real* world, morality, ethics, even legality, were situational. And so when opportunities presented themselves, Stavros made the most of them, and did so with a clean conscience. Blackmailing Judge Zanger? The guy was bent, on the take, and everyone knew it. He had it coming! Bribing a juror? It meant Stavros would keep his client out of jail, which was what he was paid to do. It was his job! Accepting illicit payments? Hey, the government had its hands deep enough in his pockets as it was. He was owed this!

But now, how abhorrent it was! How abhorrent to Stavros his crimes and his rationales, his self-righteous excuses. For a decade-plus he had lied to himself and to other people, hiding the true nature of his deeds, his words, his character. But there had been no hiding in the afterlife. In the bright light of heaven Stavros had revisited all of his lawyerly sins. Each one of them. And they had revolted him, just as the memory of them revolted him now—Stavros the shyster!

A knock came at the door, and Keller stuck his head in. "Stavros? What are you doing?"

Disgusted with himself, disgusted with the man he had been, Stavros just stared at his friend.

Keller came into the office. "Everything OK?"

"Yeah, I ... just wanted to check in."

"It's a bit soon for that, don't you think?"

Stavros was struggling. Quite frankly, part of him wanted to leave, get his sorry ass home and hit the booze. But another part of him felt like this was where he belonged. This was *his* firm. *He* had helped make this place! "How are things going with Bellingham?"

"Buddy, everything's fine. We had the kid in yesterday, along with some of the senator's staff. I wanted them to meet Sal. It went well. There's nothing to worry about."

"Do you think you guys could bring me up to speed?"

"We just had the morning meeting, Stavros."

"Just five minutes. A quick sit-down."

"OK," Keller said, relenting. "Let me see if Sal's free. I'll meet you in the conference room."

* * *

"Ooooh! Boss, it's great to see you!"

Stavros, the first to arrive in the conference room, had been gazing out the window. Turning around, he saw Sal Mahony, one of the firm's associates. Beaming joyously, and looking as though he were greeting a favorite but long-lost uncle, Sal came up and gave Stavros's hand a good shake. Then he downshifted, his thousand-watt enthusiasm fading to sorrowful concern. With deep feeling he said, "We were so worried. You gave us quite the scare."

This, of course, was complete horseshit. Sal, like all of Stavros's other employees, save Ida, hadn't called or visited him in the hospital. Nor had Sal sent flowers or even an email. Yet rather than point any of this out, as he formerly would have, Stavros said nothing. Instead he was recalling, once again, his time in heaven. There, Stavros had watched himself abuse and mistreat Sal. In this very room, in morning meetings in front of the entire team, Stavros had referred to Sal as "Vinny Gambini," after the lawyer in *My Cousin Vinny*, and had regularly hollered at Sal, browbeating him for minor slipups and threatening to fire his "fat ass." Stavros had mocked, ridiculed, and humiliated Sal, and had done it in a very public way. It was shameful, inexcusable. Why had he done it? What had he been thinking?

But before Stavros could respond, Keller entered the room. Grinning as he came, he said, "Next time you feel like calling in sick, Sal, you just remember Stavros here. Two weeks ago he's in a coma, and today he's back and ready to bill some clients."

Keller took his usual seat, at the head of the long table, and Stavros took his usual seat, to Keller's right; Sal sat to Keller's left. Wasting no time, Keller promptly summarized the previous day's meeting, naming the attendees and reviewing the main talking points. For Stavros, it proved nothing of interest.

"What else is new?" he said. "Anything?"

Sal smiled, slyly, then explained that Dickie Haggerty, the firm's private investigator, had "bagged a granny." A year prior to the alleged rape Aimee Gibblin had been hospitalized for depression, spending several weeks at the Belmont Clinic—something that was already public knowledge. What wasn't known, previously, was that while in group therapy sessions Gibblin had admitted to regular cocaine use since age fifteen. This was significant because, from the outset, the prosecution had maintained that the girl had only ever taken cocaine once in her life: the night of the alleged crime, when, it was claimed, Gibblin had been given the drug by Newt Bellingham.

"How did Dickie find this?" Stavros said.

"He tracked down Gibblin's roommate from the clinic, and with a little financial encouragement, the girl told him about the group sessions. She's also willing to testify." Sal beamed, gloating with satisfaction.

"We *can't* do that," Stavros said. "Those meetings must be protected."

"No. Gibblin and the witness talked about the coke outside the meetings too," Sal said. "Apparently they even tried to smuggle some blow into the clinic. They wanted to have a little party in their room." The sly smile returned.

Stavros looked doubtful.

"What?" Sal said.

"I don't like it."

"What's not to like?"

"It's not ... I just don't like it."

"What do you mean?"

"We're talking about a teenage girl, Sal. A kid."

"*So?*" Sal said, his face scrunching with confusion.

"*So*—this could ruin her."

"*Ruin her?* ... Are you shitting me?"

Stavros wasn't.

Incredulous, Sal turned to Keller, but Keller stayed out of it. To Stavros, Sal said, "But boss, that's our strategy—*going after Gibblin!* And you're the one who initiated it when this thing first came in, back in May! *You* did!"

"Look," Stavros said, "this is nothing. It won't change a thing."

"*What are you talking about?*" Sal cried, nearly rising from his seat. "Once Donelly finds out we got this, we might not even go to trial—you know that!" Donelly was Niall Donelly, the Middlesex County District Attorney, the lead prosecutor in the case.

"And I'm telling you, Sal, that's not going to happen!" Stavros roared back, struggling to match Sal's intensity with some of his own. "Donelly's been waiting his entire life for this case. If he puts that kid away, Senator Bellingham's son, he'll be a national hero. There's no way in hell he's going to pass on this."

"But boss," Sal said, now trying heroically to restrain himself, "think about what you're saying ... Even if you are right, which I don't think you are, but even if we announce this witness and we still go to trial, it will help us in court. And as I see it, right now we need all the help we can get."

"That's not true," Stavros said, but with little conviction. "We've got a strong case."

Again Sal turned to Keller. He was like a child looking to his father, expecting daddy to intervene and make everything right. But Keller, looking tired and dispirited, only said, "OK, Sal. That's enough. Thank you."

Sal opened his mouth, thought better of it, then left the room, shaking his head.

"What's going on, Stavros?" Keller said. "What are you thinking?"

Stavros had lowered his gaze. He didn't want to see Keller's eyes, didn't want to see his disappointment. "I don't know," he said. But Stavros did know. Aimee Gibblin possibly had been raped, and already her mental-health issues were public knowledge, and so to now release her drug problems on top of everything else seemed ... wrong. It seemed cruel. But part of Stavros couldn't believe he would think such a thing. *Wrong? Cruel?* Are you kidding? That was his *job!* To attack the other side! To destroy his opponent and win the case! He shut his eyes. What was happening to him? Was he losing his mind? "Maybe I came back too soon," he said.

"I think that's it," Keller said. "I think a month of rest and you'll be fine. It's going to take some time, Stavros. You had quite the scare." He patted Stavros on the shoulder, adding, "I've got to get going. Listen to me, buddy. Everything will be fine. I'll call you soon."

SIX

The days passed and Stavros suffered. He learned that misery can surprise you. You think you can't feel any worse, but the next day proves that you can. Holed up in his apartment he brooded and drank, ordering in food and booze. At night he couldn't sleep and during the day he couldn't stay awake. He forgot to shave, he forgot to shower, he forgot to change his underpants. He canceled the maid service. He was too embarrassed to have a stranger see him in this state. As a result, the dishes piled up, the trash overflowed, and the place began to smell.

Stavros was relieved to be away from the office, but staying home day after day was killing him. To distract himself he watched movies. Since his split with Allegra he had become a late-night cinephile. Winding down after work he liked to get into bed with a drink and roll a flick. He'd bought two-hundred-plus DVDs over the past several years, and watched films in phases. He'd had his noir phase. His Western phase. His 1970s classics phase. His Kurosawa phase. His Tarkovsky phase. And currently he was in his Italian phase. He had already gone through films by Rossellini, Visconti, and Fellini, and was now going through De Sica.

Stavros loved De Sica. The stories were real, and moving. At the end of *Bicycle Thieves*, when little Bruno cries out "Papa!" as his bicycle-thief father is caught red-handed by an angry mob, Stavros had burst into tears. He couldn't bear the kid's anguish—it was too much! And at the end of *The Children Are Watching Us*, the tears had flowed yet again. When the mother who had abandoned four-year-old Pricò comes to the orphanage to visit him, the child refuses to hug her and instead turns and walks off, alone, getting smaller and smaller as the sad music plays —oh, how Stavros had wept! Hot tears spilling down his cheeks, snot running from his nose!

Of course the sorrows of these little boys reminded Stavros of the sorrows of his own little boy. Since his return from the hospital Stavros had tried repeatedly to contact his son. He wanted to talk to Brendan. He wanted to see him and make amends. But when Stavros called, Brendan wouldn't pick up. Stavros left messages, but the boy wouldn't call back.

Finally, after a week of drunkenness and despair, a week of isolation and total hygienic collapse, Stavros decided to change course. He was, after all, a pragmatist. He phoned Allegra and, as expected, she didn't pick up. He called several more times and at last she answered.

"What do you want?" she snapped.

"I'm calling about Brendan … He's not answering my calls."

No response.

"I'm trying to connect with him, Allegra, and I thought … maybe you could help."

No response.

"Is there any way I can fix this? Any way at all? … *Hello?* Are you there?"

"Yes."

"Why aren't you talking?"

"Because part of me wants to kill you right now."

"Why?"

"*Why?* You blow him off all these years and suddenly you want to 'connect with him'? Be a father? It doesn't work that way Stavros. You've lost that privilege."

In the past this is where Stavros would have erupted. This is where he would have attacked, yelling and calling names. But now, very calmly, he said, "You're right. I agree. I've lost the privilege. But I still want to try. I called him to go to the Celtics but he never called back."

"*Oh my God,*" Allegra said. "You think taking him to a Celtics game is going to change anything? A nice night out with Dad? 'Thank you, see you again in ten years'? Give me a break. He's not stupid Stavros. He's learned his lesson."

"It's a start, Allegra. It would be something."

Silence.

Stavros said, "Is there anything I can do for him? Does he need anything? A computer? A bike?"

Allegra scoffed. "So typical," she said bitterly. "So typical. If there's a problem, just pull out the money clip. Peel off a few hundreds. That's your answer to everything."

"Allegra, this is why I called. Because I don't know what to do. I want your advice."

"You want my advice, Stavros? I'll give you some advice. Why don't you do some real parenting for once in your life? How 'bout that Daddy?"

"Why are you so mad? I don't under—"

"You're out of work for what, another month?"

Stavros didn't like the sound of that. "More or less."

"OK, then you can start driving him to school. I've been doing it forever. It's just one of, oh, a hundred other responsibilities I have. Working, cooking, shopping, going to games—you have no idea!"

Stavros calculated what this would entail: he would have to wake up very early, fight the morning-rush traffic over to Cambridge, then to the school, and then back into Boston. Doing this just once would suck. But every day, for a month? … But yes, of course; this was a chance for him to help out. And more than that, there was the boy. "I'd be happy to do it. What time do I pick him up?"

"Seven a.m. And that means seven a.m."

"Right."

"Not quarter past, not ten past, not five past—"

"I'll be there."

* * *

The following morning, at 6:44 a.m., Stavros pulled into the driveway on Champney Street. The car's headlights cut through the gray dawn and shone on the garage doors. Shifting into park but keeping the engine running, Stavros considered tooting the horn to let them know he was here. But that wasn't necessary.

From inside the house, up on the second floor in what once had been their bedroom, Allegra drew aside a curtain. Framed in a rectangle of light she peered down at Stavros, her expression neutral, sphinxlike. For five, ten seconds she stared at him, and all the while he stared back, meeting her eye.

Then the curtain swung down, and she vanished.

* * *

Fifteen minutes later, as a fiery orange glow appeared over the eastern horizon, Brendan emerged from the house. Lugging a backpack and what appeared to be a trumpet case, he trudged down the porch steps and moped to the car. With a glum, weary expression, he passed around the front of the Imperator to the passenger side, opened the rear door, chucked his stuff on the backseat, then got in the front. He said nothing.

Cautious yet hopeful, Stavros said, "Good morning Brendan … How we doin'?"

"OK," the boy said, avoiding eye contact as he put on his seatbelt.

"You ready to go to school?" Stavros said, still hopeful.

"*I guess*," Brendan said, bristling with irritation.

Stavros sighed, then said, "Brendan, about the last time I saw you … At the hospital …"

Still refusing to look at his father, the kid was now gazing straight ahead, at the garage.

"I'm sorry I lied to you," Stavros went on. "About your presents. I really regret that."

Brendan's face tensed.

"And I'm sorry about a lot of other things—"

"*Dad*, were gonna be late."

"OK," Stavros said.

"And just so you know, Mom's making me do this."

Stavros nodded. "Understood." He backed out of the driveway.

"And don't forget to pick up Sally," the boy added.

"What?"

"We have to pick up Sally French. Didn't Mom tell you?"

"No. She didn't."

"Well, we do. Mrs. French picks us up after school."

Stavros forced a smile, a patient-parent smile. "That's fine. Where does she live?"

"On Alden."

"Where's that?"

"Drive toward Kirkland."

Stavros drove toward Kirkland.

At the stop sign Brendan said, "Go straight and take a left on Cambridge."

As Stavros did this the boy took out his phone and started typing a text. He sent the text, then waited for a response. Then he started typing again. Minutes passed, and the texting continued.

When they turned onto Alden the boy said, "It's right up here, after this house."

There was no place for Stavros to pull over; parked cars lined the street. "Where do I go?"

"Right here. Just stop."

Stavros stopped.

"You have to beep."

Stavros beeped.

The house, a two-family, was close to the sidewalk. It had a porch but no yard. One of the front doors opened and out came a girl of about Brendan's age. She had blond hair and wore a newsboy cap. She skipped down the steps and loped to the car, carrying a backpack and a case similar to Brendan's. She tossed her things on the backseat, slid herself in, and flashed a vibrant smile. "Hey Mr. Papadakis!"

Stavros was delighted. They hadn't met before but the girl acted as though they had known each other for years, and that she actually liked Stavros. It certainly was a warmer welcome than he'd gotten from his own kid. "It's nice to meet you, Sally."

"Same here!"

A horn blared from behind. Stavros was blocking the road.

"*Dad*, you gotta get going," Brendan hissed.

Stavros turned back to the wheel and sped off. It was now light out and the morning traffic was picking up.

Brendan said, "You know how to get there from here, right?"

Stavros did. And as he drove, both kids focused on their phones. Sally too was texting. Stavros said not a word.

* * *

At Thoreau, there were no yellow school buses. Instead there was a long line of cars and SUVs, all luxury jobs, waiting to pull up to the main building. Stavros joined the queue.

"We can get out here," Brendan said, opening the door and stepping out.

Sally, grabbing her things, said, "Thanks Mr. Papadakis, it was great to meet you!"

Stavros smiled, feeling his mood lighten. A little. "Same here Sally. You have a good day."

"You too!"

She got out, and then Brendan reached in for his stuff.

"OK Brendan," Stavros said, "you have a good—"

The kid slammed the door, turned away, and joined the flow of students heading into the school.

* * *

Stavros was back in his apartment by 8:30, and by 8:45, after he'd eaten a hunk of salami, he began to feel uneasy. What was he going to do for the rest of the day? He hadn't a clue, and immediately he became distressed. You should be at work, the inner voice said. Because that's what a man does—he works! You should be at the office or in a courtroom, billing clients and winning trials. Making money!

But Stavros wasn't ready to return to the office. Quite frankly, the thought of it repulsed him.

Angsty and restless, he went over to the windows and looked down at the grand panorama of Boston. There it was, one of the world's great cities, laid out like a giant tray filled with choice hors d'oeuvres, waiting for him to load up his plate. Was there anything out there not available to him? Stavros had money and influence. He knew people, he knew the city. So what did he want? A new suit? A new car? How about some new furniture or maybe a new painting? Or lunch, anywhere: what did he want? Or how about he hit a spa: a massage and a steam? What about scoring some tickets: the next Celtics or Bruins? Or maybe something fancy: the Symphony? The theater? He'd done stuff like that with Allegra, in better times … But none of that appealed. It was maddening! Pathetic, even.

His mood plummeting, Stavros turned from the windows to the room, taking in all his stuff. He remembered how, when he had originally furnished the place, filling it with his many pricy purchases, he had felt a certain satisfaction. A certain *self*-satisfaction. What exquisite taste he had! How stylish and classy were all his things! The poor kid from the pizza shop, the working-class boy from Ludville—"Mudville" as it was known in the surrounding towns—was living the high life above Boston Common. That's right everybody, Stavros Papadakis had made it! Made it big!

And really, hadn't that been his goal all along, to make heaps of money? As a boy his mother had told him, "You'll be rich one day. You'll live in a big house and take care of your Mama." Stavros's father would say, "Only a bum can't make a million bucks in this country." His immigrant parents, each in their own way, had expected their son to achieve the American dream. And it pained Stavros that neither of them had lived long enough to see it, to see that their boy had indeed become a success. An American success.

Yet why, now, did his $20,000 sofa, which wasn't even comfortable to sit on, strike Stavros as somehow ugly and pathetic? Why did the $15,000 sandblasted-glass coffee table look stupid rather than chic? And what about that $30,000 painting? Technically, it wasn't even a painting as it was made not with paint but with chewing gum, of all different colors, which the artist himself had masticated and applied to the large, five-by-four-foot canvas. The gallerist who'd sold the painting to Stavros had claimed that the piece spoke to "consumerist alienation in post-Western society," and because Stavros did not want to appear unsophisticated he had nodded in sage agreement. *Why, yes. Of course.* The flirty, attractive young woman had also claimed, with winking assurance, that the painting would triple in value within five years. But what horseshit it was, Stavros thought. What a load of crap! He'd gotten played, not just with the painting but with all of it, his vanity leading him to spend spend spend! How foolish he'd been. How shallow. And how disgusted he felt. Disgusted by his crass insipid life. Disgusted by this apartment, by this stuff. He couldn't bear the sight of it, all this high-priced junk!

But then he caught himself: what was he thinking? A man needed a place to live, right? And he needed furniture and other stuff, yes? And so was it really such a crime if that apartment and that furniture and that stuff happened to be nice? And moreover, hadn't Stavros earned it? Hadn't he put in the time and the hard work? Yes he had. So then why was he being so severe with himself? Where was this self-condemnation coming from?

* * *

That night Stavros went to the Steak Club, one of his and Keller's regular haunts. Seated at the bar, he was pondering his day. The ride to school hadn't gone quite as he had hoped. But it was a start, he told himself. He was doing the right thing. And in time, well, things would go better. The boy would come around. Stavros just needed to keep showing up.

Glass in hand, he turned in his seat. Both the bar and the dining room were buzzing, crowded with after-work boozers. They were a well-dressed bunch, successful or on the make, animated and drunk-loud. Scanning the room for a familiar face, or even a sympathetic one, Stavros came up empty. But he did notice a trio of attractive young women, standing nearby. Mid-twenties, wearing suits, clutching glasses, they were laughing and having fun. One of them was quite cute, with her long brown hair, nice figure, and lively demeanor. Stavros watched the girl until one of her friends noticed him staring. The friend did not seem to appreciate his attentions. Her lips twisted nastily, and she shot him a look that said, *Go away loser!* It stung Stavros; it shook him hard. What the heck was that?

Despite his unremarkable appearance, neither handsome nor homely, Stavros had never lacked for female company. He was tall, driven, accomplished: a varsity athlete and then a college athlete; a law student and then an Assistant District Attorney. He'd always had something to bring to the table. And what's more, when Stavros desired a woman, he made the effort. He could be ardent, devoted, persistent in his amorous pursuit.

But recently he'd not done so well with the ladies. A year after his divorce, Stavros filled out a profile on Lovelorn.com and had a string of terrible first dates. One woman told him pointblank that he drank too much. She knew the type, she said, and wasn't interested. Another asked how old his profile pictures were. "Ten, maybe fifteen years," he said; "is that a problem?" It was. A third asked if he wanted to have kids, and when Stavros said "*kids?*" the woman said there was no point wasting either of their time. She stood, polished off her drink, and left the bar.

This was when Stavros began watching movies. It was easier than dating, less complicated. Movies entertained but made no demands, caused no stress.

There was some commotion near the front of the room. It was Keller, making his entrance. Unlike Stavros, Keller loved public attention. A nationally recognized figure, he was especially big in Boston. They cheered him at Fenway and asked for his autograph on the street. Coming into the restaurant, Keller was smiling and shaking hands. Mario, the Steak Club's manager, rushed over to greet him. Janet, the pretty hostess who had barely acknowledged Stavros when he'd entered, was glowing and laughing at something Keller was saying to her. Keller's face, as always in these situations, shone with a warm roguish joy, as though life were one great party and he was the happy generous host, a Gatsby to the world. He looked to the bar, saw Stavros, and made his way over. Halfway there someone reached out to him. It was the girl who had given Stavros the *Go-away-loser* sneer. Her face appeared quite different now: radiant, entranced, adoring. She and Keller exchanged a few words, then the girl nestled close beside him. She held out her phone and, as the two of them beamed for posterity, she snapped a selfie with the celeb.

Keller then came up and placed a hand on Stavros's shoulder. "Hey buddy, how we doin'?"

"Good," Stavros said, smiling. "It's good to see you."

* * *

They were shown to their usual corner table. As always, Stavros took the seat facing the wall. Keller, like Al Capone, preferred to sit facing the room; he liked to keep an eye on things. It had been that way since day one, Keller taking the prime seat wherever they went. And Stavros was fine with it, though in truth he wouldn't mind having the view every now and then.

After they ordered, Stavros told Keller about his day, about his new job as Brendan's morning ride to school.

Faintly puzzled, Keller said, "Why not just hire someone? Hell, send a cab."

"Well, the idea is that I want to spend some time with him."

"Oh. I see."

"It's just till I come back to work," Stavros added, as if to make it clear that he still had his priorities straight.

"Of course," Keller said, as if there could be no doubt that Stavros still had his priorities straight.

The two men broke eye contact, then pulled on their drinks.

* * *

Over their entrées—prime rib for Stavros, New York strip for Keller— Keller said, "So, when I came to see you in the hospital you mentioned that ... something happened."

"Yes."

"Where do things stand with that?"

"How do you mean?"

"I mean, how do you think about it now? Do you think it was a dream, a hallucination?"

"No. It wasn't a dream, Wyatt. It was too real."

Cutting off a bite of steak, Keller said, "You know Stavros, I've been thinking about this, and I feel like I might have overreacted when I said you shouldn't tell anyone. Really, it's not for me to say. In my defense, I was just thinking of the firm. But maybe I was wrong ... In fact, maybe it wouldn't hurt to talk to someone. You know—a professional. Someone who could help you make some sense of it. Otherwise, it's possible it could impact other areas of your life. Who knows, right?"

A new round of drinks arrived and they each took a slug.

Stavros said, "Allegra wants me to see a shrink. But I'm not interested."

"Hey, it wouldn't hurt. It helped Maggie's brother. Saved his marriage."

"What was the problem? Or is it private?"

"No, it' fine. He was into woolies."

"Woolies? Those big pajamas?"

"No, no. That's not it … Uh … *furries*. He was into furries."

"What's that?"

"It's this … thing. A lifestyle choice, I guess you'd call it. For Julian it started on the internet. He read about these people who dress up in animal costumes. Cartoon stuff. Donkeys, skunks, cats. Evidently they have sex parties. Kinky shit."

"What?"

"Yeah. He really got into it. He bought this rooster costume and his wife flipped. She made him get rid of it. But one day she checked his emails and saw he was active with some group. She said either he put an end to it for good, or she was leaving and taking the kids. That's when he went into therapy. True story."

Stavros nodded, sipped his drink, then said, "I'm not sure I see the connection."

"Connection?"

"Between me and some guy in a rooster costume."

"There's no connection, Stavros. I was just telling you about a therapy success story, that's all. I think it could help."

"Help with what? Your assumption seems to be … that I'm crazy."

"I never said you were crazy."

"No?" Stavros said, reaching for his glass.

"Then what about Allegra? You said she also thought you should see a shrink."

"Yes, for depression. Not this."

"Oh … I see," Keller said. "Well, what can I say? As for your story, who knows what happened? Though I did look into it a bit, and it seems lots of people have these things. Credible people. Doctors, professors. Maggie also believes—"

"You told *Maggie?*" Stavros said, hotly.

"Hey, I've been concerned."

"But you made such a big deal about this, about me not telling any-one!"

"Stavros, it was just Maggie. She was worried about you. And I told her not to tell anyone. It's not going anywhere."

Stavros stared at Keller, then averted his gaze.

"Buddy, I'm sorry," Keller said. "I shouldn't have said anything."

Slowly, the tension left Stavros's face, and he smiled. "It's nothing," he said. "It was your wife. I would have done the same thing. If I had a wife."

"Well—maybe you should get a rooster costume."

Stavros chuckled, and they both went back to their steaks.

* * *

Toward the end of their meal Keller said, "Hold on, buddy. We've got a live one." He was looking up and beyond Stavros.

Stavros turned his head.

A young woman with aqua-blue hair came straight to the table, pointing at Keller and accosting him in a shrill voice: "This man is a criminal! This man is a *pig!* A misogynist *pig!* Newt Bellingham raped Aimee Gibblin and you're helping him! You're helping that rich bastard, taking his daddy's money and telling the world he's innocent! But he's not innocent! He raped her and you're a scum for defending him! You're a *scum* and you need to be exposed! This man is a *pig!*"

The room had gone quiet. Everyone was watching. There was violence in the woman's frenzied eyes, but she kept two steps back.

"You defend rapists for money!" she shrieked. "You're a *pig!* A misogynist *pig!*"

The woman then paused, and with an air of righteous expectation, she looked around the room. It was as if she were awaiting the others to rise up and join her, to follow her courageous example and take a stand … But no one rose up. Instead, the scotch drinkers in their expensive suits just stared. There was complete quiet, and soon the young woman seemed to wilt, her brave face blanching.

"That was a fine speech," Keller said. "Very impressive."

Laughs came from nearby tables, mocking guffaws. Incensed, the young woman shot Keller a murderous glare and stepped toward him. Stavros stood, ready to intervene, but then Mario came. He took the young woman by the arm and led her away. As she went the girl raised a fist in a power salute, shouting, "Wyatt Keller is a pig! A misogynist pig! And all of you are cowards! Cowards! *Cowards!*"

And then she was gone, taken to the street. Some diners turned back to gawk at Keller and Stavros, but most resumed their meals, and suddenly the room grew loud again, filled with the clamor of excited conversation.

Smiling stoically, Keller gave Stavros a shrug. This wasn't their first public haranguing, their first run-in with an outraged citizen.

"That was pleasant," Stavros said.

"It always is," Keller replied.

SEVEN

The next morning, and all the rest of the week, there was silence on the ride to school. Silence and texting, as Brendan ignored his father. The following Monday, just after the boy had buckled in, Stavros said, "Hey … can we talk?"

Brendan turned his eyes partway to Stavros, fixing his annoyed gaze on the steering wheel.

"So, I realize you're mad at me, and I understand," Stavros said. "I deserve it … But again, I want to say that I'm sorry. For everything … You know, for being a bad father. For not spending much time with you over the years. Not going to your games. Missing your concerts. Arguing with your—"

"This is fricking embarrassing," Brendan muttered, shaking his head.

"What?"

"This is *embarrassing*," the boy said, finally looking Stavros in the eye.

"Oh … I'm sorry," Stavros said, surprised. "Well, I wanted you to know that … that I'm sorry. Very sorry. And I also want you to know that I love you, and that—"

Brendan snorted, his eyes flashing derision and contempt.

"I mean it," Stavros said. "I love you, and I'm here for you. And if there's ever anything I can do for you, if there's ever anything you need, anything at all, just let me know, OK?"

Again the boy looked at Stavros, though this time not with anger but with something like cunning. "Anything at all?" he said.

Stavros felt a chill. "Well … Yeah."

"OK. Can I have a hundred bucks?"

"What?"

"Can I have a hundred bucks? You said if I ever need anything."

"Uh … That's not quite …"

"So what you said was bullshit."

"*No.* I meant it … But didn't I just give you three hundred for Christmas?"

"That was for clothes. But that's OK. I knew you didn't mean it." The boy pulled out his phone.

Stavros wavered, then reached for his money clip. "What's it for? The hundred bucks?"

"Just stuff."

"Just stuff," Stavros mumbled. He peeled off two fifties and handed them over. Brendan took the bills, put them in his pocket, and refocused on his phone. Stavros waited for a thank you. There was no thank you. Inhaling a deep breath, a breath meant to stifle the anger that was beginning to rise, Stavros backed out of the driveway and drove to Alden Street. In silence.

* * *

The following morning there was more silence. Ditto the next morning and the morning after that. All the while, Stavros remained patient and polite, greeting the boy with a smile when he got into the car, and wishing him a good day when he got out.

On Friday, as he was backing out of the driveway, Stavros said, "You know, I'd really like to hear how things are going with you … If you ever want to talk."

Brendan glanced at his father, and his expression went slack, the tension draining from his face. It was as though he were losing his resolve to be angry. Or maybe he was just getting bored with it. "What do you want to know?" he said.

"Anything," Stavros said, brightening. "What's your favorite subject at school? Do you have a girlfriend? Whatever."

"I like science best. Science and math. I like Spanish too."

"You speak Spanish?"

"*Yes*," the boy hissed. "And Italian."

"You speak *Italian?*"

"*Dad*, I told you before. I speak it with Mom. Mom and Papa Barzetti."

"Papa Barzetti?"

"We talk on Skype."

"Wow," Stavros murmured, impressed.

"And I don't have a girlfriend. Not yet, anyway."

With this, Stavros could sympathize. "These things can take time," he said.

Brendan made a face.

"And what about Louis Armstrong?" Stavros said. "Why do you like him?"

"I don't know. Why does anybody like anything? It makes me feel good. I hear a couple notes and everything changes. I like other guys too. Miles Davis. Theo Croker. But right now I'm focusing on Louis. We've been practicing some of his songs at school, and it's fun to play them. I have some solos."

"Oh yeah? I'd like to hear you play sometime."

Brendan grew pensive, and for several long moments there was silence. Then he said, "You can if you want. We're playing tonight."

"Tonight?"

"Yeah, at school. It's free," the boy said indifferently, as if he didn't care one way or the other if this might interest his father. "Anybody can go."

* * *

Stavros was the first parent to arrive for the jazz show. The school auditorium was empty except for three people on stage. A boy was setting up a drum kit, a girl was arranging chairs and music stands, and an older guy, bald with John Lennon specs, was testing microphones. No Brendan.

Stavros took an aisle seat in the third row. From here he'd be able to see his son perfectly, and his son would be able to see him. And what Brendan saw wouldn't be, to use the boy's own phrase, "fricking embarrassing." Stavros was smartly dressed: Montalbani suit, Myshkino tie; the prosperous, respectable-looking parent.

Waiting for things to get rolling, Stavros took the place in. It was a ritzy venue—plush seats, lots of blond wood, elaborate lighting system. Very contemporary, and no doubt very expensive. At Stavros's high school the auditorium was actually the gymnasium. There was a stage at one end, and for special events they raised the baskets and set up metal folding chairs. This was at Ludville High, where the building was vandalized, the textbooks outdated, and fistfights part of daily life. But thanks to his hard work, in both sports and academics, Stavros won a scholarship to Olmsted College, a small, private school in western Massachusetts. He majored in economics and played four years on the basketball team. After this, he went.to Boston Law.

On stage, a girl appeared with a saxophone, followed by a boy with a trombone. Next came Brendan, trumpet in hand. He spotted his father in the seats, and though he didn't wave, his face betrayed the hint of a smile—a smile not of derision, but of happiness. And seeing this, Stavros felt happy too.

More kids appeared and soon they began warming up. They plucked, hit, and blew into their instruments, filling the hall with a brassy racket. Stavros loved it. All the while parents and students had begun to file in. There was a buzz in the air, a palpable energy. Watching the other parents greeting each other, chatting and laughing, Stavros realized he didn't know anyone. Not that it was a surprise. The last school function he'd attended was Brendan's kindergarten graduation.

A man and a woman, holding coats and smiling hopefully as they stood in the aisle, asked Stavros if the seats beside him were taken. A number of people had already squeezed past and the row was almost filled. Quite frankly, Stavros had been hoping that Allegra might show up, minus Young Paul Newman, and that the two of them would sit together and watch their son. For Brendan's sake. But Allegra was nowhere in sight. So, friendly as could be, because that's how school parents roll, Stavros stood to let the couple in.

The woman went through first and the man sat next to Stavros. Immediately the guy leaned in close, as if going for a kiss; Stavros flinched back, startled.

"Chas Gordon," the guy said. "And this is my wife, Corkie."

Corkie was beaming. "We're Joshy's parents. He plays the trombone."

"I'm Brendan's dad," Stavros said, shaking Chas's hand. "He plays—"

"Oh, *Brendan!*" Corkie squealed. "He's such a good kid! He and Joshy play soccer too. I'm surprised we never met you before. *Have* we never met you before?"

"I don't think—"

"And I love Allegra!" Corkie went on. "What a woman! We should have you guys over sometime!"

"That'd be nice. Except we're divorced."

Corkie went quiet.

Chas took over. He had by now withdrawn from Stavros's personal space. "You coming from work?" he said in a manly tone, taking in Stavros's suit.

"No," Stavros said, now noticing that none of the other parents were dressed up. It was a jeans and khakis crowd.

"You're the lawyer," Chas added approvingly.

"That's right."

"You got that big case coming up. The Bellingham kid."

"Actually, I'm … on medical leave."

"Oh, I'm sorry to hear that," Chas said, becoming uneasy. Now he went quiet.

Corkie said, "Did you go to the Fall Concert?"

"Uh, no … Something came up," Stavros said.

"Oh, it was amazing," Corkie said, with something like reverence in her eyes. "These kids put on such a good show."

"Zhirayr does a hell of job," Chas said.

"He *really* does," Corkie said, nodding.

Stavros nodded too, though he had no idea what they were talking about.

"And your boy," Chas added, eyeing Stavros with respect, man to man, "is quite the trumpeter."

Recalling that he'd never heard Brendan play even a single note, Stavros squirmed slightly. "Yeah, he's … pretty good, huh?"

* * *

The lights dimmed, and soon the auditorium burst into applause. From backstage came the young musicians. Brendan, astonishingly, was aglow with confidence, chin raised, walking tall and proud. It was a remarkable sight, and it gave Stavros a proud fatherly thrill.

"That's Joshy in the denim shirt!" Corkie Gordon said, leaning across her husband to inform Stavros of this important fact. Joshy was tall and skinny, with a mop of curly brown hair.

The guy in the John Lennon glasses greeted the audience, welcomed them to the Thoreau Academy Freshman and Sophomore Jazz Band's Winter Concert, and introduced himself as Zhirayr Narek. Corkie, Chas, and a handful of other parents clapped with great vigor. Pleased by this, Zhirayr made a slight bow. Then he said, "Tonight we'll be presenting selections from Duke Ellington, Louis Armstrong, Charles Mingus, and Sonny Rollins. The first piece is 'Blue Cellophane,' featuring Josh Gordon on trombone."

There was scattered applause, but Corkie went nuts. "*Yay Joshy!*" she cried.

Stepping forward to take the solo spot Joshy grimaced at the sound of his shrieking mother. The gangly boy readied his instrument and looked to Zhirayr Narek, as did the rest of the band. With much panache the maestro raised his arms and counted off *one*, *two*, *three*; and just like that, as though a switch had been flipped, there came a glorious burst of noise —unified and precise, melodic and upbeat. An instant mood-booster. Stavros had expected off notes, clumsy playing, possibly a flat-out flop. Which would have been fine; he was just here to see his boy and show some support. But Corkie was right—the kids *were* good.

As they played, some of the musicians rocked their heads, others tapped their feet, and one girl was practically dancing as she blew into her trumpet, the music moving her with rhapsodic joy. Corkie Gordon too was swaying with joy, her face alight with pleasure as she watched her son. Loud clapping and cheering came at the song's end.

And so it went, one song after the next, with Zhirayr Narek introducing the new number and the featured performer. The audience roared, loving every note, and all the while Stavros's heart throbbed with tender paternal feeling. He kept his eyes fixed on his son, and as he did, as he watched the boy bob to the beat, his fingers working the valves of his horn and his cheeks puffing like a bullfrog's, Stavros was filled with wonder. His boy, the once-tiny being he and Allegra had created not so long ago, was doing this? Making these beautiful sounds?

Zhirayr Narek said, "Next up is a medley of early Louis Armstrong songs. Our trumpet soloist is Brendan Papadakis."

It was too much for Stavros. His eyes moistened and he clapped loudly. Corkie Gordon cried out, "*Yay Brendan!*" With complete self-assurance the boy came to the front of the stage and raised the trumpet to his lips. And for the next fifteen minutes, as the band played three numbers, Stavros was in pure rapture, exhilarated by his son and his dazzling talent.

* * *

After the show family members waited near the stage for the musicians, off gathering their stuff. The Gordons had said good-bye to Stavros and were mingling with other parents. Chas was already leaning into some guy's personal space, offering his hand for a shake. Off by the far wall stood Allegra, with Dylan. They were chatting with another couple. Stavros kept an eye on them, and when Allegra finally looked his way he smiled and waved. She quickly turned her head, pretending not to have seen him. Publicly snubbed by his ex, Stavros went stiff, his cheeks flaming.

All around him the casually dressed parents were conversing among themselves like friends at a party. The vibe was festive, buoyant. The kids had put on a great show and everyone was in good spirits. But Stavros, standing alone in his expensive suit, felt self-conscious—the friendless wallflower, uptight and overdressed.

One by one the kids emerged from backstage in their winter coats, carrying instrument cases. When Joshy Gordon appeared, his face crimsoned with embarrassment as his mother boisterously embraced him. *"You were so good!"* she said loud enough for all to hear. At last Brendan appeared. Stavros waved to his son, but the boy went straight to Allegra and Dylan.

Stavros vacillated—but what other choice was there? They certainly weren't going to come to him! With a touch of trepidation, he made his way over to the three of them. Stavros said hello first to Allegra, who looked ... great. Yes, he thought, she looked great. Healthy, fit, pretty as ever—maybe even a touch prettier than he remembered. She, very politely, said hello back to him, but nothing more. Next Stavros turned to Dylan, who likewise looked healthy and fit; a young buck in his prime. Instantly, Stavros felt his mood sink. Meeting Stavros's eyes, Dylan's expression was both superior and cold. And Stavros, recalling how poorly he had treated Dylan on Christmas morning, realized he had made yet another enemy. Was there anybody in his life that he *hadn't* offended, Stavros wondered? Humbly, almost meekly, he said, "Hi Dylan."

In response, Dylan merely nodded. Then he made a cool smirk, his face betraying an unmistakable air of satisfaction. Was the young doctor enjoying this? Did Stavros's public abasement—from bumptious bully on Christmas morning to chastened outsider here tonight—please him? It looked that way.

Finally, to his son Stavros said, "Hey, I'm speechless." All the warm feelings from the concert swelled back into his chest. Stavros wanted to give the boy a hug but held off, wary of yet another rejection. "You were amazing up there," he said. "Louis Armstrong would've loved it. And the band was terrific. Really, it was great stuff."

Brendan was smiling, pleased with the praise but also reserved. "Thanks. It was fun."

"It was," Stavros said. "Well, hey, we should celebrate. Would you like that? We could go get some food. Anywhere you want. What do you say?"

"We already have plans," the boy said.

"Oh," Stavros said, his cheeks flaming yet again. God, what a fool I am, he thought! Assuming the boy wouldn't already have plans. Assuming the boy would even want to go out with him. "That sounds good," Stavros said. "I'm glad to hear it."

Brendan just looked at him. No one spoke.

Stavros said, "*All righty* ... Hey, you were great up there, Brendan. I was very proud of you. I'll see you Monday morning."

"OK."

Stavros wished them all a good night, then turned for the exit.

EIGHT

Over the following week there was a marked change in Brendan's attitude toward his father. Rather than texting on the morning ride to school, the boy was actually talking, and Stavros was getting to know his son. In addition to jazz, Brendan was very interested in physics. He was particularly interested, he said, in quantum mechanics and string theory, and was the only freshman in the Thoreau Physics Club. He was also interested in artificial intelligence, and wasn't sure if he wanted to be a theoretical physicist or a robotics engineer. "Though I might get into film," he added.

"*Film?*" Stavros said.

"Yeah, I've been working on a couple screenplays."

Stavros glanced from the road to his son, wondering if the kid were bullshitting him. A fourteen year old who was into physics and robotics and was writing screenplays, in addition to playing Louis Armstrong on the trumpet? When Stavros was fourteen, his sole focus in life had been girls and basketball and wondering how to get rid of his pimples. "What sort of movies do you like?" he asked.

"Sci-fi stuff. Things you probably never heard of."

"Try me," Stavros said.

"*Stalker—*"

"Tarkovsky?"

"You know him?"

"Sure. *Solaris, Andrei Rublev*. My favorite is *The Mirror*."

"Hm ... I never heard of that one," the boy said, looking vaguely impressed, and staring at Stavros as though he were rethinking his opinion of him. Perhaps his father wasn't such a philistine after all, his expression seemed to say.

"I'll tell you what," Stavros said. "You burn me a couple jazz CDs to play in the car, and I'll give you my DVD of *The Mirror*."

The boy mulled this, then nodded. "OK … Cool."

* * *

Things were going so well with the boy, in fact, that by the end of their second week together Stavros decided to broach the girlfriend question again. It puzzled him that Brendan didn't seem interested in Sally French. She'd been joining in on their morning conversations, and to Stavros it seemed like the two kids were a perfect match. Like Brendan, Sally was a musician: she played violin in the school orchestra. Like Brendan, she was an athlete: soccer and tennis. Like Brendan, she was involved in an academic club: both the French Club (yes) and the Political Debate Club. And on top of this she was cute and upbeat, a genuine force of positivity. The boy had said he was looking for a girlfriend, so why not this one?

"*Sooooo*," Stavros said, as they were heading toward Alden Street. "Sally French."

Brendan's face scrunched up. "What?"

"Sally French."

"What about her?"

"She's pretty cute, huh?"

"That's creepy, Dad."

"I don't mean for me. I mean for *you*."

"What are you talking about?"

"You said you wanted a girlfriend. Well, why not look in the backseat? She's sitting there every morning."

The boy rolled his eyes.

"Brendan, trust me, girls don't just walk up to guys and ask them out. At least, that never happened to me. You got to get out there. Make something happen. You know, take her for a slice, tell her a few jokes. Make her laugh."

Brendan pulled a face.

"What?" Stavros said.

"I'm not interested in her."

"Why not? You don't think she's hot, or whatever the word is today?"

"She's too young. I like older women."

Stavros chortled. "Brendan, you're fourteen. In your world, what constitutes an older woman—fifteen?"

"Sixteen."

"Oh, *sixteen*. Yeah, that's up there."

"So what about you? Mom has a boyfriend. When are you going to get a girlfriend?"

"Hey, one headache at a time, OK?"

"What does that mean?"

"It means I have a lot going on. I'm too busy to have a girlfriend right now."

"Too busy? You're not even working."

Stavros chafed at this, and went silent. Minutes later he said, "So how *is* your mother? Since we're talking about her. She seems kind of different lately. Calmer than usual. Sort of."

"It's because she's in therapy."

"She is?"

"Yep. For about a year. She's also on Pacifil."

"She told you that?"

"She told me about the therapy, but not the pills. I saw them in her bathroom."

Wow—this was big news. But it made sense, given Allegra's recent behavior. More than once Stavros had seen her hold back on her temper and refrain from going all-out ballistic. Now her eruptions were just moderately ballistic. It was something.

On Alden, Stavros tooted the horn. When Sally came out of the house, skipping down the porch steps with her backpack and violin case, Brendan seemed to pay her more attention than he normally did.

* * *

That night Stavros went out to dinner with Keller, Maggie Keller, and a woman named Lindsay Vanderberg, whom Stavros was meeting for the first time. They were at Spectaculaire, a much-hyped French-Japanese-fusion restaurant that had just opened in the South End. The chef/owner, a minor national figure who had published a popular cookbook and appeared regularly on TV, came to the table to shake hands with Keller and Stavros and charm the ladies.

After the guy left, Keller said, "We live in strange times. Ten years ago a chef was a drunk who couldn't get a better job. Today he's a celebrity."

"I think you could say the same about defense attorneys," Maggie said, giving Stavros a wry glance.

"Actually it started with Julia Child, back in the sixties," Lindsay Vanderberg said, very earnestly. "She was the first celebrity chef."

"What about Chef Boyardee?" Stavros said.

Maggie laughed, and it tickled Stavros. He'd known her for about ten years, and had always thought her a knockout: beautiful, sexy, provocative. Now in her late thirties, Maggie had met Keller just after art school, when she'd been spending her days painting at her Fort Point Channel studio and her nights tending bar at the Steak Club. At the time, Keller was married to his second wife Angela, though within a year they were divorced and three months later, on a private beach in Nantucket, Keller and Maggie were wed. Maggie stopped bartending and started painting full-time. She was very ambitious, and had expectations of art world success. But it never happened, and eventually a new passion emerged. According to Keller, Maggie was now often away, traveling. For weeks, sometimes months at a time, she was off to Europe, Asia, Latin America.

She said, "Stavros, it's amazing how different you look. You always had this tortured expression on your face, like your balls were in a vise and the world was squeezing them tight."

Keller laughed, showing his unnaturally white teeth.

"But now you look calm and relaxed," Maggie went on. "And you lost some weight too. Very nice. You look great."

An appetizer came compliments of the chef: frogs' legs in a tangy wasabi sauce.

"Oh dear," Lindsay Vanderberg said, peering at the dish.

Stavros reached for one. "Looks good."

"Lindsay's pescatarian," Maggie said.

"What's that, fish?" Stavros said.

"I couldn't give up my sushi," Lindsay said.

"It kind of tastes like fish," Stavros said, chewing. "What are frogs, amphibians? Does that count?"

"I don't think so."

Maggie cut in: "Stavros, Lindsay and I are dying to hear about your near-death experience."

Stavros shot Keller a look.

"I told her not to tell anyone," Keller said.

"And I told Lindsay not to tell anyone," Maggie said.

"I won't say a thing," Lindsay said. "I promise."

"Come on, Stavros. Tell us," Maggie said. "That's why we came tonight. To hear your story."

Stavros, who was not inclined to deny Maggie anything, said, "Maybe later. Let's eat first."

* * *

After their entrées arrived, and they were well into their second round of drinks, Lindsay said, "So what kind of name is Stavros?"

"Greek," he said.

"It means 'teetotaler,'" Keller said.

Stavros laughed. "And Wyatt means, 'Lord of the Dance.'"

Now Maggie laughed. Lindsay gave Stavros an inquisitive look, and he explained: "The three of us were at a wedding—"

"It was for one of their associates," Maggie said. "What was her name?"

"Athena Mourikis. We're at the reception and Wyatt's had a bit too much ouzo—"

"Not as much as you," Keller said.

"This is true," Stavros said. "Anyway, the band starts playing the music for the syrtaki dance, and Wyatt decides it's time to channel Zorba the Greek. He gets out on the dance floor, and the crowd parts. Kind of like in *Saturday Night Fever*—"

"Only Wyatt is no John Travolta," Maggie said.

"So he's out there like Anthony Quinn," Stavros said, "bending his knees and waving his arms—"

"People were going crazy," Keller said, relishing the memory.

"Cheering on the famous lawyer," Maggie said.

"And the next thing you know … boom," Stavros said.

"Boom?" Lindsay said.

"I fell," Keller said.

"He slipped a disk and couldn't get up," Maggie said. "He was writhing on the floor."

"Somebody called an ambulance," Stavros said.

"There was no need for that," Keller said. "But hey, it gave the couple something to remember."

"And everyone else," Maggie said.

"Oh, that's terrible," Lindsay said.

"Stavros doesn't dance," Maggie said.

"No?" Lindsay said, turning to him.

"I'm not a performer."

Keller laughed.

"I thought Greeks were supposed to be uninhibited?" Lindsay said.

"There are different ways to be uninhibited," Stavros said.

Lindsay's brow rose.

"Tell us, Stavros," Keller said. "I'm sure Angela would love to hear all about it."

"*What did you say?*" Maggie snapped, turning on Keller. "What did you call me?"

85

"What?"

"You called me Angela."

"No I didn't."

"Yes you did."

"That's crazy," Keller said.

"He's going senile," Maggie muttered, turning back to the table.

Keller's expression darkened.

There was an uncomfortable pause. And just then a cellphone started ringing, and everyone looked at Keller. Typically when dining out he kept his phone on the table, face-up beside his water glass, ready for action. But this phone was silent. Instead the ringing seemed to be coming from his person. Keller froze, went very still.

The ringing continued, and finally Lindsay said, "What's that?"

"*Oh*," Keller said, as if suddenly remembering. He reached into his suitcoat and pulled out an old flip phone, which he muted. "It's just a client," he said, looking grim. He slipped the phone back into his coat.

"Give it to me," Maggie said, holding out her hand.

"Honey, it was a client—"

"Give me the damn phone, Wyatt," she said, quiet but forceful.

"I'm telling you, it's business."

"I swear to God Wyatt, if you don't give me that damn thing I'm going to start screaming that you're a pedophile and a wife beater and I guarantee you half the people in this room will film it and it'll be on the internet before we get home."

Cornered, beaten, Keller held out the phone. Maggie took it, examined it, and gave Keller a livid glare. She then pressed some keys on the phone and raised it to her head.

"Maggie, don't," Keller said helplessly.

"*Who is this?*" Maggie snarled, addressing her new friend. There was a pause, then: "I'm his wife, that's who! But you know what, *bitch*, you can have the fat prick. He's all yours."

"Maggie!" Keller growled in a hushed voice, not wanting to make a scene. Though of course it was too late for that. Diners all around them were now gawking, taking in the show.

Maggie dropped the phone in Keller's water glass, got up, and headed for the door.

"I'll talk to her," Lindsay said.

"No, I've got this," Keller said, rising from his chair. He extracted the sopping phone from the glass, gave it a couple shakes, offered a quick apology to Stavros and Lindsay, then scampered off after his wife.

Watching him go, Lindsay said, "I wondered when this would happen."

* * *

After Stavros paid the bill, Lindsay asked if he wanted to go for a drink. He did. She led him around the corner to a place called Smooch. It was dark, trendy, and loud, pulsating with electronic dance music. Through the dense throng they made their way to the back, where Lindsay found them a cozy love seat in a section filled with couples and small groups.

A waitress came up to them, and she was beaming. "Hey Lindsay!"

"Hey Willow!" Lindsay said, jumping to her feet to embrace the girl.

And Stavros thought, She's a regular here. While the women chattered away he took in all the fashionable fops and fopettes, preening and posing. This wasn't quite his scene.

Eventually Willow took their order and left. Sitting back down, Lindsay swiveled toward Stavros and rested a knee firmly on his thigh. It sent a pleasurable sensation through his body, turning his mind instantly to sex. *Well hello ...*

"A scotch drinker, huh?" she said with flirty eyes. "I've always associated it with my father and his friends. Old people. What are you, fifty?"

"Forty-four."

"Oh. Sorry."

"It's the lighting," Stavros said. He reckoned Lindsay herself was about thirty-five, but discreetly left it at that.

She said, "Hey, this might sound odd but, do you drive a black Imperator?"

"I do."

"I think you gave me the middle finger once."

"I did?"

"Yeah. This past Christmas, on Storrow Drive."

"Oh no. That was you?"

"It was."

"Damn. I'm sorry," he said, wincing.

"It's fine," she said. "I think it's funny … Though you were kind of a jerk."

Willow came with their drinks, and just in time. Stavros needed a boost. He said "Cheers," then went straight for the burn—bottoms up! Lindsay, sipping her martini, was smiling at him. Not knowing what to say, Stavros scanned the room, nodding agreeably. "Yeah, this is a nice place," he said. "Very hip."

Lindsay put a hand on his forearm. "So, are you going to tell me your NDE story?"

"NDE?"

"Near-death experience. I'm completely fascinated by these things."

Stavros felt encouraged, and not just by the hand on his arm. For here, quite possibly, was someone who might believe his story and not think him nuts. "Do you know anyone else who this happened to?"

"My grandmother. Though hers was actually a pre-death experience."

"*Pre*-death?"

Lindsay told him the story: "It was about ten years ago. She was in a hospice and we knew she didn't have much longer. My mother was holding her hand, and suddenly she became very alert. She was staring up at one corner of the room, and she was smiling. Her whole face was glowing, and she said, 'Robert … Hello Robert.' And my mother and me and my aunt had no idea what she was talking about. There was no one else in the room, and certainly no Robert. And my grandmother started talking to this person, and it wasn't a monologue; she was listening and answering questions, like it was a two-way conversation. And finally my mother said, 'Mummy, who are you talking to?' And my grandmother said, 'Your Uncle Bob … Don't you recognize him?' Apparently 'Uncle Bob'—my grandmother's older brother—had died when my mother was in her teens. My grandmother talked to him for ten, fifteen minutes."

"What was she saying?"

"She said Robert had come to take her 'home,' and that there was nothing for her to fear. He said there were people waiting to see her, and was she ready to go. By now she was totally at peace. It was a complete change. When she'd first gotten sick, about a year earlier, I had gone to visit her and she'd actually cried, telling me she was afraid to die. She said she thought God was mad at her, because she had done bad things. To me this was crazy, because she was always such a kind and loving person. Very selfless. And when I told her this, and said she had nothing to worry about, she wouldn't believe me. She was convinced God was angry at her. So when my mother and my aunt and I saw this—how peaceful she had become—we all got very emotional. It was beautiful, and such a gift to her, and to us. And that night she died, and I swear there was a smile on her face."

There was a time, and not so long ago, when Stavros would have laughed at a story like this. Now, he was reminded of his own experience with the mystical—seeing his mother in the white light, and all the other amazing things that had followed.

He sipped his drink, then looked at Lindsay. She was watching him, waiting. But Stavros wavered, and it occurred to him that he wasn't ready to open up to a stranger. It didn't feel right. Not now. Not here. He said, "So how do you know Maggie?"

"Wait—what about your story?"

Stavros shrugged. "It's kind of personal … Maybe another time."

"Oh, I'm sorry. I didn't mean to be pushy. Sometimes I do that. I'm working on it." She tipped back her drink. "Um, Maggie … We met at yoga. We go to the same studio in Brookline. We've become really close."

"Are you the person she goes skiing with?"

"Yes. We're going to Aspen next month. We've gone the past four years. Do *you* ski?"

"Not really."

"Oh, it's a good time … Say, you don't have a thing for her, do you?"

"Who, Maggie?"

"Yeah. It's just the way you look at her. A couple times you were staring at her breasts."

"*What?* Nooooo," Stavros laughed, nervously. "We're just old friends. The three of us. They're a great couple."

Lindsay's eyes questioned him.

"I mean, apart from tonight they're a great couple," he added. "But they're solid. I'm sure they'll patch this up."

"You think?"

"Yeah … I hope so."

"How well do you know Wyatt?"

"We're like family. We've been partners for thirteen years."

"I don't like the way he treats her."

"Well, yes. What happened tonight was bad. I didn't mean to minimize it."

"I wasn't talking about tonight. I mean in general."

Stavros looked at her.

Lindsay said, "Even before I'd met Maggie I'd heard things about Wyatt. And I still do."

For years Keller had been the subject of rumor. Rumors of all sorts: legal, financial, marital. But it wasn't something Stavros wanted to discuss, so he said, "There are people in this town who like to slander him. It's just jealousy."

This did not seem to please Lindsay. She looked away, focusing on the room. For some moments there was just the monotonous coital thump of the music and the sound of everyone else talking. Stavros finished the last of his drink.

Lindsay then turned back to him, now smiling politely. "So tell me about your job."

Stavros told her the basics but soon shifted the focus to her. With women he preferred to be on the listening end. It had always been that way.

Lindsay said she had never married and was currently single. No kids. She'd grown up in Chicago, in Winnetka, and had gone to Wellesley then moved to Boston. She told Stavros about her interior design business, her work with an animal shelter, and her passion for yoga and travel. She was thinking of going to India in the fall. She wanted to meet some real yogis and deepen her practice …

And as Lindsay went on about Lindsay, Stavros realized he wasn't completely feeling it. Yes, she was interesting, intelligent, and physically appealing. Sitting close together, their legs touching, Stavros admired the beauty of her eyes, her hair, her shapely lips, and found himself wondering about the rest of her. Still, he was aware of some obscure inner resistance, a sense that something wasn't quite clicking.

After they'd finished their second drink Lindsay said, "I'd love another, but it's getting late."

Stavros agreed.

"Did you drive?" she asked.

"I took a cab."

"Let me take you home."

"No, that's fine."

"Really. I'm parked nearby. You're on Tremont, right?"

* * *

They were on the move, racing up Washington Street in Lindsay's SUV —the same vehicle that had nearly crashed into Stavros on Christmas morning. It was, he thought, a curious coincidence. Was there maybe something to it? Some providential significance?

"What are you thinking?" Lindsay said.

"Oh, nothing. I'm just tired."

"Well, I hope I can get a raincheck on your NDE."

"Sure. Maybe we'll get together sometime."

At his building she pulled up to the entrance and switched on the car's interior light.

"It was good to meet you Lindsay," Stavros said, offering his hand for a shake.

Lindsay ignored the hand. "You know, I've never been in this building before," she said musingly, as though this were some strange cosmic oversight.

Stavros withdrew his hand, and there was silence. Then he said, "Do you ... want to come up?"

She thought about this. "Well ... I guess it's still early."

He glanced at the dashboard clock. It was 12:47. "Uh, yeah ... Pretty early."

"OK," she said, as though he'd convinced her. "Why not?"

* * *

In the elevator Lindsay nestled close, giving Stavros a good noseful of perfume. It smelled like candy, and sex. Immediately he tensed, part of him saying *Yes!*, another part still naggedly unsure. He'd not done anything like this in years. Many years. Maybe it was just nerves.

They entered the apartment and he hung their coats. Lindsay went straight to the windows. "Wow, look at this!" she said, as if according to script. For a minute or two she stood in rapt silence, taking in the sights. Then she focused her attention on the room, her decorator's eye making a discreet yet thorough inspection: sofa, chairs, carpet, lamps. The whole shebang.

"Is that a Camus coffee table?" she said, impressed and maybe surprised that he would own such a tasteful, high-status item.

Embarrassed by this, but also darkly amused, Stavros fidgeted slightly. Part of his motivation in renting this apartment and filling it with pricy things, he realized, had been precisely for a moment such as this—to impress a sexually attractive female. Yet now that the moment had finally arrived, now that the fantasy scenario was finally playing out, it left him only with a sense of his own ridiculousness. How absurd it was, he thought. How absurd *he* was! Very dryly he said, "Yes. That is a genuine Camus coffee table."

"It's lovely," Lindsay said.

You can have it, Stavros nearly said, but he kept his mouth shut.

Next Lindsay stepped up to the large painting, Stavros's one major art purchase. Very studiously she began to examine the thing, as though it were a Rembrandt hanging in the Louvre. Then, in a burst of bewilderment, she said, "Is that bubblegum?"

Stavros said it was.

"Oh," she said, perplexed, and a little deflated. She took a few moments to reassess the canvas. "Well ... I like it," she said courteously. "It's got something."

"It does," Stavros said.

Giving the room and the view a final scan, Lindsay turned to Stavros with a teasing smile. "So this is your lady trap?"

"Oh yeah. It's a party up here every night."

"Your legal groupies," she said, playing along.

"All zero of them."

"All zero?"

"Actually, I'm thinking of moving," he said.

"Seriously?"

"Seriously."

"To where?"

"Maybe Cambridge."

"Isn't your ex over there?"

"And my son."

"You don't like it here?"

"No. Not really." And it was true. Over the past few days Stavros had been perusing real estate listings online. He wanted out. He'd had enough of the swank pad with the swank views, enough of living up in the sky like an astronaut on a space station. He wanted to be back on the ground. He wanted grass and trees and dirt. He dreamed of a gas grill and lawn chairs, chirping birds and hopping squirrels. The stuff he'd had on Champney Street.

* * *

When Stavros woke the next morning, Lindsay Vanderberg was at his side. She lay under the comforter in panties and one of his shirts, snoring lightly on her back. Watching her, and pleasantly pleased by the warmth and scent of her body close to his, Stavros recalled their evening together. It hadn't ended quite as expected. Once they'd started kissing, things escalated quickly, with passionate sighs and caresses and the clumsy shedding of clothes. But at some point Stavros's enthusiasm began to wane. As if intuiting this, Lindsay redoubled her efforts. Yet with her wet tongue moving around in his ear—a sensation Stavros found distinctly unerotic—he finally pulled back, saying he had to stop. "Is it me?" she said. "No. You're great. It's me," Stavros said, and apart from the tongue in the ear, he meant it. For him, this was too much, too fast. And to be honest, he still wasn't sure about her. Something was holding him back. Taking this in, Lindsay appeared confused, and abashed. Stavros said, "*Really*. It's me. You're very beautiful." Her expression softened, and she kissed his forehead. By then it was past two, and she asked if she could spend the night. Stavros would have preferred to sleep alone, but to kick her out then would have been brutish, so he said yes. And now, he was glad that he had. Very quietly he got out of bed, dressed, and left the room.

In the kitchen he made coffee and began frying bacon. The greasy, saliva-inducing aroma filled the apartment, and soon Lindsay appeared, looking booze-damaged. Wearing Stavros's shirt, which reached to her knees, she greeted him with a pained expression as she passed into the living room. She collected the rest of her clothes from the floor and sofa, then padded back to the bedroom. Minutes later she was in the kitchen, dressed in last night's outfit. Stavros poured her some coffee and she sat at the breakfast counter. "My head's killing me," she said.

"Do you want some breakfast?"

"I don't eat meat, remember? And I definitely don't eat bacon."

"How about some eggs?"

"No. I should get going. I need to call Maggie."

Stavros nodded, then tended to the bacon, popping and sizzling in the pan. He liked his bacon soft rather than crisp, with the fat still whitish. The key was low heat.

"Do you have any aspirin?" Lindsay said.

Stavros had plenty of aspirin. He got her a bottle and a glass of water, then turned back to the stove. Once the bacon was finished he cracked a couple eggs into the pan.

"Actually, I'll have some eggs," Lindsay said.

Stavros made her some eggs and toast, then made a plate for himself, and joined her at the counter.

"*Mmmm* ... These eggs are delish," Lindsay said, squirming with pleasure.

"It's the bacon fat," Stavros said, giving her a playful look.

She smiled. "So last night you said Maggie and Wyatt were a 'great couple.'"

"Yeah. I think they are."

"Did you know he was cheating on her?"

Munching on a slice of toast, Stavros eyed Lindsay. This one doesn't hold back, he thought. On anything. "I don't know who this other woman is," he said, and it was true.

"OK. But did you know he was cheating?"

"No, I didn't." Strictly speaking, this too was true. But Stavros *had* known about Keller's second phone. Over the years Keller had occasionally used the second phone in front of Stavros—at the office, at court, over dinner—and always the conversations on it were hushed and brief, and afterward not a word of explanation was given, or expected. As far as

Stavros was concerned, Keller's business was Keller's business. Of course without question Maggie herself had at one time been connected to the second phone—when she and Keller were conducting their own affair behind Angela's back.

Watching Stavros closely, Lindsay finally nodded and the subject was dropped. When they'd finished eating, she helped clean up then said she was going to leave. Stavros got her coat.

"Are you on Facebook?" she said.

"Uh, no. I am not on Facebook."

She gave him a business card. *Lindsay Vanderberg / Interior Design.* There was a web address and a telephone number. "Call me if you want to get together," she said, smiling.

"Sounds good," Stavros said, smiling back.

They hesitated, then exchanged a quick peck on the lips.

* * *

Later that morning Stavros called Keller. The news wasn't good.

"What can I say, Stavros? I screwed up. I slept in the guest room and when I woke up she told me to leave. I'm heading to the Royal Continental now."

"Why don't you stay with me? I have an extra room."

"Thanks buddy, but the office is next door. It's easier."

"You sure?"

"Yeah. Hey listen, I have to go. I have to make some calls. I need to get to the divorce lawyers before she does."

"Is it that serious?"

"It looks that way … Anyway, I've got to run."

NINE

On Wednesday afternoon Stavros was back at Thoreau Academy, parked near the main building, waiting on his son. They had agreed to meet at 4:30, following band practice, but it was now 4:47. Had one of his employees kept Stavros waiting like this, they would have gotten a good dose of fury. There would have been yelling and threats. Yet now, oddly, Stavros was calm. Or at least, mostly calm.

Finally the boy appeared. He was with a girl. Older-looking and taller than Brendan, she had a tangled mass of dirty-blonde dreadlocks, Rasta-style, and wore an old pea coat over a flowing peasant dress. Hanging from her shoulder was a colorful patch-cloth bag, which she gripped with a hand adorned with silver rings and bracelets.

Brendan was beaming. With a rapturous, overeager, somewhat servile expression, he looked as though he were thrilled just to be in the girl's presence. Her expression was quite different. Cool and knowing, like some hippy Mona Lisa, she appeared aloofly amused by the boy's attention.

The girl was heading toward the main lot, and Brendan was tagging along, oblivious to his father. Stavros hit the horn. The kids looked over and Brendan stopped, but the girl kept walking. Brendan said a few more words to her but she didn't bother to slow her stride. The boy watched her walk off, then came to the car. Without a word he tossed his things in the back and got in the front.

"How's it going?" Stavros said.

"Good."

"How was practice?"

"It was OK."

"You guys run late?"

"No. I had to talk to someone."

Stavros nodded, feeling a slight ripple of pique. *The kid had to talk to someone* ... "And who was that girl you were with?"

"Just a friend."

Just a friend. Another ripple. "Oooh-Kay ... So, are you hungry? You ready for some food?"

"Not really. I just had a candy bar."

He just had a candy bar. Even though he knew they were meeting specifically to go eat. "Not a problem," Stavros said, forcing a smile. "Anyway, there's something I want to show you."

"What?"

"It's a surprise."

* * *

Ten minutes later they turned onto Ridley, a quiet street jammed with modest houses and even some pickup trucks. Stavros pulled into one of the driveways and kept the engine running.

"So what do you think?"

"About what?"

"This house."

Brendan looked the place over. It was tiny—just one window on either side of the front door—and decrepit. Peeling paint, listing chimney, disintegrating shingles. No garage. "It's kind of crappy."

"*Noooo,*" Stavros said gently. "It's a nice house. You should see the backyard. It's big."

"Dad, what are we doing here?"

"I'm going to rent it."

"This place?"

"Yeah. I signed the lease today." It was true. Over the past few days Stavros and a rental agent had looked at a number of properties in the

Fresh Pond area of Cambridge, apartments and houses. And sure, this place was a bit … weathered. But that was part of the appeal. In fact, the home's rundown condition had given Stavros an idea, a plan. A father-son plan.

"I don't get it," Brendan said. "Why?"

"Because I want to live here."

"What about your apartment?"

"It's not for me. Too showy. And plus, this way if you ever need anything, a ride home from school or whatever, I'll be here."

"But I thought you were going back to work soon? You said you were driving me to school for just a few weeks and it's already been three."

"I decided to take another month off. It's all set."

"OK, another month. But I still don't get it."

"Brendan, it's not that complicated. This is my new home."

* * *

At Bucky's Barbecue they sat at a table with mounds of hot food. Memphis-style ribs, brisket, sausage, beans, cornbread. A cherry soda for Stavros, because he wanted to set a good example, and a root beer for Brendan.

"I love this place," Stavros said, chomping on a rib.

"I only came here once. Mom says it's not healthy."

"That's crazy. It's all about moderation."

The boy nodded. With fork and knife he began cutting meat from a rib.

Stavros watched, amazed. They were at a BBQ joint, not Buckingham Palace. He said, "You know Brendan, it's OK if you use your hands. I won't tell your mother."

The kid looked at him.

Stavros held up his almost-bare bone, to demonstrate.

Brendan set down his cutlery, cautiously picked up the greasy rib, took a bite, and started chewing.

"See? It's fun," Stavros said. "And it tastes better that way too."

The boy smiled.

Stavros sipped his soda. "So who was that girl, back at school?"

"Just a friend."

"Brendan, there's no need to be secretive. I like women too, remember?"

The kid kept eating.

"Is she the 'older woman' you were talking about last week?"

"No ... Hey, I have a question for you."

Sighing, Stavros said, "All right."

"Why do you defend guilty people?"

With the trial approaching, the Bellingham case was back in the news. This, Stavros guessed, was what the boy was alluding to. "It's a good question. It's true that not all of our clients are innocent, but a lot of them are. And it's my job to defend them. It's just a job."

"But what about when you know the person is guilty, even before the trial starts? Like that guy you represented who bombed the mall. You said he wasn't guilty, but they had video of him actually doing it. And also that Irish Mafia guy. Everybody knows he killed people."

Stavros cleared his throat. "People ask me this all the time, and I always say the same thing. In this country, if you're accused of a crime, you have the right to a fair trial. Whether you're rich or poor, you're entitled to your day in court. It's the American way. And so my job is to make sure none of my clients ends up in jail for something they didn't do. There's an old line, 'Better ten guilty men walk free than one innocent man be convicted.'"

"But that's not what I asked. If the guy is guilty, and you help him get off, don't you feel weird?"

Stavros tugged on his soda. "It's not for me to say if my clients are guilty. If the guy claims he's innocent, then it's my job to fight for him and make sure he gets a fair shake, to make sure the state doesn't abuse its power and destroy an innocent life. And trust me, it happens. Lives get ruined all the time. Sometimes by corruption, sometimes by incompetence. As for the verdict, that's for the jury to decide, not me." But saying this, Stavros felt … uneasy. And once again the inner voice whispered: shyster … *shyster!* "The bottom line Brendan is that society needs defense attorneys. Without us, the system wouldn't work. And God forbid if you were ever accused of something, but if you were, you'd be glad you know me."

The boy mulled this, nodding. "Also, it seems like a lot of your clients are rich people." It was said evenly, without accusation.

Stavros reached for a napkin and wiped the grease from his face. "I didn't know you were so interested in what I did."

"A lot of your cases are online. I read about them. And everybody knows Newt Bellingham is rich."

"Yes. Newt Bellingham's family is definitely rich. You know Brendan, when I started my career the idea was to do some good. To make a difference. Which is why I went to work in the DA's office. And I *did* make a difference. I put away some bad guys, and I helped victims and their families get the justice they deserved. And I liked doing it. It felt good. And so when I went to work with Wyatt, my thinking was that I could help people and also make some money. I had a family to support. Bills to pay. But the fact is, I *have* helped people. People who deserved to be helped. It's something I feel good about."

"But what about Newt Bellingham—do you think he's innocent?"

"I don't know … I'm not involved with that case. We'll see what happens."

"Everybody says he's guilty."

"Well, sometimes everybody's wrong."

"So you think he's innocent."

"I didn't say that."

"You think he's guilty?"

"Brendan, I don't know. But between you and me, things don't look so good. And that doesn't leave this table, OK?"

"OK. Also, Sally knows Aimee Gibblin."

"She does?" Stavros said, alarmed.

"They live near each other."

"Are they close?"

"No. Aimee's older. But they say hi and stuff."

Stavros took another slug of his soda.

"Are you going to the trial?" Brendan said.

"No. I told you, I'm not involved with that. It has nothing to do with me."

* * *

An hour later they pulled into the driveway on Champney Street. The old house was lit up, glowing in the night. Stavros thought about Allegra. He wondered how she was doing; he wondered *what* she was doing. Was young Dr. Dylan making a house call? It was an unpleasant thought. Turning to his son, Stavros said, "Well that was fun. We should do it again."

"Yeah … Hey Dad, can I have fifty bucks?"

"Didn't I just give you a hundred?"

"That was like two weeks ago."

"What's it for?"

"Just stuff. CDs. And some kids are going out for pizza on Friday."

"Is this a date?"

"I'll just ask Mom," the boy said, reaching for the door.

"OK, OK," Stavros said. He reached for his money clip.

* * *

On Friday night Keller brought Stavros up to speed on his floundering marriage. They were back at the Steak Club, sitting at their usual corner table, with Stavros as usual facing the wall. Keller explained that he was now permanently encamped at the Royal Continental and that Maggie was making threats. She'd threatened him with arrest and a restraining order if he should return unannounced to their home. She'd threatened to hire famed feminist-attorney Saroya Spike to represent her in divorce proceedings. She'd threatened to take out a full-page ad in the *Telegraph*, announcing to Boston and the world that Wyatt Keller was a philanderer and a snake.

"Maybe she just needs a little more time," Stavros said. "Another week or so."

Keller shrugged, looking resigned, and maybe a little indifferent.

"Is there anything I can do?" Stavros said. "Should I call her?"

"No, partner," Keller said, now grinning. "Thank you."

"So what's your plan?"

"My plan?"

"To get her back."

"Well ... I don't know. We'll see how it goes."

Stavros was mystified. The couple times they had spoken on the phone this week, as now, Keller had shown little remorse over his situation. There was no grief or regret, no suffering. If anything, Keller seemed ready to let Maggie go. Stavros said, "So who is this other woman? Do you mind if I ask?"

"Her name is Belén. And I met her because of you."

"Me?"

"We sat next to each other on the flight up from Florida, when I came back after your heart attack. She's Argentinian. Absolutely gorgeous. And very bright. I love being with her."

"Wow ... So it's a thing?"

"Pretty much. She's been spending nights with me at the hotel."

"Oh man."

"What can I say, Stavros? I'm obsessed with her. She's beautiful, smart, funny. Twenty-nine and not a single wrinkle on her body. She's doing a PhD at Tufts. It just feels right with her. I didn't expect this to happen, but it did."

Stavros was stunned. Yes, he had known all along about the second phone. Nevertheless he'd always thought Keller and Maggie were solid, happy, in it for the long haul. Not once in ten years had Stavros heard Keller say a single critical word about Maggie or their relationship. And whenever he saw them together, out in public or in private at their Brookline home, Stavros had marveled at the easiness between them, the enviable harmony they seemed to share, the jokey, lighthearted rapport. It puzzled Stavros that Keller would be so willing to give that up, to give Maggie up. He wanted to ask his friend what, if anything, had gone wrong with his marriage. But something held him back, and the moment soon passed.

* * *

After their meal, as they were working on a final round of drinks, Stavros said, "I don't know if you heard, but Lindsay and I got together. That night we all went to Spectaculaire."

"Really? Hm. No, I hadn't heard. That was Maggie's idea, to bring Lindsay. Apparently she's interested in these near-death things, and so Maggie thought the two of you might hit it off. I told her you probably wouldn't be interested, but I guess I was wrong."

"Why did you think I wouldn't be interested?"

"I didn't think she was your type."

"What do you mean?"

"Lindsay's very different than Allegra. Allegra's Ivy League—brainy, driven; very Type A. Lindsay, on the other hand, appears to take life more on the easy side, shall we say."

Stavros considered this. Quite frankly, "life on the easy side" didn't sound so bad. In fact, it sounded pretty good. "How well do you know her?"

"Not well, but enough. Every now and then we have dinner: me, Maggie, Lindsay, and whoever Lindsay happens to be dating. She and Maggie are pretty close. They do yoga together, go skiing. They're pals."

"You say she dates a lot of guys?"

Keller shrugged. "They do seem to change."

"She's young," Stavros said, defending her.

"True," Keller said, sipping his drink.

It appeared that Keller wasn't too crazy about Lindsay, and Stavros wondered why. For her part, Lindsay had made it pretty clear that *she* wasn't too crazy about Keller. Maybe Keller had picked up on that and was now paying her back.

"What else do you know?" Stavros said.

"She's a bit of a party girl. Likes to have her fun. But nothing too wild, from what I can tell. Maybe the word is 'adventurous.'"

"How does she support herself? She said she's an interior decorator, but it seemed a little vague."

"Yeah, I think it's a kind of hobby job. You know, if something interesting comes her way, she'll take it. I'm guessing there's some family money there. You going to see her again?"

"I don't know."

* * *

When Stavros returned to his building the night concierge gave him a package. It was a DVD, a documentary titled *Among the Angels: My Trip to Heaven and Back*. The blurb on the case described the story of a young nurse who had drowned in the ocean near San Diego and experienced amazing things in a place she claimed was heaven. It came with a note: *I thought you might find this helpful. Xoxo, Lindsay.*

Stavros got into bed with a nightcap, and was quickly engrossed in the film. He couldn't believe how similar the woman's story was to his: Leaving her body at the moment of death and observing from above the frantic scene as lifeguards tried to resuscitate her corpse. The overwhelming feeling of love and acceptance in the heavenly realm. The greeting party of deceased family and friends. But there were differences too. The woman didn't meet Jesus. Instead she met eight-foot-tall angelic beings, luminous messengers of God. Also, she didn't go to the black place, the place where Stavros had suffered unspeakable torment. For her, it was straight to the bliss. The woman also described how she hadn't wanted to return to Earth, not even for her husband and two little girls whom she loved very much, but that the angels had told her it "wasn't her time."

Afterward, Stavros couldn't sleep. He was too excited, too hopped up from the knowledge that he truly wasn't alone with his NDE. This young woman—educated, married, employed; an altogether "normal" seeming person—had experienced something very similar to him.

The next morning he called Lindsay to thank her.

"I hope you like it," she said.

"I do. I already watched it."

"You did?"

"Yeah. It was like what happened to me. Not the same, but close."

"I want to hear your story."

"Uh, sure … sometime."

"What about tonight? Are you free?"

He went silent.

"Stavros?"

TEN

That evening Stavros pulled into the driveway of an old Queen Anne in Chestnut Hill. He killed the engine and felt a flutter of nerves. The last woman he had actually picked up for a date was Allegra, back when she lived with a roommate in Jamaica Plain and Stavros drove a ten-year-old Gnome with a busted muffler. It was a long time ago—seventeen, eighteen years.

He got out of the car, walked up to the porch, and knocked on the front door. Lindsay greeted him with a bright smile. Stavros was happy to see her too, but something held him back from giving her a kiss. Lindsay was less constrained. She went up on her toes and pressed her lips to his.

"Did you find it OK?"

"Yeah," he said, catching a whiff of her perfume, the one that smelled like candy, and sex. "No problem."

In the car he said, "So what are you thinking? You want to go someplace nearby, or head into town?"

"I was thinking Pennyfeathers. It's a perfect night for it."

Stavros went still. Allegra loved Pennyfeathers. They'd gone there a number of times in the early years, including for her birthday and when her parents were in town. "I don't think that's a good idea."

"You don't like it?"

"No, I do. It's just, you know … kind of a production. The parking, the elevator—"

"It'll be fun."

"I don't know."

"We have a reservation."

"We do?"

"I called it in this afternoon."

"Oh."

* * *

At the Providential Tower they rode the elevator to the sixty-eighth floor. They entered the restaurant, checked their coats, and were shown to a window table that overlooked the Charles. Far below them, the city and beyond glimmered in the night; and across the room, a live combo played mellow jazz. Despite his initial misgivings, Stavros was enchanted. The view, the ambience, and Lindsay Vanderberg herself were all working their magic. Lindsay's lips, which he so admired, were painted a dark shade of red. In each earlobe a fat diamond sparkled with light. The top buttons of her silky blouse were undone, and the bit of skin that showed hinted at the rest of her, which Stavros knew was quite nice. Eyes shining with delight, Lindsay was poised, happy, relaxed. Stavros had to admit, this wasn't so bad.

* * *

They started with a dozen oysters and a bottle of Muscadet, and for their entrées the waiter brought baked haddock for Lindsay and scallops for Stavros. It was delicious, all of it. Stavros couldn't have been more content.

Then Lindsay said, "I really want to hear about your NDE. When you're ready."

"Sure … At some point."

"I know the basics. I know you had a heart attack and were in a coma. And that you went to hell. Maggie said it was pretty gruesome. Demons tearing at your flesh—and doing other things …" She gave him a curious look.

"Yep, that's correct," Stavros said, irked that his very personal story had been passed around like some titillating gossip. "I went to hell. Not a good time."

"I bet. But that's pretty rare in my experience. Most people just go to a heaven-like place … What did you do, exactly? Should I be concerned?"

"Lindsay—"

"I'm sorry. But what was it like? To leave your body?"

Stavros sighed. Clearly she wasn't going to give up. She was determined to hear his story. So he told her about leaving his body, and he told her about his time in hell.

"Holy moly," she said. "It's like Dante, or Hieronymus Bosch. And then what happened?"

"Then I called out for help. I called out to God, even though I wasn't a believer. And when I did the demons went into a frenzy—hitting me harder, biting me, tearing away whole chunks of my body. I thought that was it, that I was finished, this time for real. But then I saw a white light. At first it was just a dot, but slowly it got bigger, like it was coming toward me, and as it did the demons and everything else receded—the pain, the noise, the stench, it all just faded away. And before I knew it I was engulfed in the light. It was incredible—brighter than the sun, brighter than a *thousand* suns, but it didn't hurt my eyes. And it had substance, actual weight, because I could feel it. I could feel it all over me, and it felt warm and alive, like energy, but more than energy, like it was sentient, like it was intelligent and had feeling, because now I felt safe, and cared for. I felt loved, completely loved. And I saw that my body had been restored, made whole and clean, though it wasn't made of flesh; it was more like light. I had volume and strength but no real weight. And then I saw a figure approaching me and it was my mother. She died when I was young but it was like no time had passed. She was emanating love, and telling me—with thoughts, not with words—how happy she was to see me …" Stavros felt the sting of tears, the memory moving him yet again.

Lindsay wanted more.

Stavros sipped his wine, then said, "Somehow we moved from the white light to an Earthly-type place. It just happened; one minute we're in the light, then suddenly we're in this enormous, pristine park."

"A park?"

"Yes. Not like a city park, with benches and statues, but like a nature park. There were fields and ponds and streams, and lots of trees and flowers, but it wasn't like being out in the woods; there was a certain order to everything, like it had been laid out by design. And it was all very lush, very colorful—the colors were incredible, far more vivid and vibrant than they are here. By comparison, the colors here are dull and drab."

"Were there any buildings? A lot of people see a city."

"Yes, there was a city. But it was off in the distance, many miles away. It was big and bright, kind of glowing. But I didn't go there."

"You were in the park the whole time?"

"Yes, which was fine with me. It was very peaceful there, and fantastically beautiful. Imagine the most perfect spring day, when it's warm but not too hot, and the flowers are blooming and the air is fragrant, and you're thrilled to be outside and you wish it were always that way—that's how it was, only better. Much better."

"Were there any animals?"

"Yes," Stavros said, smiling. "There were all sorts—birds and butterflies and dogs and fish and deer. All sorts of animals. But it wasn't like a zoo. The place wasn't crowded with them. Everything there is calm and tranquil. And so every now and then something would appear or fly by or wander in. There were even some lions, but they were very tame. All the animals were tame. It sounds strange to me now but when I saw the lions I wasn't afraid, and in fact it didn't even occur to me that I should be afraid. It just seemed perfectly natural to be among these creatures, these beings. And I remember this giraffe walked up to me—he just came up, slow and calm, and he lowers his head down and he's looking at me, really looking at me, into my eyes like he knows me. And my mother said, 'Remember Mr. Raffy?'" Again Stavros's eyes stung, hotly. "Oh, God. This is embarrassing."

"It's fine. Go on."

"When I was little, very little, I had a stuffed giraffe. Apparently I took it everywhere, outside to play, in the car when my mother went shopping, to bed when I slept. But I couldn't pronounce 'giraffe,' so I would say 'raff,' and eventually 'raff' became 'raffy,' then 'Mr. Raffy' … And don't repeat that."

"I won't tell anyone. But what does it mean? The real giraffe was … Mr. Raffy?"

"I don't know what it means. I have no idea."

"You didn't ask?"

"No. I just accepted it—I accepted that this giraffe, this very friendly, curious giraffe, seemed to know me, in some way. It was like with the lions, how I wasn't afraid; and with seeing my mother. Everything that was happening was so extraordinary, and at the same time so unquestionably real, that my response was just … 'wow.' Pure wonder."

"Like when you were a child."

"Yes. Exactly. Everything seemed amazing and new."

Lindsay paused to take all this in, and Stavros paused to eat another scallop. It was cold.

"So were you just with your mother the whole time?"

"No. Once we got to the park other people joined us. Lots of people. But not all at once. They just sort of drifted in, one or two at a time. My father, my aunts and uncles, my grandparents, some neighbors from Ludville, some teachers and coaches I'd forgotten, some old school friends, even some former clients. And then there were many other people I'd never met but who knew me. And they were all happy to see me. All of them."

"The greeting party," Lindsay said.

"Yes."

"And did you see God?"

Stavros reached for the bottle, poured them each more wine, and took a slow drink.

"Stavros?"

"I know it sounds absurd, but I met Jesus."

"It's not absurd. There are lots of NDEs with Jesus."

He shrugged. "I don't know."

"What?"

"It's very personal."

"Oh come on. How is it any more personal than what you've already told me?"

Stavros made a heavy sigh. "OK ... So I'm with my family and everyone else, and suddenly ... *he* appears. Not out of the clouds, not out of the sky, but he just walks up to us, very ... unassuming. And instantly I knew it was him. And everything else, everyone else, just sort of went away, and then it was just the two of us. And as he looked at me, I knew this was it. I knew this was everything: truth, ultimate meaning, whatever you want to call it. And I knew that he knew everything about me, that he knew me perfectly—everything I'd ever done, thought, or felt. But there was no judgment in him. No criticism, no anger. No disappointment. There was just compassion, and love. Pure love. It was the greatest feeling I've ever known."

"Did you do a life review?"

Stavros told her about the life review, and how he had wept.

"What did Jesus say?"

"He didn't say anything. He didn't have to. Everything was out in the open. It was clear what I had done and what I had failed to do. But as I wept, he comforted me. He consoled me. And after I settled down we talked. He spoke about love and forgiveness—those were the things he stressed the most: that we should love and forgive everyone, without exception. He also spoke about not judging other people, and the importance of charity and serving others, of putting other people before ourselves. Basically, all the stuff I'd learned as a kid, at church and at Sunday school," Stavros said, laughing quietly. "And after that, after he'd finished, he told me I had to go back."

"Were you upset?" Lindsay said.

"Very."

"All experiencers say that."

"Yeah, you don't want to leave there … And soon after that I was back in my body—*this* body. It was awful. Suddenly I'm in pain again. I'm in the hospital, and I feel depressed, and disoriented, and very heavy, like some bloated lump of meat. The body is so cumbersome. You have no idea."

Watching him, Lindsay was rapt, enthralled. She asked more questions and Stavros answered them all.

Afterward he said, "So what do you think—am I crazy?"

"No! Not at all … Do *you* think you're crazy?"

"No. But sometimes … I don't know. I mean, it's pretty incredible, right?"

"Actually Stavros, it's not as incredible as you think. NDEs happen all the time. Many thousands have been documented, and many, many more haven't. You just need to talk to some people—people who've also had one, or people who study them. Talk to a hospice nurse. Or at least read up on it. Go on Amazon. Or YouTube. There are tons of NDE things on YouTube. Christian NDEs, Buddhist NDEs, Jewish, Hindu. And lots of non-denominational ones. People who just see angels or family members. You need to educate yourself."

* * *

They ordered desserts and drank more wine. And after they'd finished eating, Lindsay asked Stavros to dance.

"I don't dance," he said.

"I know. You're not a performer."

He chuckled, but made no reply.

"Come on," Lindsay said. "It's slow music. You'll be fine."

This was true. The combo was playing late-night couple's music. All Stavros had to do was hold on to Lindsay and spin around slow, like he'd done at the junior high dance when the DJ played "Suddenly" by Billy Ocean.

Grinning at the memory, Stavros dabbed a napkin to his mouth and rose from his seat. He led Lindsay to the dance floor and they danced one, and then another number. Teeming with good feelings, from the food, the wine, the conversation, and especially the feeling of Lindsay Vanderberg in his arms, Stavros realized he hadn't enjoyed himself this much in years. Many years.

On the drive home Lindsay asked if he wanted to spend the night. He did.

ELEVEN

Encouraged by Lindsay's wholehearted belief in his afterlife journey, and inspired by her suggestion that he "educate" himself, Stavros spent the next few days investigating NDEs online. He visited NDE websites, watched NDE videos, and read NDE articles. It was enlightening, but also confusing. Opinion on the subject was wildly diverse, and while some of the accounts and analyses seemed legit, or at least plausible, others did not. So Stavros decided he needed some help—an expert witness, so to speak. Someone who had done more than just post a video to YouTube.

To find this expert witness he went through the websites of several local universities, and finally honed in on one Xanthe Notaras, professor of comparative religion at the Cambridge Divinity School. Her focus was world religions with an emphasis on mystical experience. She had degrees from Sarah Lawrence, Stanford, and Oxford, and had published numerous articles and several books. The webpage also listed her campus address and office hours.

* * *

When Stavros knocked on the professor's opened door, an older woman, seated at a desk, looked up from a paper she'd been reading. Stavros introduced himself and asked if he might have five minutes of her time.

The woman leaned back in her chair. "Aren't you that lawyer?"

"Uh, yes. Among other things."

Her brow crinkled. "Is this a legal matter?"

Stavros said it wasn't; he said he had some questions about mystical experience. "For personal reasons."

The professor considered this, then said, "Well, OK. But I am expecting students. If one comes you'll have to leave. Please take a seat, Mr. Papadakis."

Stavros unbuttoned his coat and settled into a chair. It was a modest-sized office, high-ceilinged and book-crammed. On one wall hung a number of framed degrees and also an icon of the Theotokos and Christ Child. The icon jolted Stavros, brought him back to his youth. As a boy in Ludville his mother had regularly taken him to St. Nectarios, a small Greek church where he had been baptized and attended Sunday school through the sixth grade. The church was filled with icons like this one; people would kiss them and cross themselves and sometimes light a candle, making supplications or praying for the dead.

"How did you find me?" the professor asked.

"The internet."

She grimaced slightly, and Stavros got right to it. He recounted his recent health issues and his trip to other realms, and finished by saying that he'd met Jesus—Jesus who was now, as it happened, watching him from the icon on the wall. "Are you familiar with this type of phenomenon?"

The professor's face had grown curious. "I am."

"Well, that's what I wanted to talk to you about. I'd like to get a scholar's perspective."

She nodded, studying him. Then she began: "What you describe, Mr. Papadakis—a story in which a person dies, goes to other planes, and then returns to this world—appears across religions and cultures, going back to ancient times. For example, in Plato's *Republic* there's the story of Er, a soldier who awakens on his funeral pyre and tells of his journey to the afterlife. He talks about a bright light, the soul's judgment, a place of suffering for the bad and a place of bliss for the good. The *Egyptian Book of the Dead*, which is older than Plato, has a similar structure: the soul is taken to the underworld, faces judgment, and is sent either to a place of torment or to a place free of pain and sadness. I could on: the Aztec *Song of the Dead* and the *Bardo Thodol*, which you might know as the *Tibetan Book of the Dead*, also describe afterlife realms. One could also make a case for Saint Paul having firsthand knowledge of the afterlife. There's the white light and the experience of God on the road to Damascus, which some claim to be a near-death experience, and also a number of other references in his epistles. For example, in Second Corinthians he talks about 'visions and revelations of the Lord.'"

"Now when you refer to these experiences as 'stories,' what does that mean, exactly?" Stavros said. "Are you talking about something made-up? About myths?"

"Well, in general terms, stories from ancient times tended to be redacted over generations. So typically there's movement from a par-ticular event—the Trojan War, the life of the Buddha—toward a more fictionalized narrative, which is to say, the story gets edited; elements are added or subtracted, form is imposed, and so forth. Essentially the story evolves, if you will, from personal experience to communal metaphor."

"Are you saying the near-death stories are based on fact?"

"I think, based on the evidence, from Plato up to present-day re searches on the subject, that yes, some sort of mystical phenomena is literally occurring. To me the fact that the stories appear across cultures and religions, and indeed across the ages, speaks less to an archetypal narrative form than to the simple fact that something is actually hap-pening, in some cases. Certain of my colleagues would disagree, but that, at least, is my position."

Stavros pulled out a notepad and pen and asked for a list of books on the subject. The professor recommended a dozen titles, on both NDEs in particular and mystical experience in general, including *The Varieties of Religious Experience*, *The Perennial Philosophy*, *Life After Life*, and *The Mountain of Silence*.

Afterward she said, "Are you a churchgoer, Mr. Papadakis?"

"No ... Not since I was a kid."

"You stopped believing in God?"

He hesitated. "It's complicated."

"It often is," she said with a gentle smile.

Stavros smiled too. "Someone close to me died … And after that, I think I became mad at God."

"I see. This was when you were a child?"

"I was thirteen. And then when I got to college, I read Nietzsche and Freud and all the rest, and that pretty much was it."

A warm, kindly light came into the woman's eyes. "It's a familiar story, including for myself: the death of a loved one, the world of ideas, the difficulty in making sense of it all. Though I'm guessing you've maybe had a change of heart."

Stavros chuckled. "Yes."

"You said you don't go to church, Mr. Papadakis. But do you pray?"

"No."

"You might consider it. Many people find it helpful. God tends to meet us halfway." The professor looked toward the door and said, "Just a moment Kayla."

Stavros turned and saw a young woman standing in the corridor, looking in. It was time for him to go. He thanked the professor for her time and she wished him good luck.

* * *

Days later, Stavros was deep into *The Varieties of Religious Experience* when his phone rang. Seated in his favorite armchair, he had been reading about ecstatic visions—intense states of consciousness and spiritual awareness, direct encounters with the divine.

Allegra said, "Did Brendan say anything to you this morning?" Her voice was troubled, emotional.

"About what?" Stavros said, becoming concerned.

"How was he acting?"

"He was kind of quiet. But he said he had a Spanish test, so I—"

"Yesterday morning I found drugs in his room. Twenty tablets of ecstasy."

"*Ecstasy?*"

"Yes. Last night I confronted him and that's what he said."

"Are you sure they're his? Maybe another kid—"

"No. He said he bought them. He said he was going to have a party."

Stavros cringed. "OK ... I'll take care of this. I'll talk to him."

"No. I want us to do it together. He needs to know this is very serious."

"Where is he now?"

"At band practice. Patti French is driving the kids home. Can you be here by five?"

* * *

At quarter to five Stavros was knocking on his old front door. Though he was worked up over his son, it struck him that the last time he had walked into this house, he had not walked out. His body had been taken away on a gurney, while his soul had gone off to other worlds.

Allegra appeared, and she looked distraught. There was fear and worry in her eyes, and it moved Stavros. He wanted to comfort her, but he held off. They hadn't touched in years. She led him into the living room. On the coffee table was a plastic baggie with pink tablets. Stavros examined them.

"Where did you find these?"

"In his closet."

"What were you doing in his closet?"

"I had suspicions."

"What do you mean?"

"There've been a few times this year when I thought I smelled pot on his clothes."

Stavros erupted: "*What?* Why didn't you tell me?"

"Don't you dare, Stavros!" she fired back. "If you would have been involved in his life, I would have told you. But you weren't, were you?"

"All right, all right ... So you found the pills. And then what?"

"When I got home from work I showed him the baggie. I asked him what they were and he said ecstasy, and then I asked if they were his and he said yes. I was nearly in tears, but he was completely blasé about the whole thing. He said, 'That was lame that you went into my room.' I catch him with drugs and that's his response? He's fourteen!"

"Did you ask who he bought them from?"

"Yes, but he wouldn't say. He just walked away. I told him to come back but he didn't. He went to his room and closed the door. He never did that before. I don't know what to do."

"Who else is involved, do you know?"

"No. He has new friends this year. He goes out on weekends. I thought it was OK, but maybe I made a mistake. I trusted him."

"Has he mentioned any names?"

"He's mentioned 'Ottavia' a few times. And 'Blake.' But I don't know who these kids are. I've asked but he changes the subject. He's become very secretive. He was never like that. He was always so innocent and open. I don't know what happened."

Stavros looked at his watch. "He should be here soon. How should we handle this, in terms of punishment?"

"I don't know. We could ground him. I don't know Stavros, I've never had to do that before. In the past if he did something I would just make him go to his room. But that was for talking back, not drugs!"

"Does he have an allowance?"

"No. I just give him money as he needs it."

"Has he been asking for more lately? More than usual?"

"Yes. But he would say it was for pizza and CDs—I never thought it was for this!"

"Pizza and CDs, huh? That little shit."

"What?"

"That's the line he's been giving me."

"You've been giving him money too?"

"Like an ATM."

TWELVE

Brendan came into the living room with his backpack and trumpet case. He had removed his coat and boots at the door, and was now in stockinged feet. Seeing his father, the boy scowled. "I have to go to my room," he grumbled.

"No you don't," Stavros said. "Have a seat."

Brendan gazed at his father. Stavros crossed his arms and gave the boy his best courtroom stare-down. Without a word Brendan walked over to the armchair, set down his things, and took a seat. Allegra and Stavros sat on the sofa. The boy sighed wearily, as though he were already bored.

Anger rising, Stavros motioned to the pills. "So you're a drug user now, huh?"

Brendan made a put-out face, rolling his eyes.

"You've been smoking pot, and now you're taking ecstasy? Is that right?"

Brendan glared at his mother.

"Don't look at her. Look at me," Stavros said. "And answer the question."

The boy looked at Stavros. "Yes."

"And how often do you do this? How often do you smoke pot and take drugs?"

"Not that much. Just a couple times."

"You've taken ecstasy a couple times?"

The boy nodded.

"And the pot?"

"The same."

"Have you taken anything else?"

"No."

Stavros pointed to the pills. "You bought these?"

"Yes."

"Why?"

"I was going to have a party."

"And where was this party going to take place?"

"Here. Mom and Dylan are going skiing this weekend."

Stavros turned on Allegra, ready to explode.

"That's been canceled," she said, looking not at Stavros but at Brendan.

Stavros, doing his damnedest to control himself, looked back at the boy. "So the plan was to have a party, here. In this house. And then what—you were going to give these pills to your guests?"

"Yes."

"And were you going to charge money for the pills?"

"Not for the girls. But for the guys, yes."

Stavros shut his eyes and began rubbing his forehead. He and his buddies had done the same thing in high school. They'd throw a party in the woods or at someone's house when their parents were away, get a keg or two, and charge the guys but not the girls. But there was no need to share that information now. He said, "Brendan, did you know the penalty in Massachusetts for distribution of ecstasy to minors is a minimum five-year jail sentence? Did you know that? Five years in jail? You've only been alive for fourteen years, so that's more than one third of the life you've lived so far, behind bars. How does that sound?"

"I'm a minor, so it doesn't apply."

"Oh, I see. Smart guy, huh? You have some legal insight into this matter? Well let me tell you something Brendan, it's true they won't send you to prison, but they could send you to juvenile detention until you turn eighteen. And do you know how long you'd last in juvenile detention? Somebody like you? A rich preppie from Cambridge? Five minutes, if you're lucky. Trust me, I've seen it. They'll do things to you that you cannot even imagine."

Brendan smirked.

"Yeah, laugh now," Stavros said. "And did you know, if one of your guests were to harm themselves while on these drugs, maybe get in a traffic accident on the way home, or if some girl were to get sexually assaulted here during the party, that that would be added to your sentence as well? Not to mention the fallout for your mother and me. We're talking lawsuits that would wipe this family out. No more nice house, no more private school. It would all be taken away."

Again the boy rolled his eyes.

"I'm sorry Brendan, but is this not registering with you? Do you think I'm just making it up?"

"No. But if I ever did get caught, you'd get me off."

Everything stopped for Stavros. His thoughts. His breathing. The rotation of the planet. And then, he could feel Allegra's eyes on him, her hot condemning eyes. The boy had touched on an old wound, an old rift between the former husband and wife. "*What did you say?*" Stavros said.

"You'd help me if I got caught."

Stavros lost it. "*Let me tell you something Brendan,*" he roared, pointing a finger, "*you could not be more wrong! If you ever get caught by the cops with any sort of drugs, don't call me, because I will not defend you! And if I ever catch you with drugs again, I'll haul your ass down to Central Square and demand they book you on the spot. A citizen's arrest!*"

"Oh, that's nice," the boy said calmly. "You'd defend a Mafia hitman but not your own son."

Another blow. Stavros was finding it difficult to breathe. "That's different."

"Why, because I'm not paying you?"

Now Allegra lost it. "*Brendan, that's enough!*" she screeched.

The boy lowered his eyes.

"And what about the lying?" Stavros demanded.

"*What lying?*" Brendan said, now affronted.

"Twenty hits of ecstasy at, what, twenty bucks a pop? Where'd you get the four-hundred dollars?"

The kid glanced away, guiltily.

"Yeah, that's right," Stavros said. "From your mother and me. 'What do you need the money for, Brendan?' 'Pizza and CDs, Dad.' 'Oh, OK, here you go.' You lied to your mother, and you lied to me. You played us for suckers!"

"Sometimes I did buy pizza. And sometimes I bought CDs."

"Sure you did. I give you fifty bucks, you go for a slice and save the rest for drugs, and your conscience is clear, is that it?"

Finally, the boy showed some remorse. "I'm sorry I lied … But the other stuff, you're blowing it out of proportion. Pot is legal in some states, and it's going to be legal here soon too. And ecstasy just makes you feel good. Me and my friends don't believe in drug laws. People should be free to do what they want."

"*Oh my God,*" Allegra said, throwing her hands up.

Stavros tried a different tack. "Brendan, look. You say we're blowing this out of proportion, but I'm telling you, I've seen people ruin their lives because of drugs. I've seen it again and again. Somebody makes a bad decision, and suddenly they're in jail, or in the hospital, or maybe they die. I'm telling you, you could lose everything—school, friends, career. Everything."

"I get it, Dad. I'm sorry. I really am."

The words seemed genuine. Or at least, mostly genuine. Stavros turned to Allegra and they exchanged a cautious glance.

Then Brendan stood.

"What are you doing?" Stavros said.

"I'm hungry."

"You're *hungry?* We're not finished!"

"Look, I need to eat. I've had a long day."

Stavros shot to his feet. "*Sit your ass down!*"

Brendan sat down.

"You don't get it, do you?" Stavros said.

"I do, Dad. I screwed up. It won't happen again."

"Well that's nice to hear. As to your punishment, you're grounded for the rest of the school year."

"*What?* You can't do that!"

"I just did."

"Mom!" the boy cried, looking to his mother.

Stavros said, "When you're not at school or with one of us, you're going to be in this house. You lied to us, Brendan, and you made some very bad choices. So over the next—"

"I'm not gonna do it."

"*Excuse me?*"

"You can't make me stay here."

"You think I'm playing around, Brendan? Let me tell you something —if you leave this house when you're not supposed to, even once, then no more Thoreau, you got that? I'll haul your ass out of there and send you to public school, how does that sound?"

The boy was aghast.

Stavros said, "If you want to lie and engage in criminal activity and take your privileged life for granted, then you can do it on the city's dime, because I'm not going to pay sixty grand a year for someone who thinks this is all a joke."

Brendan had started to cry. "I hate you!"

"And I want to know who sold you the drugs."

"No!" The boy stood.

"Brendan, sit down!"

"*Go to hell!*" He started to walk out, but Stavros jumped up and intercepted him. He didn't touch the boy but he stood in his way, and Brendan stopped short.

"Brendan, sit down," Stavros said firmly.

"No!"

"Brendan, I'm telling you …"

"What, are you going to hit me?"

Stavros, the recipient of many blows from his own father, was tempted to do just that.

"I wish you would have died," Brendan said.

Stavros froze, and the boy darted around him and went for the stairs. Stavros didn't move. His heart was racing, and soon came the crash of Brendan slamming his bedroom door.

Allegra was incensed. *"What the hell were you thinking?* We didn't agree to that!"

Stavros said nothing.

"And you do realize if he does break his punishment, that we'll have to follow through, right? That we'll have to take him out of Thoreau?"

"Maybe I went too far."

"Yeah, maybe you did," she said, seething.

"I wasn't getting through to—"

"And if the police catch him, no problem! Dad's a criminal lawyer!"

Stavros knew that was coming. Oh, yes—without question he knew that was coming. He knew she would have to get in the dig and remind him of an old grievance. It hurt, and it pissed him off, but Stavros also knew it was deserved. And without another word, Allegra walked away.

* * *

Alone in the living room, the family pariah, Stavros remembered an argument from long ago. He and Allegra, then living near Porter Square, had just gotten home from dinner out with Keller and his wife Angela. Stavros and Keller were in talks to form a partnership and were just about there. Allegra was against it.

"Why on earth," she said, "would you want to be involved with that guy? With someone who deals with known criminals? Someone who deals with slime? I don't understand. Especially since you have other options!"

Because of his good work with the DA, Stavros had been approached by a number of interested parties, both corporate and governmental. Inquiries had been made, opportunities discussed.

"You have your pick," she went on, "so why get involved with *that?* Seriously, are you crazy? I don't understand you!"

"That's because you don't understand the law," he said. "Criminal defense is the cornerstone of our entire legal system. It's the cornerstone of democracy! The presumption of innocence and the right to a fair trial are what make us a civilized people. Without that we'd be like the communists!"

"Oh my God! That is such bullshit. If you really believe you're protecting democracy, then why not open your own office and defend the poor? Help working people. Keller deals with rich guys—criminals with money. That's justice? That's protecting civilization?"

"You don't know what you're talking about. It's not that simple. I want to do some good, Allegra, but I also want to make some money. I've earned this. *We've* earned this. Brendan will always be taken care of."

This only incited her. "So if it's about money then why not work for Cabot & Snow! They'll pay you more than we could ever need!"

"I've told you a million damn times, I am not the corporate type! I'm not a schmoozer, OK? I'm not a suck-up. That's not me! And another thing—I happen to like Keller. We get along. There's an easiness between us, and that's important. And when you get to know him better, you'll like him too."

"Stavros, I'm telling you, you're making a mistake! The guy is trouble."

"What the hell is this? Do I tell you what to do? 'Oh, don't do cardiology because brain surgery would be more prestigious'? Do I say that to you?"

"*It's not the same thing you idiot!*" The tendons in her neck strained like taut cords.

"*Don't start with the names!*" he shouted back. "This is really about you, isn't it? You don't want to have to tell your colleagues that your husband is doing criminal law. You want to say he's on Beacon Hill or shuffling paper for some bank. Well I'm sorry if my career arc is no longer fashionable to you. God forbid I should embarrass you by keeping innocent people out of jail. Why do something noble when I can hang out with a bunch of Ivy League assholes at Cabot & Snow?"

"Oh go to hell, Stavros! Go to hell you fool! *Noble!* Yeah, Wyatt Keller is noble!"

"Why don't you just admit it? Why not be honest and admit that it will embarrass you if I do criminal law? Admit it!"

"OK, Stavros, you want to know what I'm really thinking? This is what I'm thinking. How are you going to explain it to your son, when he gets older and wants to know why Daddy helps murderers and Mafiosi? Why Daddy keeps bad men out of jail? How are you going to justify that? And what do you think it's going to do to his moral development?"

"His *moral development?*" Stavros spat, incredulous. "You're a sanctimonious bitch, you know that? Looking down your nose at everybody. Brendan will be proud of his father! Yeah, go on, shake your head. Miss Know-It-All. Because it's not about mobsters and murderers. It's about helping people, everyday people who find themselves in a jam. I'm telling you, the kid will be proud!"

The kid will be proud. Stavros focused on the backpack and trumpet case on the floor beside the armchair. What have I done, he wondered? What have I done to my boy?

Stavros took up his coat and headed for the door.

* * *

The next morning, just as Stavros was about to head out, Allegra called.

"Brendan's not going to school today," she said. "He's staying home."

"Why, because he's mad at me?"

"He's upset, Stavros. You were very hard on him last night. He needs to process what happened. Being at school with his friends would just complicate it."

Stavros shook his head but held his tongue. It was too early for a blowup.

"I'm staying home too," she went on, "and I'll be here this weekend. I'm worried sick that he's going to do something."

"Like what?"

"*Like leave the house!*" she snapped. "Like force us to take him out of Thoreau! I wish you wouldn't have done that, Stavros! You should've said we'd think about it—both of us. The idea was that we were going to do this together, not you by yourself."

"I know, and I'm sorry. I just got caught up in it. He was laughing at us."

"Stavros, he's happy at Thoreau. I don't want him to lose that. But if he does something and we don't follow through, then he'll think he can get away with anything. This is a real shit situation!"

"Allegra, he already *does* think he can get away with anything, and that's the whole damn point! I don't want him to lose Thoreau either. But something had to be done. If he's into ecstasy now, and he's lying and thinking he's immune from the law, what's next? What do you think he'll be like at fifteen? At sixteen?"

"I just wish you would have included me in the decision."

"I know. You've said it a few times now."

He waited for the sharp reply, but it didn't come. Instead she said, "Could you still pick up Sally?"

"Sure. Actually, that works well. I'd like to ask her a few questions."

"Stavros, don't. I don't want Patti to get upset. Sally has nothing to do with this."

"Fine. I won't say a word."

* * *

Stavros drove over to Alden and tooted the horn. He really liked Sally. At first he'd feared she would take away from his time with Brendan, but that hadn't been the case. If anything, she enhanced the morning drive, made it more enjoyable, contributing to the conversations and starting new ones. The upcoming presidential election greatly excited her, and she'd begun wearing a "Zumpthor 2016" pin on her newsboy cap. Passionate about her candidate, Sally would lecture Stavros on how "the system" was "rigged," healthcare was "broken," Wall Street "corrupt," and the student loan system a "criminal scam," in which colleges and the government colluded to financially exploit young people. Howie Zumpthor, Sally boldly declared, would fix everything. Stavros was charmed, amused by her teenage optimism.

Coming out of the house, she bounded down the porch steps, tossed her things on the backseat, and sat in the front.

"How are you Sally?"

"Good. I have a math test and I'm going to kick butt."

"Excellent," Stavros said, shifting the car into drive. "So, Brendan's not coming today. Obviously."

"Yeah, I know."

"Did he text you?"

"No. He posted it on Facebook."

"Facebook?"

"Yeah, he also said he's grounded for the rest of the year, and that his party's canceled."

"He mentioned his party? On the internet?"

"Yep."

Stavros winced. "And did you know about this party? Before today?"

"Yeah. A lot of people did."

"Were you going to go?"

"No. My mother wouldn't let me."

"You're *mother* knew about this party?"

"Mm-hmm."

"How?"

"I told her."

Oh boy ... Stavros said, "Sally, who are Ottavia and Blake? Do you know them?"

The girl gave him a side-glance. "Not really."

"Not really?"

"No. They're juniors. They don't talk to me."

"Is Brendan friends with them?"

"Um, Mr. Papadakis, I don't feel comfortable talking about Brendan behind his back."

"Sure. I understand. And I can respect that. Nobody likes a snitch. But I'm worried about him, that's all, and this is just between us."

Eyes focused on the road, Sally kept silent. But when Stavros pulled to the curb at the Thoreau entrance, she said, "Blake is really into drugs, and so is Ottavia." She hopped out of the car, grabbed her things from the back, and was off.

Stavros wasted no time. He pulled into the school's parking lot and called Dickie Haggerty, the firm's PI. Stavros explained the situation and said he wanted the name of the dealer responsible for the drugs, and that Dickie should start with two juniors at Thoreau Academy named Ottavia and Blake.

THIRTEEN

"I haven't heard from you in a while," Lindsay Vanderberg said over the phone.

Stavros was in Cambridge, at his new place. He had decided to move in midmonth after he'd worked out a deal with the landlord. Stavros would paint the home's interior, all five rooms, in exchange for a month's rent plus the cost of supplies. Of course, the idea had been that Brendan would help out. Stavros had envisioned the project as a sort of father-son bonding experience. But thanks to the drugs fiasco, it looked as though Stavros would be painting alone.

"It's been a crazy week," he said. He omitted the part about Brendan and the twenty hits of X, and spoke instead of the big move. "I had cleaners in here yesterday, and today I've got people in my apartment, packing everything up."

"What are you doing now?"

"I'm expecting a delivery from Home Warehouse, and then I'm going to do some work."

"Why don't I come over?"

"There's no furniture here."

"That's OK. I have something for you, and I'd like to see the place."

* * *

An hour later Lindsay said, "Stavros, is this a joke?" She was standing in his new driveway, looking at his new home. She wore a white down parka and held two fancy shop bags, one in each hand. "Why would you want to live here? Why would *anyone* want to live here?"

"I like it."

"You *like* it? But you have such a nice apartment!"

"Nah. I wasn't happy there."

"And this is your solution?"

"Let me show you the backyard."

He led her up the driveway and around the house. The yard was roughly fifty by thirty feet, and was bordered by leafless trees and shrubs through which you could see the backs and sides of other tiny houses. When Stavros had first come here with the rental agent he'd envisioned the yard in spring, once the foliage had filled in: it would be Edenic, a green oasis, complete with birds and squirrels. "Not bad, huh?" he said.

Taking in the barren, snow-covered plot, Lindsay appeared bewildered. Stavros took her into the house. Entering the kitchen through the back door, she gasped. "I thought you said you had cleaners in here?"

"I did," Stavros said. In fact, the cleaners had spent several hours in this room alone, and afterward Stavros had thought it looked pretty good. But now, with Lindsay's reaction, he wasn't so sure. The stove and refrigerator, which were maybe twenty years old, appeared grimy and cheap. The ceiling and walls—cracked, warped, and peeling—had permanent grease stains. The 1970s linoleum floor was still grungy, and always would be, no matter how many times it was mopped. He said, "Let me show you the dining room."

It too was in a sorry state, in need of a complete redo. But that, precisely, was the plan. Stavros pointed to the just-delivered supplies from Home Warehouse—spackle, primer, brushes, rollers, pails, etcetera—and explained that he was going to fix the place up.

"Yourself?" Lindsay said.

"Yeah. My son and I. Hopefully."

"Have you ever done this type of work?"

"Sure, when I was a kid. We did all our own painting and carpentry. If your house needed fixing up, you did it yourself."

"Well when I was a kid, if your house needed fixing up your dad paid someone to do it. Really Stavros, there's no need to be all macho about this—it's going to take forever. Let me make a call. I know a guy who does great work."

Stavros declined, and Lindsay, looking mystified, said, "But why *this* house? And why *this* neighborhood? Do you gamble? I dated a guy once who—"

"No, I don't gamble. I just wanted something … simple."

She was scrutinizing him, baffled, and then all at once her face brightened. "This is because of your NDE, isn't it?"

He shrugged. "Who knows?"

"It is," she said, her eyes softening. "I think it's beautiful."

Embarrassed, Stavros said nothing.

"Just don't give your money away," Lindsay added, confidentially. "I know someone who did. She became very spiritual after a trip to Tibet, and one day she cashed in her trust fund and gave all the money to charity. Then about a year later she regretted it, and now she's living with her mother."

"I'll keep that in mind," Stavros said.

Gazing tenderly at him, Lindsay abruptly stepped forward and kissed Stavros long on the mouth. It surprised him—the impulsiveness of it, but also the feel. It felt good, he realized. Very good.

Lindsay then held out the two shop bags, saying, "These are for you."

In the first was a bottle of champagne, and in the second two flutes wrapped in pink tissue paper.

"Oh, thank you—a housewarming gift?"

"Actually, it's for Valentine's."

"Valentine's?"

"Mm-hmm."

"Is that today?"

"It is. Unless they changed it."

Stavros stared at her, surprised once again. He said, "I'm sorry, I … didn't realize …"

"It's not a big deal. But it's nice to know where things stand."

He was speechless.

"I'm kidding," she said, grinning. "You should see your face. Don't worry about it. It was just an excuse to see you. Anyway, let's have a toast. To your new place."

But Stavros could see she was only half-kidding. He said, "Let's do something. Let's go out."

"But you're not dressed."

He was in work clothes: sneakers and jeans. "I can change. We'll go back to my place."

"Actually, why don't we go to mine. We can order in and drink this champagne. How does that sound?"

* * *

Lindsay was very pleased, her eyes shimmering with delight. "It's yummers, no?"

They were in her dining room, drinking champagne and eating sushi —tuna, squid, sea urchin, salmon. Chopin played in the background, and on the table were several lit candles, casting a golden glow. And lying close by on the floor and watching Stavros with what seemed a disapproving gaze, was Sophie, Lindsay's rescue dog, a three-legged mutt of indeterminate breed.

"Yes, everything's yummers," Stavros said, saying the word "yummers" for the first time in his life. "This was a great idea."

"Better than spending Valentine's Day alone?" Lindsay teased.

Stavros smiled, a bit uneasily, but said "Yes," and meant it.

* * *

"I saw Maggie last night," Lindsay said, chopsticks in hand. "She was asking about you."

"What did you say?" Stavros said, munching on a piece of yellowtail.

"I said you're something of a puzzle."

"Isn't that a good thing, to a woman?"

Lindsay made a face, then said, "You're not what I expected. Not even close. I'd heard things, and I don't mean from Maggie. You and Wyatt both have some PR issues."

"Is it that bad?"

"It's worse. But unless you've been putting on an act, you're not that guy. Even Sophie likes you, which is unusual."

Stavros looked at the dog, and she, hearing her name, lifted her chin while keeping her watchful eyes fixed on Stavros.

"She does?" he said doubtfully.

"Oh yes. Generally she growls at men."

Stavros sipped his champagne. "And how's Maggie doing? I saw the *Bugle*."

Over the past week the tabloid's gossip page had given full coverage to Maggie and Wyatt's collapsing marriage. There'd been a column, with photos, speculating on Keller's past infidelities, including with his "current secret squeeze Belén Canales," whom the writer described as "a sizzling siren from South America who's been turning heads and breaking hearts at Tufts University." Another column announced that Maggie had hired Renata Hegewische, a hot, up-and-coming divorce attorney who had recently represented the former wife of Cesar Dominguez, the Red Sox's star left fielder, with successful, eight-figure results. In response, Keller had called Stavros in a rage, claiming that Maggie was feeding dirt to the press, and that Hegewische was likely going to contest the couple's prenuptial agreement.

"She's doing what she has to do," Lindsay said.

"What does that mean?"

"Wyatt's going to try and drag her through the mud. She has to protect herself."

"*Wyatt's* going to drag *Maggie* through the mud? That's a bit rich, don't you think?"

"He does it all the time, Stavros. Everything's personal to that guy. It's all about himself and his career, his fame. People are just props to him."

"Lindsay, he's my friend."

"Well, Maggie's my friend."

"Yes," Stavros said, nodding. "Maybe we should talk about something else."

"OK … Are you going to the trial? That starts this week, right?" She meant the Bellingham trial.

"Yeah. Tomorrow morning."

"Are you going?"

"No."

"Why?"

"I'm not interested."

"What do you mean you're not interested?"

Stavros just shrugged; he didn't want to get into it.

"But aren't you involved with that case? I thought you were still, I don't know, consulting or something."

"No. I'm not involved in any way."

"Really?"

"Really."

She looked at him, curiously. "So then Stavros, what exactly do you do all day?"

His defenses went up. Did she think him an idler? A slacker? "I've been reading," he said. "And thinking."

A great smile bloomed on her face. "That's great. And what are you reading?"

Reassured by this, and reminded yet again that Lindsay was his one and only NDE supporter, Stavros told her about meeting Professor Notaras and the books she had recommended. He told her about *The Varieties of Religious Experience* and William James's views on St. Teresa's visions and St. Paul's conversion. And he told her about the book he was currently reading, *The Perennial Philosophy*, and about Aldous Huxley's accounts of the similarities of mystical experience across religions and cultures: the saints, sages, and prophets of Judaism, Hinduism, Buddhism, Islam, and Christianity, all sharing common ground at the deepest, most exalted states of consciousness. Stavros spoke at length and with great feeling. "This stuff is real," he said. "Yet all my life I knew nothing about it. I'm telling you, dying was the best thing that ever happened to me."

* * *

The next morning, on the ride over to Champney Street, Stavros learned that a blizzard was heading for the city. A giddy weatherman was predicting two feet of snow and severe coastal flooding, beginning that evening. Wind gusts would likely down power lines. Stock up on bottled water and batteries, he said.

Pulling into the driveway, Stavros thought about a different kind of blizzard: a blizzard of adolescent spite. This would be his and Brendan's first contact since the family sit-down, and Stavros had a feeling it wasn't going to be pleasant.

And sure enough, the kid trudged to the car with a glowering face, making it clear he was ready for battle. His first move, oddly, was to open the front passenger door, very wide. Next he opened the back passenger door, also very wide. Stavros wondered what was going on. Very slowly Brendan put his trumpet case on the backseat, then did the same with his backpack. Meanwhile the car's interior, exposed to the elements, was filling with frigid air.

In a voice just loud enough for Stavros to hear, Brendan said, "Oh, I forgot something." He headed back to the house.

Stavros called out, "Hey, could you close the doors please?"

Brendan ignored him.

His breath puffing whitely in the icy air, Stavros got out of the car, went around to the other side, and shut both doors. Back behind the wheel, he put the heater on high but turned off the passenger-side seat-warmer. If the kid wants to freeze, he can freeze.

Minutes later Brendan buckled in. No hello, no words of explanation. No nothing.

Anger bubbling, Stavros forced a smile. "Good morning Brendan."

The boy remained silent just long enough for it to be officially rude, then muttered, "Hi."

Excellent, Stavros thought. A great way to start the day. He backed the car into the street, and immediately Brendan started texting.

Stavros sighed, and told himself they would get through this. The boy just needs a little time to be mad, then he'll get over it. Love everyone and forgive everything, Stavros reminded himself. He turned on Brendan's seat-warmer and said, "So, I'm moving to my new place today."

No reply.

"Brendan?"

"That's great," the kid said, not looking up.

"I'm going to be doing some painting too. The whole interior   I could probably use some help."

Brendan snickered with derision, and Stavros felt lost. He didn't know what to do. He didn't know how to handle this—teenage petulance, teenage scorn. Should he say something? Say nothing? At the stop sign he went through his new CDs, the ones Brendan had given him in exchange for the DVD of *The Mirror*. He slid Louis Armstrong into the stereo and the opening notes to "On the Sunny Side of the Street" rang out.

Brendan flipped. "*Don't play that!*" he screamed, burning with hate. The boy ejected the disc from the console, then tore out of his coat pocket a tangle of earphone wires, plugged them in, and turned to the window.

* * *

With a sense of relief Stavros pulled up to Sally's house. He knew he could count on her for some friendly feeling, some warmth and good cheer. But when the girl came to the car it wasn't with her usual buoyant air. Instead there was a heaviness about her, a look of grievance, her brow stern, her mouth pinched and unsmiling. As she took her seat Stavros said, "How are you Sally?"

"*I'm OK*," she snapped, avoiding his eye.

Stavros flinched. He tried again: "Did you hear about the blizzard? No school tomorrow, huh?"

She gave him a dismissive sneer, said "Whatever," then looked out the window.

Baffled, Stavros shifted the car into drive and sped down Alden. Minutes later a snippy voice came from the backseat: "Are you going to the trial today?" And Stavros thought, *Ah*, there it is. Till now the trial hadn't been mentioned on the ride to school. He glanced in the rearview; Sally was glaring at him, ready to cross swords.

"No. I'm not," he said.

"*Why?*"

"Because I'm not involved with that case. Not for a long time."

"But you were."

"That's true. Last year. But not anymore."

"Brendan said you think Newt Bellingham is guilty."

Stavros was floored. "I never said that!" He turned to his son. The boy was looking out the window, listening to music, oblivious to the conversation.

"Brendan," Stavros said.

No response.

"*Brendan!*"

No response.

Stavros yanked the left earbud out of the boy's head.

"*What are you doing?*" the kid shouted.

"Did you tell Sally I said Newt Bellingham was guilty?"

"That's what you said. At Bucky's Barbecue."

"I did not say that!"

"Yes you did. You said, 'Between you and me, it doesn't look good.'"

Stavros couldn't believe it. Couldn't believe that his son, his *blood*, would betray such a confidence.

140

Brendan put his earbud back in and turned to the window.

In the rearview, Stavros saw Sally's cross, censorious eyes.

"*Yes*," he admitted, "I did say that it didn't look good for Newt Bellingham. I said that. But it doesn't mean I think he's guilty; they're not the same thing."

"But if you think he's guilty, why are you representing him?"

"*Sally*," Stavros said, his patience straining, "I just said that I *didn't* say he was guilty."

"But Brendan said you did."

"Brendan misunderstood me. What I said, and what I meant, was that things don't look good in terms of … various legal issues. The law can be very complicated, very technical, and it would take a long time to explain. But the point is, I never said Newt Bellingham was guilty. I only think this is going to be a close trial. That's all I meant. And also, I am *not* representing him. Like I told you, I'm not involved with that case anymore. Now, if it turns out Newt Bellingham did indeed commit this crime, then I'll be the first one to say he should be punished. But until all the facts are presented, until both teams have made their case, we can't say for sure either way, can we? It would be irresponsible to do that. Otherwise, what's the point of having the trial? What's the point of having a democracy? You believe in democracy, right?"

She nodded.

"We just have to be patient and see what happens," he said.

While not entirely appeased, the girl seemed less upset.

Stavros said, "How well do you know her? Aimee Gibblin?"

"She's older, and we have different friends. But I see her around and she's nice. I've known her since I was little. She didn't deserve this."

FOURTEEN

The next morning, Stavros woke in Cambridge. He was in his new home, surrounded by a jumble of boxes and furniture. Because the plan was to paint the bedrooms first, he had instructed the movers to set up his bed, television, and stereo in the dining room. The rest of his furniture they crammed into the living room and basement.

In the kitchen he made coffee and scrambled some eggs. He was buttering a slice of toast when the phone rang.

"School's been canceled," Allegra said, "though that's probably obvious."

Outside the window everything was white—the ground, the trees, the roofs of houses. "I appreciate the call," he said.

"So how did it go yesterday?"

"How did what go?" Stavros said. It had been an eventful day: The ride to school. The move from Boston. His first trip to a supermarket in roughly fifteen years. His night spent unpacking.

"The ride with Brendan."

"Not so good. He gave me the silent treatment, then he screamed at me when I tried to play Louis Armstrong. How's he been with you?"

"Pretty much the same. He stays in his room a lot."

"Have you talked to him? About what happened?"

"Yes. I told him that he's jeopardizing his future, and that he could lose everything if he does this again."

Stavros was stunned. "That's what *I* said."

"I know."

He was flabbergasted. Allegra had criticized his performance at the family sit-down, but now it sounded like she was endorsing it. "How'd he take it?"

"Better than he did Thursday night. I think it's starting to sink in for him, how serious this is."

"And what did he say about his punishment?"

"He thinks it's unfair."

"What did you say?"

"I told him that you and I felt it suited the crime, and that we were together on this. I told him we didn't want to pull him out of Thoreau but that we would if we have to."

"You said that?"

"I did. At first I thought the punishment was too much. But something drastic needed to be done, and you did it. I would've kept him home for a week and then he would have gone right back to it. You did the right thing, Stavros ... And I'm glad you did."

He was amazed—Allegra was praising him?

"Well, I should go," she said.

Go? This was the best conversation they'd had in years! "Wait," he said. "Did you, uh, hear that I moved back to Cambridge?"

"Yes. Brendan told me."

"Yeah ... It's nice over here ... And I'll be closer to him."

Silence.

"Hello?"

"I have to go, Stavros. Good-bye."

* * *

All that day Stavros worked. He shoveled out his car, finished unpacking the kitchen stuff, then started the big painting project. He laid down drop cloths in the two bedrooms and began scraping loose paint and crumbling plaster. Though his muscles soon tired, Stavros was reminded of how much he enjoyed this type of work. Using his hands, using his body, doing actual, manual labor, was very agreeable to him. It felt good.

Around four o'clock his phone rang. It was Dickie Haggerty, calling about the drugs thing: "So I traced the names you gave me to a dealer out of Southie. The guy's supplying most of the colleges in the area, and also some of the high schools, including Thoreau. Big operation."

"You have a name?" Stavros said, brushing white plaster dust off his shirt.

"Yep. But you're not gonna like it."

Stavros waited.

"Kenny Bracken."

"Who?"

"Kenny Bracken, aka Kenny Sunshine."

Stavros shut his eyes, pained. Some years earlier he had gotten Kenny off on a charge of possession with intent to distribute. Two Boston beat cops had caught him with a kilo of blow in the trunk of his car, but in court Stavros had successfully argued that the search was conducted without probable cause, and Kenny Sunshine walked. "Are you sure about this?"

"Yeah. It's him … What do you want me to do?"

"I want the names and addresses of the kids who deal for him. Just the college kids; the guys in the frats and clubs. As many names as you can get."

"Anything else?"

"No. Just call me when you got it. And Dickie, bill me personally on this one. Don't send anything to the office."

Stavros hung up, and for several long seconds he considered smashing his phone. He'd done it often in the past—destroying the thing in a rage, at the house, at the office, and one time in a crowded dentist's waiting room, causing people to gasp and a baby to start crying. Now though, Stavros controlled himself. He slid the phone into his shirt pocket, went down to the kitchen, and poured himself a drink.

* * *

On Friday morning, after a week of simmering animosity, Brendan got into the car with his earbuds already plugged in—something he'd not done before. Without a word or even a glance to acknowledge his father's existence, the boy buckled in and began texting.

In silence they drove to Sally's. Things weren't much better with her either. Since the start of the trial she had been peevishly aloof with Stavros. Today was no different. Avoiding his eye, she took her seat with a perfunctory "Hi Mr. Papadakis," donned her earbuds, and began texting.

At Thoreau, Stavros decided to take a chance. As Brendan was unbuckling, Stavros gently took him by the arm. The boy recoiled and shot his father a furious look. Gritting his teeth, Stavros forced a smile, his patient-parent smile, and with both hands made a gesture like he was extracting imaginary plugs from his ears. Brendan sneered and removed one of his earbuds.

Stavros said, "This weekend I'm going to be doing some painting at my new place. If you want, I could pick you up and you could give me a hand. We'll do a little work, then go get some food. What do you say?"

"*Are you kidding me?*" the boy cried. He jumped out of the car and slammed the door. Then he got his things from the backseat and slammed that door too.

* * *

Back on the road, Stavros decided he needed a little treat, something to take the edge off this crappy morning. He was thinking maybe a stack of banana pancakes, with syrup and whipped cream. And possibly some bacon and sausage too. Yet as the Imperator sped across Cambridge, the idea of the greasy feast that awaited Stavros wasn't enough to entirely distract him from his various problems and concerns. One by one they pressed down on him: The situation with Brendan. The situation with Allegra. The situation with Lindsay. His job. His health. His whole damn life, come to think of it. By the time he found a parking spot,

Stavros had begun to wonder if going back to work might not be such a bad idea. Reuniting with Keller, losing himself in his cases—would that really be so bad? Or, to put it another way—would it be any worse than continuously taking shit from an angry fourteen year old? It was something to consider.

He went to Augie's, in Inman Square, his favorite breakfast spot from the old days. He and his family had gone there over many Sunday mornings. As a little boy Brendan would sit in a booster seat, doodling on a paper placemat with crayons brought by the waitress. Allegra would say, "Draw an elephant, a frog, and a caterpillar," and the boy, very diligently, would get to work.

Settling into a booth, Stavros ordered his food and asked for a *Telegraph*. Prior to today he had been avoiding the trial; he'd wanted nothing to do with it. But no more.

The waitress returned with coffee and the paper. The headline was a stunner: "Bellingham Accuser Breaks Down on Stand." The story began, "The 18-year-old Cambridge woman who accuses the 23-year-old son of Republican senator Clay Bellingham of Pennsylvania of date-raping her in JFK Park was unable to finish giving testimony Thursday following hostile questioning by defense attorney Sal Mahony." The article noted that the "unnamed accuser" had repeatedly burst into tears and that Judge Nathan Chinlund had "twice cautioned Mahony on his 'excessively aggressive' approach." The judge then called a recess and ordered the proceedings to resume the next day. The article also mentioned that some observers had questioned why lead defense attorney Wyatt Keller had assigned the cross-examination of the accuser to his second chair, Mahony, rather than do it himself.

At this last bit, Stavros smiled darkly. Keller was no fool. His cross-examination skills were second to none. But if it served his purposes Keller wouldn't hesitate to hand the job off to someone else. And for the past thirteen years that someone else had been Stavros. Stavros had been Keller's attack dog, the designated witness bully, the yeller, the screamer, the guy who intimidated and got results. Stavros's verbal smackdowns had broken many witnesses. Such witnesses had wept and begged judges to intervene. Most famously, one guy had literally pissed his pants under a Stavros cross-examination. But this time it was Sal who was sent in to rough up a vulnerable witness, not Stavros.

And just like that, the thought of driving Brendan to school did not seem so bad. Stavros had no complaints. He tossed the paper aside, sipped his coffee, and smiled as the waitress brought his food.

FIFTEEN

On Monday morning Stavros was expecting more drama, more filial abuse. But when Brendan got into the car there was no hostility on his face. Instead the boy appeared anxious, even a little frantic, and immediately he turned to Stavros, saying, "Did you hear what happened?"

"About what?"

"Aimee Gibblin's dad said they're done with the trial. He said Aimee wasn't going back to court."

"Where did you hear this?"

"On the news, just now. It's on all the channels. He gave an interview last night and said Aimee's been getting death threats and that people have been harassing her. He also said the lawyers were bullying her and that the judge wasn't doing anything to stop it, and that's why she didn't go to court on Friday—"

"Hold on—she didn't go to court on Friday?"

"You didn't know that?"

Stavros didn't. Since he'd read the paper at Augie's on Friday morning, Stavros hadn't seen or heard any news of any sort. He hadn't gone online all weekend or watched any television, nor had he spoken to Keller. Apart from dinner out with Lindsay on Friday night, he'd spent the last three days at home, reading and working on the two bedrooms.

Brendan explained: "After Aimee didn't show up on Friday the judge said she was in contempt of court, and that if she didn't show up today she would be arrested. But Mr. Gibblin told the reporter that the judge would have to arrest him too because he wasn't letting Aimee go back.

It's pretty wild. Could that happen, though? Could they arrest Aimee and her dad?"

Stavros said they could.

* * *

When Sally got into the car Stavros turned in his seat to greet her, face-to-face. He wanted to connect with her, let her know that he was no monster. He said hello, but she ignored him, looking away.

"How are you doing?" he added, gently.

Still not looking at him, she said, "People are such assholes!"

"Yes," Stavros sighed. "Sometimes they are."

Now she turned on him, fiercely. "It's not fair! Aimee got raped. But people are saying stuff about her online as if it was *her* fault! And they're saying really nasty things, that she should die and that she should get raped again! It's disgusting! And the lawyers made her look really awful. Why did they have to talk about her using drugs before? What does that have to do with anything?"

"Well," Stavros said weakly, "it shows a pattern of behav—"

"*But what does that have to do with getting raped?*" Sally shrieked. "If a person uses drugs it's OK to rape them? But if they don't, it's not? Does that even make any sense?"

"I think the idea is that—"

"I don't want to talk about it, Mr. Papadakis! I don't!" She put her earbuds in. The conversation was over.

* * *

That evening Stavros clicked on CNBN for the latest. There was an ad for antidepressants and another for hemorrhoids, and then appeared the familiar face of "America's most trusted newscaster," Yul Bixby. With a grave, portentous air, Bixby announced that all charges against Newt Bellingham in the "sensational Harvard Square date-rape trial" had been dismissed. Earlier in the day, Bixby explained, Judge Nathan Chinlund had announced to his "stunned Cambridge courtroom" that the prosecution had decided to drop its case. Bixby noted that there was "widespread outrage" over the result, and also that there were "unconfirmed rumors" that the governor of Massachusetts had intervened on the Gibblin family's behalf.

As the screen switched to footage of Keller and Sal Mahony facing the press on the courthouse steps, Stavros's phone rang. It was Keller himself. He was exuberant, and Stavros congratulated him on the big win.

"Thank you buddy. These past few days have been crazy, but we got the job done."

"So what happened? I saw the headlines, but what really happened?"

"What really happened is that the Gibblin family turned on Donelly. There'd been tensions there all along, from what I've been hearing, and finally they decided they'd had enough. The father, Colin Gibblin, called in some favors on Beacon Hill, and that, basically, was that. Chinlund wasn't about to take on the governor and the Twitter mob, and of course neither was Donelly."

"What about the girl?"

"Apparently she was talking suicide, and for her family that was the last straw. I heard something today that she may have spent the weekend at the Belmont Clinic. If that's true, it was a smart move, legally. Either way, she never should have been put on the stand. Donelly really screwed up. He's finished. The key, though, was Esquibel. That's when everything turned."

Stavros had no idea who Esquibel was, but he kept that to himself.

"Anyway, the reason I'm calling is because Donelly's scheduled a presser for tomorrow morning. He's in a heap of shit and I have a feeling he's going to try and dump it on us. So we're having our own right after, and I'd like you to be there."

"You want *me* to come?" Stavros said.

"Yes, I need you."

"Why?"

"Well, for one thing because you're a partner in this firm, Stavros. And there are only two of us. I want to present the whole team. You, me, and most of the associates."

"What about Sal?"

"Sal's the most hated man in America right now. He's gotten death threats. Trust me, he won't be anywhere near the cameras tomorrow. But it's important that you're there."

Stavros was quiet.

"OK?"

"Yeah, of course. Whatever you need."

* * *

After he got off the phone Stavros poured himself a drink. The first of the day. Since he'd started driving his son to school, Stavros had cut back on the booze. Not because he'd finally decided to heed Dr. Martinez's warning that continued abuse of the hard stuff would kill him, but rather because Stavros no longer felt the desire for alcoholic oblivion. That craving had all but left him. Tonight, though, he feared the desire might return. He finished off the glass, poured out another, then sat at the kitchen table with his laptop.

According to the *Boston Telegraph* website, 'Esquibel' was twenty-six-year-old Julio Esquibel, a convicted felon who had come forward at the start of the trial claiming to have seen both the defendant and the accuser on the night of the rape. A recent parolee of MCI-Cedar Junction at the time of the incident, Esquibel had been passing through JFK Park around 12:30 a.m. when he saw a young white couple emerge from a darkened area of the park onto a lighted path. Esquibel stated that the couple, whom he identified as Newt Bellingham and the "unnamed accuser," "seemed happy, like they'd just been together." He added that "they both seemed kinda wasted, especially the girl, like they'd been doin' some partying." When asked by the defense if he thought Bellingham had just raped Gibblin, Esquibel said, "No. They looked like two people who just enjoyed themselves, you know what I'm sayin'? Like they was into each other." Esquibel was seen at approximately 12:35 a.m., heading toward Harvard Square, on video taken from a surveillance camera one hundred yards from the scene of the alleged crime. It was the same camera that had captured Bellingham and Gibblin walking in the direction of the park just before midnight, and which also captured Bellingham walking away from the park, alone, at 12:45. The prosecution questioned why Esquibel hadn't given evidence sooner. "Because I have a record and I'm not white," he said; "You think I'm stupid?" "Then why have you come forward now, at the last minute?" DA Donelly demanded. "Because I don't want to see an innocent dude go to prison," Esquibel said. "Well," Donelly said, "that's very noble of you, Mr. Esquibel— that you would care so much about the son of a Republican senator whom you've never met, that you would come forward at the very last minute to provide testimony vouching for his innocence. Very noble indeed!" Donelly then attacked Esquibel's credibility, making much of his criminal record, and questioned, again and again—over repeated defense objections—whether he had in any way been compensated for his testimony or even forced or intimidated into providing it. But Esquibel didn't budge. Again and again he said that coming forward was "the right thing."

* * *

The next morning Stavros suited up and drove to the Pell Building. Stepping off the elevator, he saw a cop standing guard inside the Keller, Papadakis reception area. Facing the glass doors, the cop watched with mild interest as Stavros approached and entered the office.

From behind the big desk Michelle greeted him with a nervous smile. Stavros asked what was going on.

"Things are pretty crazy," she said. "Sal's gotten death threats the past few days and today Wyatt got one, so we called the police. People are pretty tense."

Before Stavros could respond he heard Keller call out, "Hey buddy!" Coming from his office, eyes gleaming, Keller was pulsing with energy. "You ready for this?"

Quite frankly, Stavros had his doubts. But he said, "Oh yeah."

"Come on then. I've got everyone in the conference room. Donelly's going on any minute. CNBN's running it live. Ours too. Let's go."

As they started down the corridor Keller said, "You glad to be back? Ready to get out there and kick some ass?"

"Wyatt, I'm not prepared to speak to this case."

Keller laughed. "No one's expecting you to speak, Stavros. I'll make the statement and answer the questions."

"There is one thing," Stavros said, stopping just outside the conference room.

"What's that?"

"Where did Esquibel come from? Did Dickie find him?"

"No. It was Bellingham's people."

"The senator was involved in this?"

"Yeah. His legal team. They've had their own investigators working this. But we'll take it, right?" He slapped Stavros on the shoulder and turned to go.

"Hold on," Stavros said. "Is there any proof that Esquibel was actually in the park? That surveillance camera is down the street. He could have come from anywhere."

Keller looked bewildered. "Are you serious?"

"I'm just curious," Stavros said.

After a pause Keller said, "Come on. Let's go in."

* * *

The associates were gathered around a large television. First one, then another, and soon all of them turned to face Keller and Stavros. The ones closest to Stavros, the ones that couldn't gracefully get away, stepped up to say hello: "Hey Stavros, it's good to see you"; "Hi Boss, are you feeling better?"; "When are you coming back?"

And as he shook their hands, Stavros saw and felt how stiff everyone was, how forced their smiles and their words. But he understood.
Stavros had hired every person in this room, and some had been with the
firm for years. Yet Stavros hadn't connected with any of them; he hadn't
established any bonds or sympathies or close human feeling. Instead,
with his employees Stavros had been distant and demanding, intimidat-
ing and overbearing. He had browbeaten some, and humiliated others.
And what's worse, part of him had enjoyed doing it. Part of him had
reveled in wielding his power and making those beneath him squirm.
He had inspired fear and respect, and it had given him a rush, had made
him feel important and strong. Yet now, how pathetic it seemed. How
appalling, and how disgraceful! The shame of it was overwhelming, and
as they all looked at him, making their false, wary smiles, Stavros grew
speechless. He didn't know what to say.

But then Keller said, "It's starting," and everyone turned to the television.

* * *

At the podium, backed by staff and grim-faced law enforcement, stood
District Attorney Niall Donelly. Tall and wiry and ablaze with righteous
indignation, he glared at the cameras, glared at his audience, then fired
off his opening salvo: "The system failed, ladies and gentlemen! The
system failed! It failed the victim; it failed her family; it failed all of
us! Today, women across the state of Massachusetts should be very, *very*
concerned."

With a menacing scowl, the DA paused to let his words sink in. And
once this was done, he proceeded to make his case. First, he reviewed
the evidence: the victim's bruises; the positive drug test; the testimony
of a highly respected trauma specialist affirming that the victim "without question" had been assaulted; and the sworn testimony of the victim
herself stating that she had "begged, *begged*" the defendant not to engage in sexual intercourse with her. "Given this plethora of damning

evidence, how is it," the DA asked, "that a sexual predator has been allowed to walk free? How is this possible? Is it justice for all—or justice for the rich and powerful? Justice for all—or justice for the privileged few?" Second, the DA discussed Julio Esquibel, asking, "What is the real story behind the appearance of this young man? Mr. Esquibel's testimony turned the trial, yet how credible was he, and what was his true motivation in coming forward? Does it make any sense at all that he acted on his own? Then who, or what group, was behind him? Who, or what group, has perverted the cause of justice?" Third, the DA took aim at the defense, and even obliquely at the judge. "Why," the DA asked, "was Mr. Mahony allowed to get away with his savage cross-examination of the accuser? Why was he permitted to wage such a brutal attack on a vulnerable young woman? Do Mr. Mahony and Mr. Keller have no ethics? Do Mr. Mahony and Mr. Keller have no *shame?* And to what extent have these men damaged the integrity of our legal system, and the cause of women's rights?"

In conclusion the DA said, "This case has raised many disturbing questions, questions that go to the very heart of our democratic society, and until such questions are answered, until such questions are *investigated and resolved*, the people of Massachusetts will know no peace. But I can assure you, I can assure every one of you, that this case is not over. Our fight has just begun! We owe it to the state, we owe it to ourselves, and most importantly, we owe it to the victim ... This brave young woman has endured untold suffering, and I want her and her family to know that she is ever in our thoughts and prayers—"

"*Turn it off,*" Keller growled. The screen went black, and everyone turned to the big boss. "What an asshole," he muttered. To Stavros he said, "I'm going to bury that bastard."

* * *

Two hours later Stavros stood at Keller's side, along with five of their associates, facing the lights, cameras, and inquisitive eyes of a massive press corps. From among the dense crowd Stavros recognized the usual Boston faces, local print and TV reporters, as well as national figures from the major networks. But there were also news teams from overseas, Asia, Latin America, Europe. The room was charged, crackling with a sense of drama and anticipation.

Following DA Donelly's remarks, Keller, Papadakis & Associates had come under fire. There'd been a barrage of hateful emails and phone calls, and finally a bomb threat was made and the Pell Building evacuated. Yet Keller, leaving the office by the back stairwell per police orders, was euphoric. Embattled, attacked from all sides, his whole being throbbed with life. Ecstasy shone on his face! "Well, buddy," he said to Stavros, "if this doesn't make you want to come back, nothing will!" Out on the street, in the swelling crowd of the emptying building, Keller said he would meet up with everyone soon. And then he vanished.

Now, from the podium in a packed conference room at the Royal Continental, Keller projected a serene confidence. With one hand resting casually in his trouser pocket, he took some moments to make eye contact with each of the many gathered reporters. And as Keller did this the room slowly hushed, growing quieter and quieter until there was only the sound of clicking cameras. Then, with his audience at full attention, he said, "Ladies and gentlemen, thank you for coming out today. Generally I don't respond to prosecutorial attempts to retry a case in the press, but in this—"

From the opposite end of the room came a sudden commotion, an eruption of movement and sound. A handful of young people had burst in, yelling, pumping their fists, holding signs. With great fervor they were each repeating a different slogan, creating a chaos of voices and messages. The cacophony was mostly unintelligible, but Stavros made out the following:

"Keller defends rapists! Keller defends rapists! …"

"Justice isn't a commodity! Justice isn't a commodity! …"

"Destroy white patriarchy! Destroy white patriarchy! …"

The protesters were marching toward the podium, pushing through the press, but were immediately met by police. Amid the frantic bustle one of them caught Stavros's eye: a young woman with aqua-blue hair, holding a sign that read "Keller defends rapists!" It was the woman who, back in January, had accosted Keller at the Steak Club.

The cops tried to usher the protesters out the side doors but they refused to go. Some sat on the floor, shrieking their slogans with greater intensity. Of them all, the blue-haired woman was the loudest, and angriest. When a cop grabbed her, she resisted, tried to pull away, then fell to the floor. Undeterred, the cop lifted her up and carried her toward the door. With wild eyes she kept yelling, "*Keller defends rapists! Keller defends rapists! ...*"

Once by one the young people were removed. And all the while, Keller was grinning. He was tickled, thrilled by this festival of controversy, this bounty of free publicity for himself and the firm. He gave Stavros a mirthful wink.

Of course the cameras were still rolling, capturing the mayhem as it occurred; this was, after all, a live broadcast event. And so even before the last of the protesters had been hauled off, Keller sought to regain control, to lure the focus back to himself. "Ladies and gentlemen ... thank you," he said into the microphones, smiling at the buzzing crowd. "You know, I look at those kids and I see future clients." Some people laughed, others smiled. Keller waited, and soon the room was quiet.

And then, he began. Coolly, methodically, he responded to each of DA Donelly's charges and insinuations. First, the cross-examination of the accuser. "Was it really as 'brutal' or as 'savage' as the DA alleged?" Keller asked. "Or was it merely spun that way by the losing side and their many allies on Facebook and Twitter?" Keller paused, making the faintest of smiles. "Certainly there was some spiritedness to the questioning," he continued, "some energy and some vigor, but no more than the law allows. Judge Chinlund, a man well-known for his prudence and fairness over a long and distinguished career, saw to that. But the larger question, ladies and gentlemen, is this: is the truth not worth fighting for? ... The founders of our great nation certainly thought so. Which is why, in their inestimable wisdom, and to the great envy of the rest of the world, they gave us the Sixth Amendment and the right of every citizen, rich or poor, to question their accuser in a court of law. Now, District Attorney Donelly might have a problem with the Constitution, but fortunately for the rest of us he's in no position to do anything about it."

Second, the "mystery witness," Julio Esquibel. Keller reminded his audience of recent events in Baltimore, Maryland, and Ferguson, Missouri, in which "young men of color" had been "gunned down by police," and he cited statistics highlighting the "vast discrepancy" in incarceration rates between black and Hispanic men and their white counterparts. "Ladies and gentlemen," Keller said, "I ask you: given the systemic bigotry that Julio Esquibel confronts on a daily basis, a bigotry that most of the people in this room have never experienced and never will, is it not understandable that he might be reluctant to come forward in a case such as this? And indeed is there not in fact something *brave* in his deciding to come forward as he ultimately did? Something, dare I say, *heroic?* And so, rather than questioning this young man's motives, as District Attorney Donelly repeatedly has done, should we not instead be *praising* Julio Esquibel for having had the courage to do, as he himself said, 'the right thing'?"

Third, the question of consent. "What," Keller asked, "are the facts? Two young people, both highly intoxicated, meet at a college party. The young woman claims to the defendant that she is eighteen and a freshman at Harvard—neither of which was true. The pair leave the party together and go to a park late at night. The pair start kissing and things escalate. The accuser claims she did not want to have sex; the defendant claims she did. An eyewitness, Julio Esquibel, testifies that the accuser, after the sex, appears 'happy' in the presence of the man who supposedly just raped her. The accuser goes home and is confronted by her mother—the mother who had strictly forbidden her daughter from going to college parties. The mother questions the daughter as to why she is two hours over her curfew. The daughter panics, and claims she was assaulted. A medical exam shows only light bruising on the accuser's wrists and nowhere else, leading one medical expert to testify that, physically, there was no evidence to suggest nonconsensual sex. *Those*, ladies and gentlemen, are the facts—not the *opinions*, but the facts ... And I think they speak for themselves."

Having addressed the case, Keller turned his focus onto the DA himself: "According to District Attorney Donelly, 'the system failed.' But the system did *not* fail—the system *worked!* It's *because* of the system that an innocent young man is now home with his family rather than sitting in a prison cell. Now, you might not like Newt Bellingham, for any number of reasons—because of his wealth, because of his father, because of his gender, because of his race—but that does not mean, ipso facto, that he is a rapist! Feelings are not facts, and wanting something to be true does not make it so. No, ladies and gentlemen, the system did *not* fail.

"And so the only question that remains is ... *why?* Why would District Attorney Donelly push forward with a case that lacked sound merit? Why would he risk wasting the public's time and money on a case that any first-year law student could see was headed for dismissal? And why indeed would District Attorney Donelly force a vulnerable young woman to take the stand, knowing full well that she was not up to it? A young woman with a history of substance abuse and mental illness?"

Keller paused. Like a great stage actor he was in complete control—of himself, his role, his audience. Supremely self-assured, and with a cheery sparkle in his eye, he said, "Ladies and gentlemen, the unfortunate truth here is that ... this case was never about rape. At least, this case was never about rape for District Attorney Donelly. For District Attorney Donelly, this case was about District Attorney Donelly! This case was about District Attorney Donelly shoring up support for his next run for office—be it for governor, the senate, or even possibly the presidency of the United States ... And why not? What better way for him to win over whole swaths of voters than by presiding over the high-profile conviction of a Republican senator's son for the crime of rape? A brilliant stroke!

A master stroke! An *ingenious* stroke! Only, there was one problem … Newt Bellingham did not commit the crime that District Attorney Donelly charged him with. Yet like the power-hungry politician that he is, District Attorney Donelly pushed ahead, blind to reason, blind to common sense. He pushed ahead and he pushed that young woman to a disastrous end!

"My friends, I ask you: given what we now know, that District Attorney Donelly would sacrifice the lives of not one but two young people and their families for his own political gain, does it not seem curious that he would accuse the *defense* of lacking 'shame'? That he would accuse the *defense* of lacking 'ethics'? District Attorney Donelly likes to claim, particularly around election time, that he has 'always fought for the rights of women' … Not in this case. If District Attorney Donelly has fought for anyone, it was for himself and his political career. But what District Attorney Donelly seems to have forgotten is that he is a public servant. District Attorney Donelly was elected to serve not himself and his ambition, but the working men and women of Middlesex County. And in this, District Attorney Donelly has failed. He has failed his constituency, he has failed the office of the district attorney, and he has failed the young woman whose best interests he was entrusted to protect. Ladies and gentlemen, the people of Massachusetts deserve better. Thank you."

The press exploded. Questions, camera flashes, even some cheers came from all directions. The room was electrified, quaking with a release of energy. Remaining calm amid it all, the center of this storm, Keller glanced at Stavros and made a slight smile.

SIXTEEN

Brendan moped to the car and took his seat. "We don't have to pick up Sally anymore."

"What do you mean?"

"She's riding with Ute Klonk from now on."

"Ute Klonk? … Why?"

"*You know.*"

"I do?"

"Because of the press conference! She saw you on TV yesterday. Everyone did." The boy put his earbuds in, and turned to the side window.

* * *

At Thoreau, Brendan was in no hurry to get out of the car. Which was odd. Stavros had expected the boy to bolt out, to skedaddle off as fast as possible. But he remained seated, with a long face.

"What's wrong?" Stavros said, loud enough to be heard through the earbuds.

"I don't want to go in." This was said to the windshield.

"Why?"

"They're going to give me shit."

"Who?"

"*Who do you think?*" the boy snapped, now glaring at his father.

"The other kids?"

"Very good!"

"But why?"

"Haven't you been listening to me? Because of *you*."

"Listening to you? You haven't said a word the whole time!"

"For the past few weeks I've been getting it, about the trial. And I'm sick of it."

"What do they say?"

"All sorts of things … 'Dude, why does your dad defend rapists?'" This was said in a dumb-male voice. "Or, 'Does your dad hate women or something?'" This was said in a bitchy-female voice. "One guy asked me if it was true that Bellingham's father paid off the judge. He said you'd know."

"That's ridiculous."

"Maybe it is but I'm the one who has to deal with it. I had to go off Facebook because people were writing stuff about you."

Stavros winced. "Look—what can I do? Do you want me to go in there and talk to someone?"

"No!"

"Then I don't know what to say."

"Why did you do it, Dad? Why did you stand up there yesterday? At Bucky's Barbecue you said you weren't involved with that case. You said you had nothing to do with it, and that's what I told people. And now I look like a liar."

"Brendan, I'm sorry. I'm very sorry."

"Why did you do it?"

"I had to."

"Why?"

"Because Wyatt is my friend, and because we're partners and it's my job. I owed it to him. Sometimes we have to do things we don't want to do."

Brendan got out of the car, shut the door, then opened the back door to get his things.

Turning in his seat Stavros said, "Brendan, I really am sorry, I—"

But the boy wasn't interested. He slammed the door and walked away.

* * *

"I'm sure Wyatt's thrilled," Lindsay said. "He's all over the news."

"Yeah, he's happy," Stavros said, sipping his wine.

"And what about you?" Lindsay said, giving him a wry look.

"Well …"

"You don't want to talk about it."

"No, I'm happy to talk about it."

"Just don't ask if you think Newt Bellingham is guilty, right?"

"To be honest, I don't know what to think," Stavros said mildly. "There's strong evidence both for and against."

They were on the sofa in Lindsay's living room, with two logs burning in the fireplace. Stavros sat facing the flames while Lindsay sat facing him, leaning back against the armrest, knees up, her stockinged feet under his thigh. Off to the side on the floor, lying on a doggie bed, was Sophie, keeping a quiet eye on Stavros. In the morning Lindsay and Maggie were flying out to Aspen for their annual ski vacation, and Stavros had come to see her off.

"Well, I know one thing for sure," Lindsay said. "You didn't look comfortable on the podium. The whole time the camera was on Wyatt, you were on the screen too, right behind him. You looked like you had a bad case of gas."

"I never liked press conferences. When I was younger I did, but not … lately."

"Not lately?"

"Say ten years."

"Stavros, can I speak frankly?"

"You always do."

"I'm not sure I see you as a lawyer. And I certainly don't see you as a criminal defense lawyer."

"What do you see me as?"

"That's the thing. I don't know what I see you as."

"I always wanted to write."

"Really?" she said, excited.

"No. I'm kidding."

She laughed, and nudged him with her leg.

He reached for the bottle on the coffee table, filled her glass, then filled his own.

Once he'd settled back in, Lindsay said, "So … there's something we need to discuss."

Stavros turned to her, his eyebrows ascending.

"A guy I know, Randall, is going to be out in Aspen."

"A guy you know."

"Yes. I used to date him. He's a nice guy. A lawyer too, in fact. Entertainment law, out in LA."

"OK."

"Well, the thing is … I'm not sure how to say this."

Stavros waited.

"I guess I don't know where things stand with us."

"In what sense?"

"In the sense that … what are we doing, exactly? You and me?"

"Well … right now we're sitting on your sofa, drinking wine, and soon you'll have your tongue in my ear."

"Stavros."

He was grinning.

"What I want to know, Stavros, is why haven't we had sex?"

"Ah … You mean in the Biblical sense."

"Stop joking. You know what I mean."

"We've certainly done other things."

"Yes, and it's been very nice. But what's holding you back? It's been over a month now and we've spent several nights together, but you always have an excuse. To tell you the truth, I'm starting to get a complex. The last time a guy refused to have sex with me was freshman year in high school, when I was chubby and had braces. Are you not attracted to me?"

"Of course I am. I think you're beautiful," he said, placing a hand on her knee. "You're very desirable."

"Then what's going on?"

"Nothing," he said, shrugging. "What's the rush?"

"Stavros, a man only says 'what's the rush?' for one of two reasons. Either he's not really interested, or he has feelings for someone else."

Stavros felt his gut tense.

"I have a theory," Lindsay said.

Now he sighed. "OK."

"You're still in love with your ex."

"Lindsay—"

"Let me finish. Maggie said you were devastated by your divorce. She said Wyatt was concerned about you, that you became very depressed and started drinking. More than usual ... And that's why you gained weight."

"Wow ... You guys don't hold back, do you?"

"Also, I haven't heard you say one bad word about Allegra. Not one. It's not a good sign."

Stavros had no response.

"Are you still in love with her?"

He paused. "I don't know."

"You don't know," Lindsay said, looking hurt ... "Do you still think about her?"

"Yes."

"A lot?"

"Well ... look. Sometimes I wonder if it's love I feel, or guilt."

"Guilt?"

"Yes. I didn't treat her well. Not like I should have, and I feel bad about that. It's something I think about."

"Have you apologized?"

"I tried. She didn't want to hear it."

Lindsay frowned. "And what about us? Do you have feelings for me?"

"Of course I do. Why else would I be here?"

Now she shook her head.

"Lindsay, of course I have feelings for you. I like you very much. I enjoy spending time with you."

Annoyed, exasperated, she turned her attention to the fire. In the stone hearth the flames crackled and hissed.

Stavros said, "What, does this Randall want to get back together with you?"

"He's a nice guy."

"I know. You already said that."

"Stavros, I just want to know if … you see some sort of a future for us."

At this, the two of them looked into each other's eyes. And Stavros … faltered. His mouth opened, but no words came. The silence lengthened, and it felt strained.

From the floor Sophie rose from her cushion. With mournful, dejected eyes, the dog gazed briefly at Stavros, then turned and left the room, hobbling off on three legs.

Now flustered, Stavros said, "Lindsay, I don't know where this is heading … I'm sorry."

* * *

"Hey buddy, how we doin'?" Keller said, as he came up to Stavros in the lobby of the Royal Continental.

For days Stavros had been stressing over this dinner. He had some news to deliver, and he feared it wasn't going to go down so well. But seeing his old friend now, the mischievous eyes, the jovial Keller grin, Stavros had a feeling that maybe everything might turn out OK. It possible.

They shook hands and walked over to the hotel's restaurant. On the way a man in a suit stopped Keller for a quick hello. Keller joked with the guy and the guy laughed and walked away with a smile. At the maître d' stand there were more greetings and more laughs. As they were shown to their table many of the diners paused to watch. And Stavros could see that Keller was loving the attention, every bit of it. And why not? With all the media coverage from his Bellingham triumph, Keller was no longer just the country's most prominent defense attorney; he was also, at this very moment, and possibly for another day or two, one of the country's most talked-about celebrities. He was trending.

"You heard about Donelly?" Keller said, taking his seat.

"No."

"He resigned today. Everybody turned on him—the governor, his party, the media, the 'student activists'—and finally he caved. I was just watching the presser. It was grotesque. Wife and kids at his side, and him blaming everyone but himself, and doing it in front of his family. He even took a shot at Gibblin's father. A real 'class act,' as they say." Keller was smirking, but there was also a sparkle of jubilance in his eyes, as he reveled in the downfall of his adversary. "But he'll be back. He'll lay low for a year or so, plotting his return like Nixon after Kennedy. If I had to bet, I'd say he runs for Senate in '18. And I wouldn't be surprised if he won."

"Any word on who's taking his place?"

Keller grew more serious. "Well, there's some talk the governor's going to appoint Marty Dolloff as acting DA. I don't know how true it is, but that's what I'm hearing."

A flicker of panic passed through Stavros. Was more trouble heading his way? An investigation? A trial?

Keller said, "Have you heard from him? From Dolloff?"

"No. Not since January."

"That's good," Keller said, nodding but breaking eye contact. "I'm sure he's moved on."

"What do you know about Zanger?"

"Well … I heard someone in Donelly's office was looking into him."

The panicky feeling returned, intensified. Stavros was thinking not just of himself but of his son, of what a trial would do to the boy—the shame, the disgrace, the public ridicule from his peers.

"But now that Donelly's out," Keller said, "who knows what's going to happen. It's nothing."

"But if Dolloff takes over—"

"Buddy, it's just speculation. And even if Dolloff does become DA, and even if Zanger does talk, what? Compared to a judge, you're a small fish, Stavros. And on top of that, it's just your word against his. I'm telling you, it's nothing."

* * *

"So how've you been? How's the ticker?" Keller said.

They were sipping their drinks, waiting for their food.

"Good. I feel better than I have in years."

"Well you look good. Actually, you look *different*. Not like the Stavros I remember—the intense guy who was always ready to drop the gloves. People used to fear you, Stavros, inside the courtroom and out. Now, I don't know; it's like you're a eunuch or something. Do they have you on drugs?"

"No."

"Nothing? Hm," Keller said, giving Stavros a quizzical look. He pulled on his drink, then said, "So what have you been up to anyway? I've been trying to imagine your life outside the office, but I keep drawing a blank."

Stavros told him about the painting project and also about his problems with Brendan, including the role of Kenny Sunshine. Keller asked what he was going to do about it, and Stavros said, "You know what I'd like to do, but as that isn't possible I'm just going to turn him in."

"Turn Kenny in?"

"That's right."

"Are you sure that's wise?"

"This is my son, Wyatt."

"I realize that. But Stavros, how does it look if we're turning in former clients?" Keller said, breaking into a sudden laugh, struck by the preposterousness of the idea.

Stavros tipped back the rest of his drink and made no answer.

"Buddy, I understand," Keller said, now commiserating. "Go after Kenny. Of course. But could it be done anonymously? A call to the tip line? An untraceable email to the drugs unit? Because the thing is, no matter who you tell over there, word will leak. And you know it."

"OK. Sure ... I'll get Dickie to take care of it."

"Good. Thank you."

* * *

Over their steaks, Keller said, "What's going on with Lindsay? Did you ever see her again?"

"Yeah. Several times."

"Really?" Keller said, surprised.

"Yeah."

"And are you still seeing her?"

"Well ... I'm not sure."

"OK," Keller said, now confused.

"And what about Belén?" Stavros said, wanting to change the subject. "How's she doing?"

"She's doing well," Keller said, and as usual he offered no more.

"And Maggie?" Stavros said.

Keller grimaced. "You know, I never wanted things to get ugly. For a time there I was even thinking of tearing up the prenup, making her life comfortable. But she's been so bitter, and so calculating. I'm sure that stuff in the paper was Hegewische's idea, but Maggie OK'd it, and that was a big mistake. She never should have gone to Hegewische. If she would have just come to me and said she'd had enough, I would've taken care of her. But she chose another route, and now she's going to pay."

"What do you mean?"

"I put Dickie on it and he found some stuff. Stuff I would've preferred not to know."

Stavros became curious. Very curious. But he discreetly held back, said nothing.

At last Keller said, "This doesn't leave the table."

"It never does."

"She's been banging her yoga teacher," Keller said, fire coming into his eyes. "Can you believe it? A yoga teacher! And this is a guy who came to my house. Maggie had him and his wife over for dinner, about a year ago. It was the four of us, and all the while this skinny little prick is sitting at my table, eating my food, and thinking what a fool I am, that he's screwing my wife and I don't have a damn clue. I'm telling you, it fries my ass ... And yes, I realize these things happen. Obviously. But to bring it into my *house?* To rub it in my face like that? That's unforgivable."

Stavros said, "Yeah, that's tough ... Though you kind of rubbed it in her face too."

Keller just stared, thunderstruck. Clearly he'd not expected Stavros to say something like that, to question him, to challenge him. But he pondered the comment, and his expression grew thoughtful, even a bit chastened. "Well ... I suppose I did," he said.

"It's just something to consider," Stavros said.

"Yeah," Keller said, now focusing on his plate, cutting off another piece of meat.

"So what are you going to do?"

"Do?" Keller said, distracted.

"About the yoga teacher."

Keller shrugged, uneasily. "It's all set," he said, waving a hand as though he didn't want to get into it. "Dickie found something on the guy. Financial stuff. He'll sign something admitting to the affair, which will trigger a clause in the prenup, and that'll be the end of it ... It's finished."

* * *

After their meal the waitress came and cleared the table.

Leaning back in his chair, pleasantly sated by the food and the drink, Stavros said, "So ... the trial."

Keller's face brightened. "Yeah. It's been a good week. Cover of the next *Time* magazine, from what I'm told."

"How's the girl?"

"Gibblin? I don't know. I haven't heard anything."

Stavros nodded. "So what's next?"

"There was some talk about a defamation suit, but that's not going to happen. The senator wants this to go away as fast as possible."

"And what about Esquibel? What's the real story there?"

"There's nothing, Stavros. People are saying there was a conspiracy. 'Backroom dealings!' 'A high-level fix!' But that's just the politics of it. This case has been a gift to both sides. For the left, it's been a chance to have a go at Republicans and the rich, a chance to babble on about 'powerful white males' and all the other predictable lefty clichés. For the right, it's the same. The trial was further proof of the 'vast left-wing conspiracy'; it's because of the feminists, the media, political correctness, and who knows what else, the Illuminati, that polls show a majority of Americans still think Bellingham raped Gibblin. So there it is—something for everyone! People use the case for their own ends, the facts be damned. Partly it's because this is an election year. But mainly it's because this is the age we now live in. The social-media age. The age where opinion trumps fact. Facts are inconvenient, Stavros. Evidence, truth, objectivity, rational thought—they're all on the way out. We're a decade away from mob rule in this country. Hopefully I won't be around to see it when it all comes crashing down. But hey, America had a good run. I've got no complaints."

Stavros could tell Keller was a bit tipsy. His views tended toward the cynical, but they only came out in private, and then only after he'd had a few drinks.

For some moments they were quiet, and Stavros tensed, realizing it was time. He said, "Wyatt, there's something I need to tell you."

Keller looked at him.

"I've decided I'm not coming back. I'm leaving the firm."

Keller's expression softened, and he smiled.

"You knew?" Stavros said.

"Buddy, I've known since December. The day I came to see you in the hospital."

"Really?"

"I had a feeling."

"Why didn't you say anything?"

"I was hoping I was wrong. Hoping you'd maybe change your mind. But then when you didn't show for Bellingham, I thought that probably was it."

"You're not mad?"

"Hell no. Stavros, what do I always say? It's just a game—work, life, everything. And we've done well. Both of us."

A great feeling of relief came over Stavros, but also some surprise. Keller's response was far more understanding than he'd expected. Stavros had feared disappointment. Possibly anger. But Keller's expression was cheery and blithe, free from any distress.

Nodding uncertainly, Stavros said, "Oh ... OK."

Keller smiled, but said nothing. He sipped his drink.

Stavros also sipped his drink.

The silence grew, and as it did Stavros realized he was waiting. He was waiting for Keller to say something. He was waiting for Keller to acknowledge in some way the end of their thirteen-year partnership. And the longer Stavros waited, the more uneasy he became. For a decade-plus the two of them had worked together, battled together, putting in countless hours, side by side. Was that not worthy of some comment? Some feeling? Something?

Stavros said, "So we're good, right? We're still friends?"

And Keller, who loved nothing more than to talk—in courtrooms and in press conferences and with random well-wishers on the street—would only say, "What do you think?"

What do I *think?* Stavros thought.

Keller's eyes were gleaming, as if to say, "Of course we're still friends." But Stavros wanted more. He wanted ... words. Honest, meaningful words. And they didn't have to be Shakespearean! A simple "I'm sorry you're leaving, buddy; I'll miss you" would do. Stavros would take it. And so he waited.

Finally, Keller responded. He held up his glass and said, "You want another one? They're going to be closing soon."

Stavros looked at him. "Uh ... no. I'm all set. Thanks."

* * *

Early Monday morning, Allegra called to say Brendan wasn't going to school. "He's sick," she said.

"What's wrong?" Stavros said. He was in the bathroom, shaving, his face half covered with white cream.

"He seems to have a cold."

"He *seems* to have a cold? Allegra, you're a doctor—is he sick or not?"

"He said his throat was sore."

Stavros felt the irritation rising. "This is about the press conference, isn't it? The kid decides he doesn't want to see me and suddenly he gets sick. I don't like it. This isn't how you handle problems. You don't run away from things."

"Oh my God!"

"What?"

"*You're* talking about not running away from problems?"

She always had to get a jab in, Stavros thought. She couldn't resist. "Look, I told him I was sorry. I apologized."

"I know. He told me."

"OK, then tell him to get ready. I'll be there at seven."

"Actually Stavros, there's something else ... He doesn't want to ride to school with you anymore."

"What? Allegra, I had to do it. I had to go to that press conference."

"Maybe so, but this is the second time he said he doesn't want to ride with you."

"The second time?"

"The first was right after you grounded him. After we grounded him."

"What happened?"

"I told him he didn't have a choice."

"Well tell him again!"

Silence.

"You can tell him again, right?"

"I don't know. I don't know what to do. He's becoming more moody and aggressive. Maybe I'll just start driving him. You're going back to work soon anyway, right?"

"Uh, no. I'm not."

"What do you mean?"

"I quit."

"You quit?"

"I left the firm."

"You left Keller? You're joking!"

"I'm not. It's over."

"What happened?"

"Nothing … I've changed."

"You've *changed?*"

"Yes."

She scoffed. "Unbelievable … Unbelievable. Stavros, I have to get off the phone."

"*Why?* Can't you talk to me?"

"*Now you quit?*" she said. "*Now you quit Keller?*"

He understood.

"And to do what?"

"I don't know. I'd like to spend more time with Brendan."

"Unbelievable."

"Why are you mad?"

"*I'm not mad!*"

"You sound it."

"I have to go."

"So I'll pick him up tomorrow?"

She paused, said "*Fine*," then hung up.

Grumbling to himself, bothered, frustrated, Stavros finished shaving and rinsed his face. Then he got his keys and his phone, put on his coat, and went for the door.

SEVENTEEN

He was on the road. Yes, Stavros was going to see his son—some face-to-face interaction was required there—but right now he had to work out some things regarding Allegra. For instance, what exactly was going on with them? Clearly he was still attracted to her. Physically, emotionally —there was still something there. But what of it? What, realistically, could come of it? The thought of them getting back together was ludicrous. You can never go back, right? Certainly not after you couldn't make it work over, what, fifteen years? No, it was unthinkable. Yet, their early days had been bliss. Allegra was, had been, the love of his life. Her personality, her mind, her body, everything. In those days, Stavros thought she had it all. She was vibrant, funny, smart, alluring, thoughtful, affectionate. Being with Allegra was fun, and exciting. She made Stavros laugh and think, and sex with her was thrilling, a heart-pumping joy. Seeing her naked, taking in her scent, feeling her in his embrace, filled him with rapture.

But against the few blissful years were the many painful ones. The years of hostility and rage. In her words, Stavros had been selfish, egotistical, irresponsible; a coward who refused to face his problems. He wasn't a real man, she had said. Stavros retaliated by calling her a bitch, a harpy, a pain in the ass. What began as badgering and bickering escalated to frenzied meltdowns. Screaming and shouting. Broken plates and fist-dented walls. Sleeping in separate rooms or spending days away from the house.

The fights took their toll, and eventually they tried a separation. Stavros spent a month at the Warwick Hotel on Memorial Drive, but this improved nothing. So he took the apartment overlooking Boston Common. If he was going to suffer, then at least he would do it in style. He and Allegra didn't speak for weeks at a time, and when they did their words quickly became heated. Finally, drained and exhausted, they simply gave up. They could take no more. Allegra asked for the divorce and it went down fast. She wanted just the house and money to raise Brendan. Stavros objected to nothing.

At the Middlesex Probate and Family Court in Cambridge, on the day of their divorce hearing, Stavros bumped into Allegra and her attorney in the crowded lobby. Husband and wife for another hour, they were startled to see each other. Expecting malice or hate in Allegra's eyes, Stavros saw only sadness and defeat. Was this actually happening, he wondered? Had it really come to this? At one time they had been in love; they had been happy, very happy. Yes, they'd had that. They'd had what everybody wants—love and happiness. But somehow they'd lost it, squandered it. Stavros wanted to say something. *Maybe this doesn't have to happen ... Maybe we could ...* But before he could settle on the right words, before he could say anything, Allegra's lawyer led her away.

Inside the courtroom, filled to capacity for the afternoon's many hearings, the two of them sat well apart. The proceedings went fast, as the judge, a man known to Stavros, worked with great efficiency. By the power vested in him by the State of Massachusetts, he dissolved one union after the other. Again and again, man and woman stood before his honor, and within minutes the marriage was terminated. *Next!*

When their case was called, Stavros stepped forward and explained that he was representing himself. The judge then turned to Allegra's attorney, and as the two of them went through the formalities, Stavros choked up, his eyes watering, his chest convulsing. It was wholly unexpected—a sudden, uncontainable sorrow. But he quickly suppressed the emotion, stuffed it down, buried it deep, and fifteen minutes later the hearing was finished. Stavros and Allegra were no longer married. She and her lawyer headed for a side door, and she was gone.

For more than a year afterward Stavros was a wreck. All he did was work, and drink. He had no desire, no will. He avoided Brendan, and argued with Allegra whenever she called to see why he wasn't spending any time with the boy. For Stavros, things were bad. And without Keller they would have been worse. Keller took Stavros out for meals, and even met up with him on free weekends for a drink or a game—the Celtics, the Sox. But still, he suffered. That year had been hell, the worst of his life.

And yet here Stavros was now, wondering about his feelings for his ex-wife. Was he crazy? Was he mad? Hadn't they suffered enough? *Yes*, he thought with feeling—they *had* suffered enough. Both of them. Getting back together was preposterous. It was absurd.

*　*　*

When he pulled into the driveway Stavros thought it best to give them a heads-up. He called and Allegra answered. He explained that he wanted to see Brendan, then waited for the antagonistic response. But she said, "I think that's a good idea. Do you want to come here?"

"Actually, I am here. I'm in the driveway."

"Oh … Well, I'll meet you at the door."

There, he expected a stern greeting. But instead Allegra met him with a smile. A warm, pleasant smile. Stavros was shocked! "Come in," she said. "I'll let him know you're here." And as she turned to go she gave him a look that was borderline affectionate—which shocked him even more! What was this, he wondered? What was this cordiality, this seeming goodwill? Was it because he was finally showing an interest in the boy? Because Stavros was finally acting like a father to their son? Cautiously pleased, he followed her into the house. He even wiped his shoes.

But the good feelings didn't last. As Allegra went up to the second floor, Stavros stopped near the foot of the stairs. Through the archway into the dining room he saw Dylan, seated at the table, eating breakfast. Instantly, Stavros felt awkward, like an unwitting intruder. Yes, as he stood in the home he had bought and was still paying for, the home in which his ex-wife and son still lived, Stavros felt like an interloper, an unwanted guest. And how different it was from the last time he'd met Dylan in this house! Then, on Christmas morning, it was Dylan who had seemed the intruder. Almost apologetically, Stavros held up a hand and made a passably friendly smile. "Hi Dylan."

Dylan, with noticeably less friendliness, just said, "Hi," then went back to his food.

Apart from the sound of chewing, there was silence. Stavros turned his attention to the living room, looking at the sofa, the chairs, the windows, as though this might ease the tense feeling. It didn't.

Mercifully, Allegra started down the stairs. And again she smiled at Stavros—warmly, pleasantly. "Brendan's in his room," she said. "He's waiting for you."

"He's *waiting* for me?"

"He didn't want to come down," she said, now standing on the floor, an arm's-length away from him. "And just to warn you, he's a little grumpy."

"What else is new? I took his crap all week."

Allegra laughed. It was a brief, restrained laugh, but genuine nonetheless, her eyes twinkling with a merry light. Stavros was elated. When was the last time he had seen her laugh? When was the last time he had *made* her laugh?

She said nothing more, and aware of Dylan's observant gaze, Stavros said, "Well … I guess I'll go up." With a jaunty step he started for the stairs. The wooden treads creaked familiarly under his weight, just as they'd done in the old days. And as Stavros took the steps two at a time, he experienced a full-body frisson, a heady feeling like he was … home.

Turning down the hall toward Brendan's room, he heard his name called from behind. It was Allegra, ascending the stairs in a hushed, furtive manner. He waited for her and she came up close, just inches away. Looking into her eyes, the eyes he remembered so well, Stavros saw the black pupils expand within the green irises.

In a near-whisper she said, "Don't say anything about him not wanting to ride to school with you. He doesn't know that I ..."

But Stavros was no longer listening; his mind had gone elsewhere.

* * *

It was June, many years earlier. Stavros was young and ambitious and had a full head of black hair. He and a buddy from the DA's office, a guy named Milos Wildzumas, were out drinking and had decided to crash the party of a friend of a friend of Milos's who had just graduated from medical school. They arrived around midnight at an old Victorian in Mission Hill. The place was rocking, house and yard filled with drunken doctors. There were kegs and jello shots and speakers set up in the windows playing live Nirvana.

Milos's friend Katrina, a tall blond and a first-year resident at Boston General, was sozzled. She wore a pork-pie hat and an Aloha shirt. Seeing her friend she cried, *"Milos Wildzumas! Milos Wildzumas!"* She leapt onto him, encircling him with arms and legs as the two of them nearly fell to the ground.

While Milos and Katrina stumbled and laughed, Stavros noticed Katrina's friend. Tall, slender, attractive, she had a bounteous pile of red hair that she'd pinned up, with loose strands playing fetchingly around her face. She wore a white linen top, high-water cargo pants, and bright red sneakers.

Katrina, still laughing, untangled herself from Milos. She said hello to Stavros, whom she'd met before, then introduced Milos and Stavros to the girl with the red hair. Stavros held out his hand and Allegra shook it, firmly.

"Stavros works with Milos," Katrina said. "He's a lawyer."

"That's too bad," Allegra said.

Katrina cackled. "Nooooo. They're good lawyers! They help people."

Allegra made a faint, impish smile then walked off. Stavros watched her go into the house. "She's pretty," he said.

"She's single," Katrina said. "Men are afraid of her. She eats them alive. Vagina dentata." She laughed again, then told Milos she wanted to dance. They went into the house and Stavros followed.

The place was jammed and sweaty. Loud music, loud voices. There was a keg stacked atop another keg and strands of Christmas lights hanging from the walls. Stavros told Milos he'd get them a beer. Katrina said she wanted one too. When Stavros returned with three filled plastic cups, Milos was alone.

"Where'd Katrina go?"

"She said she was going to change the music. But I think she went to puke."

"Nice."

Milos took one of the beers and left Stavros double-fisted. The Nirvana gave way to Prince. Ecstatic female shrieks rang out and people started dancing, causing the floor to shake.

Allegra came up to Stavros and Milos. "Are you two dating?"

"We just broke up," Milos said. "Do you know where Katrina is?"

"She went upstairs."

Milos headed for the stairs.

Stavros, holding a beer in each hand, looked at the red-haired beauty.

"Do you have a drinking problem?" she said.

"One's for Katrina."

"Oh. You go for blonds, eh?"

"Not always. Sometimes I go for brunettes."

She gave him a smirk.

"But I am flattered," Stavros said.

"By what?"

"You've insulted me three times already. It can mean only one thing."

Her eyes flashed. "And what's that?"

Ignoring the question, he said, "So are you in the Army?"

"Excuse me?"

"The pants. Very G.I. Joe."

"*What?* These are cool!" she said, glancing down. "Are you kidding?"

He was laughing. "No, I like them. And I like your sneakers. They remind me of kindergarten."

"I love these sneakers," she said, punching him on the arm.

They talked for a while, joking and ribbing each other, and then "1999" came on. There was another burst of female shrieks, ear-piercing squeals of pleasure. The mob of moving bodies went into a frenzy and the floor began to bounce.

"Oh! We should dance," Allegra said.

"I don't dance."

"No?"

"Sorry."

"Not even when you're drunk, like most guys?"

"Nope. Not even then."

She made a face that said, "Oh well," and joined the pulsating throng. Stavros watched. The girl wasn't particularly rhythmic, but she looked happy, joyful in her body as she moved to the music.

Milos came back and told Stavros he was going to head out.

"What about Katrina?"

"She's making out with some guy."

"There are other women."

"It's almost one."

It was a Thursday night and they both had to work the next day. Stavros could either catch a ride home with Milos, who was driving, or stay here, try his luck with this Allegra, and call a cab if things didn't work out. He decided to leave; he didn't want to be dragging at work. He told Milos he was ready to go but had to use the bathroom. There was one upstairs, down the hall, Milos said. Stavros found it, did his business. When he opened the door, Allegra was standing there.

"Oh ... Mr. No Dance," she said, startled, as if they were meeting by chance.

"Miss Army Pants," he said, stepping toward her and stopping just inches away.

Her head jerked back, but she stood her ground. Her eyes questioned him, playfully, and Stavros thought he also saw the trace of a dare, a look that challenged him to make a move. He took her in his arms and kissed her full on the lips. She resisted, pushed back, and slapped him on the face, hard. "What the hell are you doing?" she said. "Are you crazy?"

Unfazed by the slap Stavros stared at her, his face flush, blood pumping. Allegra didn't move. Her pupils were dilated, her lips parted. She gazed at him, bewildered, wondering. He leaned toward her and the two of them came together.

* * *

Now, in the upstairs hallway of the old house on Champney Street, Stavros became unsteady on his feet. He felt lightheaded and started to wobble.

"What's wrong?" Allegra said. "Are you all right?"

"No ... I'm a little ..." His legs went limp, and as he went down Allegra grabbed his arm and prevented his head from smacking the wood floor. She rolled him on his back and straightened his limbs. He had briefly lost consciousness but now was alert.

Kneeling at his side Allegra said, "Stavros, what are you feeling? Is it your heart? Do you have any pain?"

"No I'm ... just dizzy." He tried to sit up.

"Don't move," she said, holding him down. "Are you sure—no pain anywhere? Your chest, your arm, your jaw?"

"No."

"What about nausea? Do you feel like vomiting?" she said, now holding his wrist and taking his pulse.

"No. It's just my head. It's spinning."

She said she'd be right back, then returned with a chair. She lifted his feet and placed them on the seat. "I think you just fainted," she said. "This will get blood into your brain." She was kneeling again, gazing

183

down at him, her pretty green eyes focused and caring. She was concerned for him—Stavros could see it! He broke into a smile, a happy grateful smile. But then, abruptly, he realized they weren't alone.

Standing near Stavros's head, and looking down from what seemed a great height, was Dylan. Stavros thought the lad's expression was less than sympathetic. And near the chair supporting Stavros's feet stood Brendan, his face showing an odd mix of worry and disdain. Now abashed, finding himself in a weak, laughable position, Stavros waved. "Hi Brendan."

Without a word the boy held up a hand, cheerlessly returning the wave.

And Stavros wondered if he really had just fainted. Because of the memory of his first kiss with Allegra? It was too embarrassing! He rested his head back on the floor, gazing up at the ceiling. To no one in particular he said, "I'm probably coming down with something. The flu maybe."

"It's possible," Allegra said. "Did you eat this morning?"

"No."

"That doesn't help. Are you dehydrated? Were you drinking last night?"

"Maybe one or two. I *am* a little thirsty."

From her knees Allegra looked up to Dylan. "Could you get him some water?"

For some reason this made Stavros grin, and he saw a wrinkle of displeasure come over Dylan's face. But Dylan said, "Sure," and obediently went off, down the creaking stairs to the kitchen.

Allegra said, "Stavros, when was the last time you saw your doctor?"

"January. After I got out of the hospital."

"What did he say?"

"He said I'm lucky to be alive. Like everybody else."

"I want you to make another appointment. Or you could go to the ER right now."

"No, I'm fine. I'll be in there all day, and then they'll say I just need to drink more water."

"Then make an appointment with your doctor. I'm not joking. This may be heart-related."

Stavros smiled, savoring the irony. Turning to the boy he said, "So how are you? I hear you're sick."

Brendan made a sulky face, but said nothing.

"Is that a yes or a no?"

"*Yes,*" the boy hissed.

"Well, I'm sorry to hear that," Stavros said, thinking his son looked fine; certainly better than his old man.

Dylan returned with the water. Stavros pulled his feet off the chair, sat upright on the floor, and drank down half the glass. He said he felt better, then rose to his feet with help from Allegra.

"Do you want to lie down?" she said.

"No, I'm fine. You two go back to your breakfast. I'm sorry I interrupted."

"I have to leave. My first patient's in half an hour." She patted Stavros on the arm, almost absentmindedly. "Please call your doctor, Stavros, OK?"

"OK," he said, beaming at the pat on the arm.

Allegra and Dylan started down the stairs and Stavros watched them go. Once they'd disappeared from sight, he turned to Brendan. The boy was looking at him, waiting, and it hit Stavros that he was here for a reason: to have a father-son chat.

* * *

Brendan's room, Stavros noticed, had greatly changed. Gone were the super-hero action figures, the Harry Potter bedspread, and the crayon drawings of space ships and aliens that had once covered the walls. Now there were posters of jazz men and soccer players and women in bathing suits. Shelves packed with books, CDs, and a sound system. A desktop computer with a large monitor.

Stavros examined one of the posters, a fit blond in a bikini. "Who's this?"

"Alana Seyfried."

"A model?"

"Surfer."

"Oh yeah? Not bad … When I was your age I had a poster of Cindy Cooper in my room. Do you know who she is?"

"No," the boy muttered, looking bored.

Stavros went over to the bookshelf. There were classic novels, *Crime and Punishment*, *Seize the Day*, *As I Lay Dying*, as well as books on jazz and physics. There were four books alone by Stephen Hawking. "Did you actually read these, or are they just to impress the ladies?"

"*Yes*, I've read them."

"Well, that's good. I've been doing some reading myself lately."

Brendan yawned, was uninterested.

Stavros just wanted to connect with his son. He was trying. He tried again. "So why *do* you like physics, anyway? It's pretty complicated stuff, no?"

"It's fun."

"OK. And how did you become interested in it? Where did it start?"

"I don't know. School. Teachers. Mom buys me books and DVDs on science and we talk about them."

"You talk about physics with your mother?"

"Yeah. Physics, astronomy, biology. She's pretty smart."

Stavros was struck by this. Not to hear that Allegra was "pretty smart" —she was in fact very learned, far more so than he—but rather that she was so engaged in the boy's intellectual development. In addition to everything else, work, chores, life, etcetera, she found time to hold science seminars with their kid? What parent does that? It was very impressive.

"Well … should we sit?" Stavros said.

Brendan nodded and sat on the side of the bed. Stavros took the chair from the desk.

Done with the small talk, he came right out with it: "So, are you still mad at me?"

The boy looked away.

"It's OK if you are," Stavros said. "But at the same time I'm thinking maybe we should move on. Put this thing behind us."

"*We? Us?* What did I do to you?"

"OK … Then maybe it's time for *you* to put this thing behind you."

Brendan shook his head.

"Brendan, I know you don't hate me, deep down. And do you want to know why I know? Because I saw how upset you were, when I had my heart attack."

The boy looked at him.

"Yes. You were very upset," Stavros said. "And it's probably why I'm still here, why I'm still alive—because of you."

No reply.

"That's pretty significant, don't you think?"

The kid shrugged.

"Well, *I* think it's significant. That whole experience made me realize how important you are to me. It made me want to be a better father."

Brendan snickered.

"Laugh if you want, but I mean it."

They were silent, then Stavros said, "I have a question for you, since we're talking … Why did you buy the drugs? Why did you really do it?"

Brendan made a face.

"I'm just curious," Stavros said. "It's something I've been wondering about."

"I don't know."

"You don't know? The guy who reads books by Stephen Hawking doesn't know why he bought twenty hits of ecstasy?"

"I just wanted to have fun."

Stavros wasn't so sure. It seemed odd to him that the kid who loved jazz and soccer and academics would also be interested in drugs. True, teens like to experiment, and there may have been an element of peer pressure, but something seemed off; the motive, Stavros felt, was a little fuzzy. But maybe he was overthinking this. Maybe—

"Nobody likes me."

"What? *Nobody likes you?* Why? Because of the trial?"

"*No.*"

"Then what are you talking about? Who doesn't like you?"

"Some of the older kids. At school. And some kids in my class. They're jerks."

"Did something happen?"

The boy gazed out the window.

Stavros waited, then said, "Look Brendan, I've got all day. Believe me."

"There's this girl I liked."

"OK."

"She's a junior."

Ah, Stavros thought: Brendan had said he liked "older women." "What's her name?" Stavros asked.

"Ottavia."

Right: Ottavia. Sally had mentioned an Ottavia, and Stavros had mentioned an Ottavia to Dickie, and Dickie had used the name to track down Kenny Sunshine. "And what's she like?"

"She's cool. And pretty. She's different."

Stavros remembered the afternoon he had gone over to Thoreau to take Brendan to see the house on Ridley. Brendan had come out of the school with an older girl who indeed had looked "different." Stavros said, "And does Ottavia by any chance have dreadlocks?"

The boy erupted: "*Are you making fun of me?*"

"*No!* I'm just trying to get a picture of her. That's all. So how did you meet her?"

There was a long pause, then: "I wrote her a poem."

"You wrote her a poem?"

"*Yes*," came the testy reply.

"OK … That's cool. A poem. And when was this?"

"Last fall. I kept seeing her at school, and I liked her. But we were in different classes and none of my friends are friends with her."

"Did you talk to her?"

"No. I didn't know what to say."

Stavros shrugged. "It happens."

"That's why I wrote her the poem."

"I see … So was this, you know—a *love* poem?"

"*Dad!*"

"Right, forget that. Dumb question. So you wrote her the poem. And how did you get it to her? Did you mail it? Email? How's that done these days?"

"I went into her class and gave it to her. On a piece of paper."

"You walked into the middle of a class and gave a poem to a girl you didn't know?"

"No, I went before the class started. When people were getting there."

"And then what?"

"She put it on Facebook."

"What does that mean?"

"It means she took a picture of the poem and put it on the internet. And by the next day everyone at school was laughing at me."

Oh, boy, Stavros thought. "I'm sorry to hear that, Brendan."

"I don't care. They're just assholes."

"Did your mother know about this?"

"Yes."

"Did the school do anything?"

"No. But she felt bad."

"Who?"

"Ottavia. She said sorry."

"Well that was nice."

"Yeah," Brendan said, missing his father's sarcasm. "She started talking to me. We became friends."

"Friends."

"Well, sort of. I mean, she did start talking to me. And sometimes I ate lunch with her and her friends, and they invited me to a couple parties. But she also asked me to start doing her geometry homework."

Stavros cringed, though he tried to hide it. "And did you do it?"

"Yeah, but now I wish I didn't. I think she was just using me. She liked somebody else, this guy Blake, and she would talk to me about him, about how much she liked him. It's like she thought I was her little brother or something."

Oh, man, Stavros thought, rubbing his face. "Yeah, that's never a good sign."

Brendan said nothing.

"And so was that why you wanted to have the party? To show her you're not her little brother?"

"I don't know. Maybe. I just wanted them to like me."

"Who?"

"Ottavia and the older kids."

"What's wrong with the kids your age?"

"They're boring. They talk about stupid shit all the time."

"What about Sally French? She's not boring."

"I don't know."

"Hey, she seems pretty darn smart to me. And on top of that she plays sports and speaks French and plays the violin. If you ask me, that's pretty cool."

"I guess."

"So where do things stand with Ottavia?"

"I don't really talk to her anymore."

"Why?"

"After I got grounded, she and her friends thought it was funny and they started giving me shit, so I told her I wasn't going to do her homework anymore and she got pissed. That's why I think she was using me."

Again Stavros rubbed his face, trying with all his might to contain himself. "*Of course she was using you, you numbskull!*" he wanted to yell, but he said nothing.

"But I'm done with her," the boy said. "She's a jerk."

Thank God, Stavros thought. His impulse was to give the boy some advice, lecture him on how doing a girl's homework probably wasn't the best way to get her to think of you as a prospective boyfriend. But Stavros had a feeling that any paternal words of wisdom might not go down so well. So he opted for a more indirect approach, saying, "I like how you handled that. You saw that she was trying to play you for a chump, and you put an end to it. Very good. And as for the poem, I think that showed a lot of balls. I respect that. And I'm sure the next time you do it, you'll actually, *you know*, meet the girl first, to make sure she's worthy of it."

"I already thought of that."

"OK, good."

"So does this mean I'm not grounded anymore?"

"*What?* Why would you think that?"

"Why else would you come here?"

"I came here because I wanted to talk to you."

"But I've been grounded for almost *three weeks!*"

"That's right. Which means there's only about three months left."

"Fuck, Dad!"

"Hey—watch your language!"

"It's not fair! Nobody at my school gets grounded! When Ottavia's parents caught her smoking pot they just said don't do it in the house."

"Brendan, look. My guess is that Ottavia and her parents have their own problems, OK? As for your punishment, you're grounded till June, and that's the end of it. So just drop it."

Throbbing with hostility, Brendan refused to look at his father. And Stavros felt … conflicted. He wanted to say, "All right, you're not grounded. Let's be buddies." But that would be wrong. So he said, "Do you want to get some breakfast? We could head over to Augie's."

"I don't want to do anything with you. Ever."

The words cut Stavros. They stung. They shouldn't have, but they did. "OK," he said. He stood and put the chair back as he'd found it. "But I will say this, Brendan: nothing good comes of being angry and holding grudges. It's a waste of time and it just pushes people away. So if you want to be alone all your life, keep it up."

"You should know."

Stavros went still. "That's right, I do know. Which is why I'm telling you, so you can learn it now rather than when you're forty-four ... Good-bye Brendan, I'll see you tomorrow morning."

The boy made an acid face, and looked away.

"Brendan, I'm talking to you. I'll see you tomorrow."

"OK."

EIGHTEEN

Later that week Stavros went back to the office. In reception, Michelle greeted him with a somber smile. She said she was sorry to hear he was leaving the firm. "We'll miss you," she said.

This annoyed Stavros. Not the white lie—he knew nobody would miss him—but rather that news of his departure had been leaked. He had wanted to make the announcement himself. "Who told you?"

"Mr. Keller, yesterday. He had everyone in for the morning meeting. We were all pretty stunned."

"Is he in?"

"No, Mr. Keller's in court this afternoon."

Walking down to his office, Stavros saw Ida. She was at her desk typing, innocent and unawares. In the past, Stavros had had no problem letting an employee go. In fact, in the past there had been times when he'd positively relished canning somebody's ass. But not now.

Looking up from her computer, Ida said, "Hey stranger. I was wondering when I was going to see you."

"How are you Ida?"

"Good. I've been getting a lot of writing done," she grinned.

She was referring, Stavros surmised, to her poetry. "I guess things have been pretty slow for you these past few months."

"Yeah, it's been great. Two-hour lunches. Long chat sessions with friends. A couple new poems per week. I'm going to miss it."

He asked her to step into his office, and he shut the door. Stavros sat at his desk, still cluttered with papers and food-stained takeout menus, and

Ida sat across from him, in the client's chair. She wore a vintage polka-dot dress with short sleeves that revealed her Popeye tattoo, a Jackie-O-1960s-type headband, and very thick mascara. It took Stavros a few moments to process her getup; but once he had, he said, "Well Ida, as I'm sure you've heard, I've decided to retire."

"Wyatt told us yesterday. It was kind of like the principal telling you in front of the entire school that your boyfriend was dumping you."

"Ida, I am sorry. I only just learned of that meeting now. I was hoping to tell you first. That was very insensitive."

She looked at him, perplexed. "Did you just say—'insensitive'?"

"Yes. It was my fault. I should have come in sooner, or at least called."

Mulling this, she studied him. Then she said, "Well, everything turned out OK, I guess."

"It did?"

"Yeah. I mean, I liked working for you. It certainly was never boring. Sal is more … *normal.*"

"Sal?"

"Yeah. You know, he doesn't scream at people. He doesn't really drink. He seems fairly stable, basically. But who knows, maybe now that he's a partner that might change. One can only hope."

"*Sal … a partner?*"

"You didn't know?"

Stavros shook his head.

"Oh. That's weird."

"When did this happen?"

"Yesterday, at the meeting. After Wyatt told us about you he said Sal and Inés were being named partners. It's going public next week. And after the meeting Sal asked if I wanted to be his secretary, and I said sure. I'm already here, right?"

"Yes," Stavros said distractedly, stunned by the news. "Well, that's good. I was thinking I was going to have to let you go."

"Nope. I'm staying … And actually, that reminds me. Sal wants to know when you're going to clean out your stuff."

"My stuff?"

"Yeah, he's taking this office."

"Sal's taking my office," Stavros said, in a daze.

Ida nodded.

"I see … Maybe this weekend."

"He was kind of hoping you could do it by Friday. He wants to move in here on Saturday, to be ready for Monday."

"Right … Well … I guess I could do it now."

There was a long silence, then Ida said, "What's wrong?"

"Nothing."

"Are you having second thoughts?"

"No. I think it's just the finality of it. It's starting to hit."

"If you're going to change your mind, now's the time to do it."

"No, I'm done here."

More silence.

"So what's next? Do you have something lined up?"

"I have no idea what's next."

"There's always the Peace Corps."

"That's a thought."

Ida smiled, tenderly. "So this is it, huh? The big departure scene?"

"I suppose it is … You know Ida, I don't think I've ever thanked you. For all that you've done for me."

A playful light came into her eye. "No, I don't believe you ever did."

Now Stavros smiled, feeling a pang of affection for her. "I'm sorry about that, Ida. I've been a selfish man. Selfish and weak. But I am grateful to you. You've been incredible, day after day."

"Thank you."

"And about the times I may have lost my temper. Yelling on the phone, yelling at the associates, sometimes yelling at you—"

"Don't forget the pizza guy."

"What?"

"That night you tore into the pizza delivery guy. You ordered a pepperoni and sausage but he brought a pepperoni and onions, and you went ballistic, remember? You chewed him out and then you smashed your phone. People around here still laugh about it."

"Oh."

"But don't worry about it. It never bothered me. To be honest, I kind of felt sorry for you. You always seemed unhappy. I hope you don't mind me saying that."

"Uh, no. It's fine."

"Plus, I actually liked the craziness. The drama. Like I said, it was never boring."

"Well … good."

"So, should I get some boxes? I'll help you pack up."

He nodded. "I would appreciate that."

*　*　*

Hours later Stavros was pushing a cart through the aisles at OrganaFood, feeling numb. Not only was he now officially unemployed; he was now officially without the life he had known for the past thirteen years. The office, the clients, the cases, the trials, working alongside Keller—it was all gone. Finished. Had he done the right thing in leaving? Yes, he was sure of it. But then why did he feel so damn sad?

In his distress Stavros went over to the cheese cooler, looking for something to ease the pain. He took in the selections—the cheddar, the Brie, the Gruyère—then reached for a fat wedge of manchego. He loved manchego. He might even have a bite right here.

"Stavros," said a voice, and it sent a tingle down his spine. He turned and saw Allegra. And beside her, Brendan, manning a cart filled with groceries. Like a lost sailor spotting a verdant island, Stavros locked eyes on his ex-wife. "Hey!" he said happily. "What are you doing?"

"Shopping," Brendan deadpanned.

"Right," Stavros said. He focused on Allegra. "How are you?"

"I'm fine. But what about you? Did you call your doctor?"

"Not yet."

She made a face. "Has the dizziness come back?"

"No."

"You're very pale. Are you eating well?"

At this, the three of them—father, mother, son—looked into Stavros's cart. There was a pecan pie and a box of sugar cookies with sprinkles. A pint of pistachio ice cream. A pint of black raspberry ice cream. A pint of chocolate chip ice cream. Several packages from the meat counter. And, oh, look at that: a case of wine.

He shrugged. "I cleaned out my office today. I guess you could say I'm celebrating."

"Sounds like fun," Brendan said.

Stavros looked at his son. Following their sit-down up in the boy's room earlier in the week, relations between them had actually improved. On the ride to school Brendan was no longer giving Stavros the silent treatment. Instead he was actually saying "Morning" and "Bye." It was something.

Turning back to Allegra, Stavros said, "What are you guys doing for supper? Do you have plans?" His tone was hopeful—cautiously hopeful.

Allegra became uneasy. "Yes … we do."

"Dylan's cooking for us tonight," Brendan said. "Tacos."

Stavros nodded. "That's great." He looked at Allegra, and she looked at Brendan. Brendan looked at Stavros. Stavros said, "Well, I should get going. I've got some stuff to do." He said his good-byes, then turned his cart toward the checkout lanes.

* * *

On Saturday, just before noon, Stavros's doorbell rang.

It was Brendan, bundled up in hat and coat, standing on the front steps. "Hey Dad."

Puzzled, Stavros said, "Hey there … What's going on?"

"Not much."

"OK," Stavros said, still puzzled. Holding the door open to the cold winter air he looked to the driveway. Allegra sat behind the wheel of her idling Nostromo station wagon, watching them.

"Are you still painting today?" Brendan said.

"I am."

"Can I help?"

Stavros was floored. Yesterday morning on the drive to school he had asked Brendan, yet again, if he wanted to come over this weekend to help paint, but the kid, yet again, had declined. "Is your mother making you do this?"

"No."

"She's not?"

"No ... So is it OK?"

And Stavros thought: is this really happening? Had Brendan finally worked through his daddy hate? Or was this some sort of ploy—the kid acting nice now, only to later hit him up for some cash, or make another case for his punishment to be dropped? How confusing this was, Stavros thought; how confusing, and how draining, to be a parent! He didn't have the energy for another round of adolescent histrionics. Not today. Guardedly he said, "Well, if you want to help out ... I think that's OK."

"There's just one thing."

Ah-ha, Stavros thought: the catch. "And what's that?"

"Can you give me a ride home?"

"A ride home?"

"Yeah."

"Sure. I can do that."

"OK, I'll tell Mom," he said and started toward the car.

"You know what," Stavros said, "I'll tell her." He let Brendan into the house, then walked to the driveway.

Allegra lowered her window. "This is your new place?"

"Hi, yes—do you like it?"

"Well ..."

"I'm fixing it up. Do you want to come in?"

"Oh, I can't. I have to get back."

He nodded. "So," he said, giving her a knowing smile, as if he were on to her, "you're making him do this, right?"

"No."

"This wasn't your idea?"

"No. He asked me."

Stavros didn't believe her. But he wanted to believe her, and so part of him did. He told himself that his son had forgiven him, and he instantly felt relieved, and spent. Thank God he only had one kid!

"Are you OK?" Allegra said.

"I'm just tired ... How's he been with you?"

"This week was better than the ones before. You coming over on Monday really helped, whatever you said to him. He's been less angry."

"Good," Stavros said, pleased. "Are you sure you don't want to come in? I can make some coffee."

"No, I have to go."

"OK. So I'll drive him home ... Hey, if things go well, would you mind if I took him out for supper?"

She said it was fine, then said good-bye. Stavros waved as she drove off, but she didn't turn to see him do it.

* * *

Brendan looked uncomfortable. He had removed his coat and was standing in the dining room. "Nice place, Dad."

Over the previous few weeks Stavros had finished painting the two bedrooms, which were now furnished, and had begun work on the living room. Thus his sofa, armchairs, and all the rest of his furniture, along with some still-unopened moving boxes, were now crammed and piled here in the dining room. The place was a shambles.

"It's temporary," Stavros said. "So, you ready to do some work?"

"Sure." It was said blandly, with zero enthusiasm.

"Have you ever painted before?"

"No."

"Well … it's easy."

No response.

"*All righty*," Stavros said in a chipper voice. "Let's get to it."

He led the way into the living room, which he'd already scraped, spackled, and sanded. On the floor, covered with a drop cloth, were all the tools and supplies. Stavros gave the boy a gallon can of primer, half-empty, and told him to start shaking.

"What?" Brendan said, his brow wrinkling.

Stavros retrieved the can and demonstrated, holding it with two hands and energetically moving it up and down. The boy nodded and took over. Stavros then went into the dining room and turned on the stereo to a local jazz station, and raised the volume.

Re-entering the living room he said, "It's important to play music when you paint."

The boy smiled. "How long do I have to shake this?" he said, his hands moving like pistons.

"Keep going," Stavros said. He set up two plastic paint trays and got the brushes and rollers ready. A minute later he said, "OK, that should be enough." Stavros took the can, removed the lid, and poured some of the primer into each tray. Next he gave a brief lecture on the proper way to lay down paint, providing an example by running a paint-soaked roller up and down the wall. "You see that? No streaks, no bubbles. A nice smooth finish."

The boy nodded with easy assurance, as if to say, "I can do that," and they began. At first they worked in silence, listening to the music. But ten minutes in, after a new song came on, Brendan said, "This is Theo Croker." Stavros concentrated on the sounds. "Yeah, it's pretty good. Can you play this too?" And with that, the gabfest began.

Brendan said he could play Theo Croker, "pretty much," and he talked about the new material he was practicing for the school jazz band's Spring Concert, which was coming up in May. Stavros said he couldn't wait. Then they talked sports and physics. Though Stavros knew nothing about quantum mechanics or the Leicester City "football" club, it didn't matter. Just being with his son, listening to the boy chatter away about things that interested him, gave Stavros a deep pleasure.

On top of this Stavros was amazed at the kid's work ethic. Brendan showed no laziness. He kept painting as they talked and, best of all, took pride in his work. "Am I doing this right?" he'd asked, and, "Does this look OK?" Stavros had expected dawdling and lollygagging, bored faces and weary sighs. But it was just the opposite. So what happened to the sullen, mopey, disinterested character Stavros had come to know these past few months? What happened to *that* kid?

When they finished priming the walls they did the ceiling, and because the work went faster with two people, they even had time to paint the trim with a finish coat of white. By now it was getting close to five, and Stavros was getting hungry. "Do you want to get some food?" he said.

Brendan mulled the offer. "Where do you want to go?"

"Name it."

"Have you ever been to Gemma's?"

"The pizza place?"

"Yeah."

"Your mother and I used to take you there when you were little."

"Really? That's weird. Mom says she doesn't like it. I go there with my friends."

Stavros scratched his head. He and Allegra had loved Gemma's and had gone there often, before Brendan was born and after.

"So can we go?"

"Sure. Just call your mother to let her know. And don't mention Gemma's."

Stavros cleaned the brushes and rollers at the kitchen sink. When he returned to the dining room, he saw Brendan examining his books, piled on the table beside the armchair.

"What, are you religious now?" the boy said.

"Me?"

"Yeah. *The Lives of Saint Paisios and Saint Porphyrios*? And what's this, *On the Afterlife: Stories from Heaven*? … You don't believe in that crap, do you?"

Stavros was alarmed, and torn. Allegra had told him not to mention his NDE to their son. But how could Stavros deny it? How could he deny the most important, most impactful event of his entire life? Where was the honesty in that? The integrity? And what kind of lesson was it for the boy? No; it was time to talk, time to spill the beans. "Brendan, why don't you have a seat."

Brendan sat on the armchair, Stavros on the sofa.

"Remember when I had my heart attack?"

"Of course."

"Well, something happened."

"Like what, you saw Jesus or something?"

"Uh … well—"

A sly smile came over the boy's face. "Dad, I know."

"You know?"

Brendan laughed. "Mom told me."

"She did?"

"She said she told you not to say anything, but she thought you would, so she told me to warn me. She said you thought you went to heaven, and that's why you were acting so weird."

"When was this?"

"Right before you started driving me to school."

"You're joking."

"Nope."

"Why didn't you say anything?"

"I don't know. Mom said not to. But now we're talking about it, so I guess it's all right. What happened?"

Stavros told his son about his NDE—minus the gruesome attacks he'd suffered in hell. There was no need to scare the kid.

Afterward he said, "So what do you think? Is your old man nuts?"

"Not necessarily."

"OK," Stavros said.

"In a way it's kind of funny."

"*Funny?*"

"Yeah. It reminds me of how primitive we still are. I mean, think about it. We don't even know who we are or why we exist. They're the most basic questions there are, but really we don't have a clue." A merry smile broke over the boy's face, and he laughed.

Stavros went silent, unsure how to respond.

"OK, take physics," Brendan said, as if to clarify. "Most of the older generation of living physicists, including Stephen Hawking and Carlos Corelli, deny God outright. But to me that doesn't make any sense. *Obviously* something created the universe. Something doesn't just happen out of nothing, particularly something as complex as life. So for me the real question isn't *is* there a God, but rather *what* is God? Who or what made the universe, and why? I told you one time about the Simulation Theory, about how our world is a sort of video game created by a superior intelligence. What you described, about going to a black empty place, seeing your mother, going to heaven, and talking to Jesus—that could all be explained by the Simulation Theory. And basically, the Simulation Theory could explain religion in general and miracles in particular —because if everything's digital, then what's walking on water, right? It's nothing. Quantum mechanics could also explain what happened. I actually found this interesting paper on an aerospace website. A paper on NDEs, explaining them through astrophysics. The white tunnel is explained as a wormhole, for example. And heaven and the other realms are simply other dimensions, which are pretty much a theoretical given at this point."

"Who says this?"

"An astrophysicist. Someone you never heard of. But it's just a paper, meaning it's only a hypothesis. Nothing's been proved. But it's pretty interesting to read."

Stavros's head was spinning. "So Brendan, what are you saying, exactly? Do you believe me or not?"

"Sure. Why would you lie? As to what actually happened—whether it was just in your brain or in your mind, meaning your consciousness, which is separate from your brain according to some theories, or in another, actual space or dimension—that's the interesting puzzle. Either way, it's pretty cool." The boy fell silent, and his expression seemed to say that he was finished.

"So that's it?" Stavros said.

"Yeah. Pretty much. The key is to have an open mind, right?"

* * *

Gemma's, a small place, was crowded and noisy with conversation. Between Stavros and Brendan was a fragrant pizza, topped with sausage, Kalamata olives, onions, and extra mozzarella. The boy's choice. To drink, Stavros had a cherry soda, Brendan a root beer.

Chomping away Stavros said, "This is good, huh?"

The boy agreed, then said, "So what was Pappous's pizza shop like?" Pappous was Brendan's grandfather, who had died when Brendan was a toddler. Heart failure at the shop on a busy Friday night.

"It was nice," Stavros said. "Nothing fancy. Not like this place. But then a soda cost you fifty cents, not three bucks."

"Did you like working there?"

"It was OK. Though it made your clothes stink, all the grease. Imagine walking around Thoreau every day smelling like a pepperoni pizza."

"Did you have video games?"

"Yep. And a jukebox. It was a popular place—Papadakis Pizza and Subs. Kids would come in and hang out."

"What kind of music did you have on the jukebox?"

"Oh, you know ... the Stones, Aerosmith, Journey. Whenever I hear 'Don't Stop Believin' I'm back at the shop, making a sub. *'OH, large meatball to go! Lettuce and provolone!'*"

Brendan laughed. "What were the video games?"

"Donkey Kong, Pac-Man, Centipede. They changed every few years. You rented them. Asteroids was my favorite. I was pretty good."

Brendan smiled as he chewed. Stavros reached for another slice. As he took a bite he saw a pensive expression come over his son, as though an idea were germinating. Stavros waited.

The boy said, "I can tell you like Mom."

"What? Of course I like your mother … She's a good woman."

"No, I mean you *like* like her."

"I *like* like her?"

"Yeah, I could tell by the way you looked at her."

"When?"

"When you passed out the other day. Everyone could tell."

"*Everyone?*"

"Yeah. Me, Mom, and Dylan."

"They said that?"

"No."

"They didn't?"

"No."

"Then what are you talking about?"

"I don't know. Nothing."

Stavros sighed. "You know, Brendan, your mother and I were together a long time. Many years. And we were in love."

"Do you want to get back together?"

"Me and your mother?"

"Mm-hmm," Brendan said, chewing and staring at his father.

"Well, I don't know. I hadn't thought about it, really … And plus, there's Dylan. She's happy with him, right?"

"Yeah."

"*She is?*" Stavros said, stung.

"Yep."

"She told you?"

"No, but you can tell."

"How?"

"It's like they're married."

"*Married?*"

"Yeah, they're always touching each other, and they laugh at dumb stuff. It's embarrassing."

Concerned, Stavros pondered this. "Well … to me that sounds more like dating. Believe me, there's a difference."

"Maybe."

"And do they fight?"

"I think you asked me this before."

"But do they?"

"Sometimes."

"About what?"

"I don't know. Though I know Mom doesn't like his friend. This guy Jake. She gets mad when he hangs out with him. Also, she kind of bosses him around."

"Your mother bosses Dylan around," Stavros said.

"Yeah, and I can tell he doesn't like it. She tells him to do something and he makes this face, but then he says OK or whatever and he does it."

Faintly, Stavros smiled. "And what do you think about Dylan?"

"He's all right," Brendan said, frowning slightly.

"I thought you guys were buddies?"

"No, I like him, but … he comes over too much. At first it was just once in a while, but then he started sleeping over, and now it's like he's here all the time. Sometimes I go to the TV room to watch something and he's in there lying on the sofa. It kind of pisses me off. He has his own place."

* * *

In the driveway on Champney Street, Stavros thanked Brendan for coming over and helping with the painting. "You did a great job," he said. "I was very impressed."

"Thanks. And thanks for the pizza."

"You're welcome."

As the boy reached for the door Stavros said, "Hey, quick question."

Brendan looked at him.

"Your mother made you come over today, didn't she."

The boy hesitated. "Pretty much."

"Well, I'm glad she did. I enjoyed seeing you … Did you have a good time?"

"Yeah. It was fun. Better than spending the day in my room."

Stavros nodded. "I can see that."

"And I liked talking with you too."

"You did?"

"Yeah."

"Oh," Stavros said, feeling a bloom of happiness. "That's good to hear. I liked talking with you as well."

The boy shrugged. "I should go in."

"OK. You have a good night."

"You too."

Stavros felt the desire to say, "I love you Brendan," but something held him back.

The boy got out of the car, shut the door, and passed through the headlights' bright glow. And once Brendan had disappeared into the house, Stavros's gaze went up to the second floor. In his old bedroom the curtains were closed, and illumined by a soft, interior light.

NINETEEN

When his phone rang, Stavros was moving furniture. He had finished painting the living room the day before, a cheery shade of yellow, and was now arranging the space—sofa, armchairs, books, coffee table. Afterward, he was going to run out and get some plants, some big green ones. Bring some life into the place.

Keller said, "How are ya, buddy?"

"Hey Wyatt, how've you been?"

"Good, good. Hey, I was thinking, we should get together."

"Sure. Name a day."

"How about tonight?"

"Uh, yeah. That works," Stavros said, detecting a slight trace of urgency in Keller's voice, and wondering if something were up. "You want me to come in? I could meet you at the hotel."

"No, there's been a problem there."

"What do you mean?"

"I'll tell you later. Actually, I'd like to get out of the city. How about I come to Cambridge?"

"Why don't you come here? To my place? I'll cook."

"You'll cook? Do you even know how?"

"I'm getting there."

* * *

Hours later, the two men were sitting in Stavros's living room, drinks in hand. Stavros had just given Keller a tour of his new home, pointing out all the work he had done or was going to do—the painting, the plastering, etcetera. Taking everything in, Keller had displayed a range of emotions: shock, horror, bewilderment, incomprehension. Now, as though the shock had passed, he was grinning, his eyes curiously amused. From the sofa, in his bespoke suit and hand-made shoes, he said, "Is there something you want to tell me, Stavros?"

"About what?"

"This house. I know how much money you make. I sign the checks, remember?"

Stavros rubbed the stubble on his jaw. "It's kind of hard to explain."

"Are you in financial trouble?"

"No. Not at all. I wasn't happy in my apartment. I needed a change."

"OK. But why this place? It's a little rundown, don't you think? A little small?"

"Nah. It's fine. And how much space does one person need, really? A whole family could live here. It's comfortable. I like it."

Keller nodded, sipped his drink, and said no more.

"So what was this problem you mentioned on the phone?" Stavros said, wanting to shift topics.

"I had dinner last week with Allen Moscowicz, in the restaurant at the hotel, and on Tuesday it was mentioned in the *Bugle* gossip page—along with the fact that I currently live there."

"Oh, great."

"Yeah. So that same night I'm back in the restaurant, eating by myself, and some crazy off the street comes up to my table and says he wants me to help him sue 'the Internet.' That's what he said, 'I want to sue the Internet. They're spying on me.' I said, 'Sir, I'd love to help you, but I'm a defense attorney. If the Internet ever sues *you*, give me a call.' A real nutter. Anyway, security came and they walked him out. I'm told a few other people have come in, asking for my room number at the front desk."

"That's a little disturbing."

"It's because of Bellingham," Keller said, brushing it off. "It'll blow over soon."

* * *

"Hey, this is pretty good," Keller said, putting away his first bite. "Very tasty."

They were in the dining room, its walls still cracked and unpainted, seated at the table. For their meal Stavros had broiled two T-bone steaks, tossed a salad, and cooked up two potatoes and some asparagus. To drink, Keller had brought a bottle of McLagan, and for dessert, Stavros had picked up a pecan pie from the OrganaFood bakery. All in all, things were going well.

"So what else is new?" Stavros said. "Anything?"

Cutting off another bite of steak, Keller said, "Well … I proposed to Belén."

"Hey, congratulations!"

"She said no."

"Oh … I'm sorry to hear that."

Keller shrugged, chewing his food and averting his gaze.

Stavros recalled how Keller had seemed eager to meet tonight. Now he knew why. "What happened?" he said.

Keller grew uncomfortable, visibly abashed. "She said she thought I understood we were just having a fling; that it would end in June, when she goes back to Argentina."

"She's finishing her degree?"

"Yeah."

"And you knew she was going back?"

"I did. But I thought she'd want to stay. I thought she'd be excited to stay. She was always saying how much she loves Boston, how she thought it was great for an academic, and how there was so much opportunity here. I thought we could have a nice life together, the two of us. But I misread the situation." Keller reached for his glass, and suddenly shook his head, becoming irritated, cross. "It was a complete farce, Stavros. The whole thing. I actually got on one knee."

Stavros screwed up his eyes, struck by the idea of it—Keller on his knee? "When was this?"

"Friday night, at the hotel. We'd just got back from dinner. I told her I had something to ask her, and she sat on the sofa. Then I bended the knee ... I thought she'd appreciate the gesture ... Her family's very Catholic."

"OK," Stavros said, his eyes still screwed up.

"At first she just stared—at me, at the ring—then she said, 'What are you doing?' And I said, 'I'm proposing to you,' and then I did. I made my declaration. And the whole time she's got this look on her face—like I'm offering her a turd. Not a diamond ring, but a turd. And after I'd finished, she blushed. And not from joy. She was embarrassed, Stavros. She was embarrassed for *me*. I could see it in her eyes, the pity. Then she said, 'I thought you understood—this was never about commitment.' She kept saying that, 'I thought you understood.' By this point I realize it's time to get off the knee, but when I tried to get up ... my leg sort of gave. I don't know what it was, a cramp, some weakness in the thigh. But it took some effort to stand ... I'll never forget that. She's sitting there, watching me, and I'm struggling to get to my feet like somebody's grandpa. I felt ridiculous, Stavros. Old and ridiculous. And then she left. She said she had to go, and she left."

Stavros was stunned. He couldn't believe what he was hearing: Keller rejected, Keller humiliated, and most of all, Keller actually admitting to it. He said, "So that's it? Have you talked to her?"

"I called her the next day but she didn't answer. Then on Sunday she called and said we shouldn't see each other anymore. I said 'Why?' She said, 'It's for the best. I don't want to hurt you.'" At this, Keller cringed, the pain showing on his face. "Can you believe that? A twenty-nine year old, Stavros. A graduate student."

Stavros wasn't sure if he was supposed to laugh or commiserate; but Keller wasn't laughing, so Stavros said, "That's terrible, Wyatt. I'm sorry."

"I just don't know what I was thinking," Keller said. "Every day on the job I see people do stupid things. Every damn day. Now I'm the idiot."

"Hey ... join the club," Stavros said.

Keller knocked back the rest of his drink and poured another—his fourth of the evening. He asked Stavros if he wanted a refill but he said no.

"Yep, here I am buddy," Keller went on, his voice now tinged with self-mockery, "sixty-four next month, alone, and living in a hotel. It's not quite how I had envisioned my twilight years."

Observing Keller, Stavros thought of Maggie. Charming, vibrant, beautiful Maggie. Maggie whom Keller had left for someone less than half his age. Had it been worth it, Stavros wondered? Did Keller now have regrets? Stavros, who knew something himself about regret, would love to know. But this wasn't the moment for such questions. Maybe another time. He said, "You'll meet someone else."

* * *

Over dessert Keller said, "Where's your drink?"

Before he'd brought in the pie Stavros had cleared the table, removing the dinner plates and his glass. "I've had enough," he said.

"You've had *enough?*"

"Yeah. I've cut back."

Keller was incredulous. "Since when?"

"Late January, early February. I'm down to about two drinks per day."

"Come on."

"I mean it. I let my health go when I was working. I'm trying to get it back."

Keller stared at him. "Stavros, you've been in Cambridge for a month, and now you're on the wagon, living in a shack, and wearing blue jeans. I would not have predicted any of this."

Stavros held up his hands as if to say, "What are you going to do?"

"So you're serious."

"Yes."

"Well, then I guess I'll drink alone," Keller said, pouring out the last of the McLagan.

Stavros felt a twinge of guilt, as though he were being a poor friend. Unsupportive. Keller was hurting, after all. He said, "I suppose I could have one more."

* * *

When Stavros entered the living room with a bottle of Glengowrie and two tumblers, Keller was already seated in the armchair. He was grinning, his tipsy eyes sparkling with mischief. "I've been looking at your books, Stavros. Near-death experiences, a Bible, lives of saints. What's next, are you going to enter a monastery? ... St. Stavros the Sober?"

Stavros chuckled. "I don't think they'd take me," he said. Yet in his mind Stavros acknowledged that Keller wasn't entirely off base. Since his visit to Professor Notaras, who had first suggested it, and since he'd begun delving more deeply into his reading list, including books on the lives of saints and mystics, Stavros had begun to pray. It had proved easier than he'd thought it would. He'd started with the prayer from his youth, the Lord's Prayer. But lately he'd begun to pray more spontaneously, more conversationally, randomly thanking God for some blessing—his son, his life, his home—or saying he was sorry for some sin: his crimes, his mistreatment of Brendan, of Allegra, of many other people. It felt good to do this, Stavros realized, and natural. It felt right.

After he'd poured them each a drink, Stavros placed the bottle on the coffee table and sat on the sofa.

"So you're sticking with your Jesus story?" Keller said, still grinning.

Stavros said he was, and he sipped his drink.

"Now, you told me about the hell part, about the demons attacking you and doing sexual things, but we never did get to the part with Jesus. What exactly did the two of you talk about?"

There was more than a trace of derision in Keller's tone, but Stavros attributed it, mostly, to the scotch. He said, "We talked about a number of things."

"I see. Presumably this was in English, and not Aramaic?"

"Yeah. My Aramaic's a little rusty. Actually, Wyatt, we didn't really talk. We communicated more by thoughts."

"By thoughts," Keller said, his brow rising with interest. "Like something on *Star Trek?*"

"Basically, yes."

"Interesting. And these thoughts were in English?"

"I guess. Yeah."

"You don't remember?"

"What I remember is that I understood everything perfectly. There was no ambiguity."

"And how did you know it was Jesus? Did he look like Jesus? Did he introduce himself?"

Stavros smiled, patiently. "No, there were no introductions. No handshakes. I just knew it was him, and he knew who I was. I could *feel* it. I could feel from his eyes that he knew everything about me. As for what he looked like, it was just what you'd expect. Long hair, beard, Semitic features."

"And his clothes? Let me guess: robe and sandals?"

"That's right."

"OK, so the fact that he looked just as you'd expect him to look, the Jesus from art and kitsch culture, that doesn't raise any flags for you?"

"No, because this wasn't just a vision. If it had been, then sure—I would agree that it was probably something my brain had cooked up from things I'd seen in the past. But it wasn't a vision. It was an actual, physical experience. And quite frankly, his appearance was the least memorable thing about him. What really struck me, and what stays with me now, is what he said, and most of all, how he made me feel."

"Which was what?"

"Loved. He made me feel loved. It was overwhelming."

"How so?"

"It's hard to explain. It's beyond description."

"Try."

"It was the best I've ever felt, Wyatt. Period."

"Better than sex? Better than drugs? Better than booze?"

"There's no comparison. In heaven you're completely lucid, and aware; you're in the present, not in some blissful state of forgetting. And what you feel is complete acceptance, complete fulfillment. A joy that's boundless yet calm. You realize, for the first time, that you're home. That you're where you're supposed to be."

"And yet … here you are. In Cambridge, Massachusetts."

"That's right. But I didn't want to come back. In fact, I pleaded with him to stay."

Keller laughed. "That's funny—you pleaded with Jesus. Apparently it didn't go so well."

Stavros said nothing.

Now bristling, exasperated, Keller said, "You do realize how crazy this sounds, right?"

"Of course I do. And if I hadn't experienced it myself, I'd think it was crazy too. But I did experience it. It happened, Wyatt."

"What does Allegra say? I'm sure she has an opinion."

"She thinks it was a biochemical process. That it all took place in my brain."

"And you disagree."

"Yes. She's a doctor. She deals with measurable facts, and that's fine. It's how she was trained. But what happened to me is entirely beyond that. It's a whole other realm, with a whole other set of rules. It's just something we don't understand yet. Just like at another time we didn't understand gravity or nuclear fission."

"*Well*—nuclear fission," Keller said. "So we're talking hard science now."

"Wyatt, look. I knew from the beginning that you and Allegra both thought I was nuts. And it bothered me. But now? I don't mind. Like I say, I understand how crazy it sounds. But I've had time to think about it, and I've had time to study it and talk to people, and I'm comfortable with my position. I've read all the different theories, about how a lack of oxygen or the abnormal functioning of dopamine can cause hallucinations; how a surge of endorphins in the moments before death can cause a sense of well-being; how drugs like ketamine and DMT can reproduce NDE symptoms; etcetera. I've read all of it. And as theories, they're plausible. They're reasonable. But to someone who actually experienced it, they're meaningless. They're inadequate. Because what I experienced there, in that other world, was infinitely more real—more vivid, more memorable, more profound—than anything I've ever experienced here. The fact is, *this* world is the dream; the other world, *that's* the real one, that's the place we belong. Earth is just a temporary stop. Think of it this way: when you were in your mother's womb, you had no idea that there was anything else, that there was a whole other world waiting. No idea. It's the same with life on Earth. It's temporary, and its purpose is to prepare us for the next life, just like life in the womb prepares us—"

"OK, OK," Keller said, holding up a hand. "This is starting to sound very New Agey. Very Cambridge. Let's just stick to the facts. So you talked to Jesus—*telepathically*. And what great mysteries did he reveal? Did he tell you the meaning of life?"

"He didn't have to."

"No?"

"It was obvious. When you go there, you understand."

"I see. *Love*."

"Yes."

"So the Beatles were right after all, huh?" And with a grin, Keller sang the opening lines to "All You Need Is Love."

Stavros felt a twitch of irritation.

"I'm just joking, Stavros. You look upset."

"I'm not upset, Wyatt."

"You know, it's a nice sentiment—'love is the answer'—which is another song, by the way. England Dan and John Ford Coley, I believe. An admirable ideal. Something to teach the kiddies. But what about the adults? Do you have anything for us, Stavros? For the folks who understand that simplistic world views do more damage than good? For the folks who deal with life as it is rather than walking around with our heads up our asses, clinging to feel-good illusions? The world is a brutal place, buddy, and you know it. We've seen the worst in men, day after day on the job: petty things, cruel things, horrific things. All manner of ugliness. As for love, it's just a trick we play on ourselves and on others to get something we want: sex, food, shelter, money, companionship. Our primary impulse is selfishness, not love. People are greedy and vengeful. They want power, they want control. And the only thing that keeps them in line is fear of retribution: from other people, from the law, and from a belief in hell, if they're weak or ignorant enough to believe in such nonsense. That's it, partner, and you know it."

Stavros understood; Keller's beliefs had been his once too. "You're right, Wyatt. The world *is* brutal. I won't argue with that. But still there's love. Love that changes lives. You say love as 'the answer' is simplistic, childish. Sure, as a *concept* it's simple. But to actually live it? To actually love your neighbor? It's very difficult. At least for me it has been. To be honest, I don't think I've ever genuinely loved anyone, ever. Not in the way I now understand it. I thought I did; I thought I loved Allegra, and Brendan, and *you*. But now, I'm not so sure. If it was convenient, or if I felt there was something I could get in return, I would give of myself. But in the end, it all came down to me, to my needs. It's just like you say: our primary impulse is selfishness. We want and we want and we want. But where does it lead? Where does this nonstop craving lead? In my experience it leads to loneliness. It leads to depression, and anger, and fear. And I'm done with that. I've been miserable for most of my life, Wyatt. From childhood on. But I've had a taste of love, and I know it's the way out."

* * *

Keller's glib smile had vanished. He struggled to his feet and reached for the bottle. "You want some more?"

Stavros did not.

Keller filled his glass, placed the bottle back down on the coffee table, closer to himself, then sat. After a meditative sip, he said, "What's interesting to me, Stavros—and by the way, I thought you expressed yourself quite well there, talking about love; it was very moving—but most of what you said, and I mean no offense of course, but most of what you said could have come from these books." He glanced at the stack of volumes on the table beside him: the Huxley, the James, the NDE books, the Bible, the several books on saints.

Stavros said, "That's true. But I've never claimed to have said anything original or new."

"As you say. But you see, buddy, the problem is this. Since your words sound like they come from books, what's to say they didn't?"

"Wyatt, you know I don't have any proof. Only my word."

"Right. Your word that you left your body, went to hell, and then went to heaven and met Jesus Christ."

"Yes."

Keller sighed, looking both frustrated and resigned. "Then what exactly did you talk about, Stavros—you and Jesus? You still haven't told me."

"We talked about my life, about how I'd lived it. And after that he … instructed me, basically."

"Jesus instructed you," Keller said, now amused. "Your own private Sermon on the Mount?"

"Essentially, yes. He talked about the great precepts. Love. Forgiveness. Compassion. Charity. Putting other people before yourself—"

"The kiddie stuff," Keller said with a smirk, his eyes mocking Stavros.

And with this, Stavros finally lost his patience. "Wyatt, let me ask you something: why are we here? Why does the universe exist? Do you know?"

Keller's smug look faded.

"Answer me," Stavros said. "Do you know why we're here?"

"Well, according to scientists, it starts with the Big Bang."

"OK, the Big Bang. Sure. But what caused the Big Bang?"

"Stavros, I'm no physicist and neither are you—"

"I understand, but my point is that something happened to me that might shed some light on these questions, yet rather than take an interest in it you just want to laugh and sneer."

"Stavros, where's the proof? Where's the proof of God? Where is it?"

"It's everywhere! You're the proof; I'm the proof; existence itself is the proof—it's all around you! Just open your eyes and look. Life is a miracle! It's a gift—a gift we've been given. And if that's not enough, there are the saints; the mystics and prophets who've experienced God firsthand, through actual, personal experience. The saints talk about God in detail, but you don't know about this because you haven't studied it in any meaningful way. Imagine someone who's never experienced love saying, 'I've never been in love, so love doesn't exist.' Is that a credible position? Do you think it would hold up in court?"

"Fine," Keller said, "I know nothing about God. You're the expert. Then let me ask you this: if heaven was so damn wonderful, then why did you come back?"

"I had to."

"Yes. You 'pleaded with Jesus.' But why did he make you come back?"

"He said it wasn't my time. He said I was still needed here—"

"Oh come on, Stavros. Come on!" Keller spat with sudden feeling.

"What?"

"It 'wasn't your time'? If it wasn't your time, then what the hell were you doing there in the first place? God made a mistake?" Keller cackled, his whole body shaking with laughter.

"What about Brendan?" Stavros said. "I told you about the drugs."

"Right," Keller said dryly. "Jesus wanted you to come back to Earth ... to keep Brendan off drugs. You really believe that?"

"I don't know. Sure. Why not? To keep him off drugs. To be a better father to him. To let him know that he's loved. I don't know. Maybe it's something else. Maybe it was so *I* could know love."

"Stavros, I'm sorry," Keller said, his tone now reasonable, even sympathetic, "it's too much. The whole thing: Jesus, hell, it 'wasn't your time.' It's ludicrous."

"Wyatt, why would I make it up? What's my motive?"

"I don't know, buddy. But the burden of proof is on you, not me."

Aggravated, Stavros finished off the last of his drink.

Keller said, "Look, you said you were miserable before this, correct? You were miserable for most of your life?"

"Yes."

"OK. Naturally, if someone's miserable, they want to make a change. So answer me this: how much did you know about near-death experiences before you had yours? Had you ever read a book or seen a movie on the subject?"

"What? No!"

"Never? Even though these stories are out there?"

"Well … of course I'd *heard* about them. But had I read books on them? Had I investigated the subject? No. As for movies, who knows? I've seen too many to remember."

"So you *had* heard about them."

"*Yes.* Everybody has."

"What I'm thinking, Stavros, is this. Imagine a person, a depressed person, a *miserable* person, a person who, for whatever reason, feels he can't take anymore. He's had enough. Too much pain, too much suffering, too much loneliness, whatever. Life has become unbearable. And so, sensing an existential threat, the subconscious takes over and creates a situation—call it a dream, call it a hallucination—that is so powerful, so seemingly irrefutable in its reality, that the person now feels enabled or justified to make a change, a radical change. In effect, the subconscious gives the person 'permission' to alter his life, gives him a 'higher rationale' for doing so … To me it seems perfectly reasonable."

"You think I *tricked* myself?"

"Stavros, how many jailhouse conversions have we seen?"

"Come on Wyatt!"

"Hey, you've seen it just as much as me. Howie Goettz. Dwayne Beggens. These guys go in the clink, meet Jesus or Allah, and come parole-hearing time, they're model inmates. How many times have we joked about this? We may have even encouraged it ourselves once or twice, no?"

Stavros was livid. "How could you compare me to those guys?"

"I'm not comparing you to them, Stavros. And I'm not doubting anyone's sincerity. Sometimes these conversions are genuine, and the person really does change. Which is all for the good. But who knows what's really happening? The brain is very complex. And when it comes to self-preservation, it can be very cunning, very inventive. I think under the right amount of stress, and given a certain predisposition, a person can imagine just about anything."

"Wyatt, I'm telling you, it happened, OK? It *happened*."

"And I believe you, Stavros. Which is to say, I believe that *you* believe that something happened, something profound and otherworldly. I believe that. But as to the actual reality of the things you describe, I'm sorry buddy, but I'm just not there. It's nothing personal."

TWENTY

It was mid-April. With Brendan's help, Stavros had finished painting the rest of the rooms in his new home. They both thought the place looked great. Outside, in the backyard, the snow had melted and the trees were beginning to bud. Three goldenrod bushes had bloomed, and a scattering of crocuses had pushed up from the wet ground. There were singing birds—robins, blue jays—and a pair of gray squirrels. In sudden bursts of activity, the squirrels would chase each other across the grass, up the trees, and along shaky branches. Whether they were playing or fighting, Stavros wasn't sure. It was hard to tell.

* * *

On the ride to school Brendan said, "Hey Dad?"

Stavros glanced from the road to his son. The tone of the boy's voice —hesitant, humble—made it clear a request was coming. "Yeah?"

"I want to go on a date."

"A *date* date?"

"Yeah."

"With who?"

"Sally French."

"Hey, that's great! Excellent! … Oh, wait a minute—you're grounded."

"I know."

"Well …"

"You said if I'm with you or Mom I can leave the house."

"I did. But if you recall, the idea is that you're being punished. And to me, a date with a pretty girl doesn't really sound like punishment."

"But you said you liked Sally. You said I should go out with her."

"True."

"So … can we do it?"

"We?"

"Yeah, would you drive us?"

"I see. I've been elected chauffeur."

"Is it OK?"

"What are you guys going to do? Or rather, what are *we* going to do?"

"I don't know. Something."

"Something."

"I never went on a date before."

Immediately, Stavros dropped the sarcastic attitude. A boy's first date, he knew, was serious business. All sorts of emotional scars could result. "OK. Well … do you have any ideas? What does she say?"

"I don't know. I haven't asked her yet."

"You haven't asked her what she wants to do, or you haven't asked her out?"

"I haven't asked her out. But she'll say yes."

"Oh yeah?"

"Definitely."

"And how do you know that?"

"I can tell. She laughs whenever I make a joke."

"Wow … You're pretty cocky, huh?"

"What do you mean?"

"I mean, you're pretty sure of yourself."

"I just think she'll say yes, that's all."

"And do you like her, or is this just … you know."

"No, I like her. We've been texting and stuff. She's really smart."

"Oh, OK. Good. Well, what about bowling?"

"Bowling?"

"Yeah, it's fun. The three of us can do it."

"Ah …"

"You know, you're moving around when you're bowling. Playing a game. It'll make things easier for you. You'll be less nervous."

"I won't be nervous."

"You won't be nervous on the first date of your life? What are you, Casanova?"

"No."

"What about a movie? A movie then dinner. That's what I used to do. Your mother and I went to the Brattle Theatre."

"That's kind of corny."

"You got a better idea?"

"Not really ... Could we get pizza after?"

"Sure. Though there is one problem. Sally, I believe, doesn't like me. Otherwise she'd be in the car right now, remember?"

"I know. But she feels bad. She wants to see you and say sorry."

"She said that?"

"Yep."

"Well ... yeah, I think we can work something out. Let me run it by your mother first."

"I already asked. She said it's OK if you say it's OK."

"I should probably still call her. Just to touch base."

* * *

That night Stavros made the call.

"How are you?" he said.

"I'm well," she said. "Busy."

"OK ... good. So, uh, I was calling about Brendan. I wanted to check in about his date with Sally."

"It's unbelievable, isn't it?"

"It is."

"It goes by so fast."

"Tell me about it."

"But I'm glad it's Sally."

"So then you're fine with this, even though he's supposedly grounded?"

"Well, I think it's a good idea. He's been behaving and I really like Patti French. She's a good mother, and Sally's a good girl. I think she could be a positive influence on him."

"That's what I thought. But I also don't want him to think we're backing down on his punishment. Even though we kind of are. It sends a bad message."

"We're not backing down, Stavros. Life's not black and white. He knows he's still grounded till June. Let's just see how things go."

"OK."

"Also, before I go, I was wondering if you could do me a favor."

"Sure," Stavros said. "Anything."

"Dylan and I would like to visit his parents in the next month or so. They're in New Jersey, and I've never met them. I was hoping you could take Brendan for a couple days. Would you mind?"

Stavros felt a sudden tightness in his chest, a pain in his heart. His eyes shut, and he made no response. Then, calmly, he said, "The parents, huh?"

"Yes."

"Sounds ominous," he joked.

She didn't laugh.

He said, "Uh, no … I wouldn't mind. Brendan's welcome any time."

"Thank you, Stavros. I'll let you know when we settle on a date."

They hung up, and for ten, fifteen minutes Stavros remained where he was, seated in the armchair. He felt very tired, very weak. His heart was racing, but eventually it slowed. Then he stood, went into the kitchen, and refreshed his drink.

* * *

On Friday evening, he drove over to Champney Street to pick up his son for his first-ever date. It was, Stavros thought, a big deal, a momentous day for the kid. And maybe it was a big deal for Stavros too. He was sharing something important with his son, something they would both remember.

When Brendan got into the car he appeared eager but tense. Freshly scrubbed, he smelled strongly of ... something. Aftershave or cologne, applied very liberally.

"How we doin'?" Stavros said. "Are you excited?"

"Sort of."

Stavros laughed. "Sort of?"

The boy smiled bashfully. "Yeah, I am."

"Good. You should be."

The plan was to see the seven-thirty showing of the just-released *Return of Neptune Nine*, in 3D, at the Fresh Pond Megaplex, then go for pizza afterward at Gemma's.

"You have enough money?"

"Mom gave me twenty."

"Twenty? For a movie and dinner?"

"It should be enough."

"Really? And what about your date?"

"What about her?"

"You think it's Ladies' Night at the movies?"

"What?"

"How are you going to pay for her ticket and yours and still have money for pizza, with twenty bucks?"

"I don't know. She'll have money."

"Is that right."

"Yeah."

"Brendan, when you take a girl out, you pay. For everything. The tickets, the popcorn, the drinks, dinner. Everything. You got that?"

"I don't think people do that anymore. Girls pay for themselves now."

"That's baloney. Trust me, this is on you. And if the girl says she wants to chip in, don't believe it. It's a trap."

"A trap?"

"Well, not a trap. A *test*."

"Of what?"

"Who knows? It's just how it is. But the bottom line is, you pay. And if she insists, you just politely say, 'Thanks, but I've got this; you can pay another time,' and that puts an end to it. Now, if it becomes a regular thing, a boyfriend-girlfriend thing, then it's different. She can pay sometimes. This isn't the 1950s. But in the beginning, it's all you. Anyway, I'm going to give you a little loan for tonight." Stavros reached for his money clip and peeled off a fifty. "And after you buy the tickets, ask her if she wants popcorn or something. A soda, licorice, whatever. And like I said, that's a loan. I'm not your personal ATM anymore. We're going to get you a job this summer."

"You think fifty's enough? For everything?"

"You just said your mother gave you twenty, so now you have seventy, and yes, that's enough. And that includes my pizza too. Tonight you're the big spender."

"OK ... You're going to give us some space, right?"

"That is correct. You won't even know I'm there."

Stavros backed out of the driveway and sped toward Sally's.

"Now, when you're waiting in line for the tickets, talk to her, all right? Ask about her day. Say something funny."

"Dad, I know how to talk to girls."

"You do?" Stavros said doubtfully, thinking of the Ottavia-poem debacle.

"*Yes*," Brendan said, affronted.

"Well, I'm sure you do," Stavros said. "Just remember to listen when she talks. Look at her eyes and not ... other places. Do you understand? Listen to what she's saying, and nod your head every now and then to show you're interested."

"*Dad*."

"OK, OK. The main thing is, just be relaxed. Have fun. She wouldn't be with you if she didn't want to be. There's no reason to be nervous."

"I have no idea what you're talking about."

"I'm just saying, have fun. That's all."

"I will, so long as you're not telling me what to do every five seconds."
Stavros got the hint.

* * *

When they pulled up to Sally's house, Brendan didn't move. Stavros waited.

The boy said, "You should beep the horn."

Stavros couldn't believe it. Very patiently he said, "Brendan, when you pick up a girl for a date, you go to her front door. Also, her father's going to want to meet you. And when you shake his hand, give him a good firm grip, not one of these limp-noodle jobs, OK? You shake his hand and let him know you're a man, you got that?"

"Dad, Sally's father doesn't even live here. He moved to Maryland with some guy."

"Well, then you go in there and you shake Sally's mother's hand. But not too hard."

The kid exploded. "But I already know her!"

"Brendan, that's not the point! The point is that you're showing respect to Sally, and you're showing respect to her family."

Steaming, and shaking his head, the kid didn't budge.

"Brendan, please. Just trust me on this. Get your butt out of the car and go knock on that door. It's what a man does."

"*Fine*," the kid whined. He got out of the car, slammed the door, and moped up Sally's front steps. Seconds later, Sally herself appeared on the porch, her face luminous, radiant with anticipation. She was in her coat and newsboy cap, ready to go. The kids exchanged a few words then went into the house. Five minutes later, they reappeared, and were followed by what had to be Patti French—blond, slender, and with a smile just like her daughter's. She was coatless, and had her arms crossed over her chest against the cold evening air.

Stavros leapt out of the car and went around to the sidewalk.

"Hey Mr. Papadakis!" Sally said.

"Hi Sally. How are you?"

"Good. Sorry I stopped riding to school with you. I feel bad."

"Oh, there's nothing to feel bad about. I'm just happy to see you." Stavros turned to Patti French and introduced himself, extending his hand.

"It's nice to finally meet you," she said as they shook. "And thanks for taking the kids. I have to say, I was very impressed that Brendan came to the door. I didn't think that was done anymore."

Pleased by this, Stavros gave his son a look as if to say, "Did you hear that, hotshot?" To Patti he said, "It's just good manners."

"Oh, I agree," she said grandly. "My father never let me out of the house unless he met the boy first."

"Really?" Stavros said, unsure if she were kidding.

"No. But looking back on it, maybe it wouldn't have been a bad thing," she said, laughing.

Stavros laughed too. He thought she was charming.

Brendan looked mortified. "*Dad*, we need to get going."

"OK … Well," Stavros said to Patti, "we should have Sally home by eleven or so, if that's all right. They want to get some pizza after the movie."

"That's fine. It sounds like fun."

Good-byes were said all around, and when Stavros got into the car he noticed that Brendan had slipped into the backseat with Sally, and that there wasn't any space between them. The boy looked pretty pleased with himself.

"Hey," Stavros said, giving his son a meaningful look in the rearview, "put your seatbelts on." Stavros then fired up the Imperator, pulled into traffic, and tooted the horn as Patti French waved from the sidewalk.

* * *

At the cinema, Stavros parked the car and the three of them got out. But before locking up he said, "Oh, you know what? I have to make a call. I just remembered."

"Dad, there's already a line. We're gonna be late."

"You guys go ahead. I'll meet you inside. And if this call runs too long and I miss you, then let's meet back here after the movie, OK?"

Brendan hesitated.

"Go on," Stavros said. "I'll see you inside."

The kids started for the cinema, and Stavros got back in the car. He ignited the engine, turned on the heater, and watched as Brendan and Sally walked away in the darkening light.

* * *

Twenty minutes later Stavros entered a crowded auditorium. Holding a bucket of popcorn, a large cherry soda, and the 3D glasses that came with the ticket, he ducked into the first empty seat, two rows from the lobby. He didn't want to see the kids, or have the kids see him. Let them be, he thought. But not long after he'd settled in—after putting his drink in the cup holder, removing his coat, and turning off his phone —Stavros spotted them. They were on the same side of the aisle as he, four rows ahead and to the right. Stavros frowned, then chomped on a handful of popcorn. Yet despite his desire not to meddle or snoop, he couldn't help glancing over at his son. Brendan kept turning in his seat, looking all around. He was likely watching out for his old man, worried that Stavros might be spying on him, which was not good. In such a state the boy would never enjoy himself. And plus, did Stavros really want to see Brendan and Sally start necking, should it come to that?

Letting out a weary sigh, he donned his 3D glasses, gathered up soda, popcorn, and coat, and said, "Excuse me, sorry," as he squeezed past the couple to his left, then proceeded down the aisle. Walking slow, and slurping his soda through the straw, Stavros hoped to make it very clear to his son that old pops was passing safely down to the front, away and out of sight.

* * *

Surrounded by kids—talking, laughing, and, yes, texting on their phones —Stavros settled into his new seat. He was three rows from the front, and had to crane his neck to see the screen. As the coming attractions rolled he was reminded of his first date with Allegra. It too had taken place at the movies. It was June, a week after they'd met at the boozy med-school party in Mission Hill. They had kissed that night, when people had been drunk and reckless and the mood was sexually charged. An end-of-school-year blowout where anything might happen. Stavros had gotten her number, but given the circumstances of their meeting, he wasn't so sure she was serious about seeing him again. He wasn't even sure she had given him her real number; he'd gotten fake ones before. But he called and she answered.

"This is Stavros. From the party."

"Stavros from the party?"

"Yes."

"Which party?"

"The one from last Thursday."

"And which Stavros?"

"Which Stavros? Are you joking?"

She was. The next evening he drove his rusty Gnome sedan over to Jamaica Plain. Allegra buzzed him into her building and Stavros took the stairs to the third floor. She was waiting for him, standing in her doorway. And seeing her—the animated eyes, the playful smile, the luxuriant red hair—Stavros was instantly hit by desire, knocked over by it. He realized loud and clear that the strong feelings she had aroused in him at the party weren't just from the booze and the debauched late-night setting. She wore a spaghetti-strap top that showed off her chest and arms, and a pair of cargo pants, similar to the ones she'd worn at the party. Stavros thought her gorgeous but she didn't seem like the type for compliments, so he said, "What's up with the cargo pants? Was there a sale at the mall?"

Provoked, she seemed to glow with pleasure. Regarding him coolly she said, "I can't tell if you're a wolf or a lamb. But I'm leaning toward lamb."

They drove to the Brattle Theatre in Harvard Square to see *My Night at Maud's*. Stavros had picked the film. He'd thought it would impress her, something European. And though Allegra had never heard of Éric Rohmer, the story did seem to interest her. Munching on popcorn, she focused intently on the screen. Stavros however was more interested in his date. He kept glancing at her, and twenty minutes in he put his hand on her knee and began caressing it. Very calmly, and without looking from the screen, Allegra removed his hand. Five minutes later he tried again. Indignant, she snapped: *"What are you, twelve years old?"* Muted laughter came from the seats behind them. Stavros froze, his cheeks burning. Allegra turned back to the movie, and her popcorn. For some minutes Stavros sat still ... What the hell, he thought? He hadn't expected *that*. Slowly his embarrassment gave way to anger. Who did she think she was, anyway? A *doctor?* Big fricking deal! *He* was an Assistant District Attorney of Middlesex County! He had status! He had prestige! He didn't have to put up with this crap!

At last the film ended. Stavros assumed she would want to go home directly. Maybe she'd even want to take the subway and just say good-bye here, which would be ideal. It was still early. He could call his buddy Milos and see what he was up to; they could hit a party or a bar.

But Allegra surprised him. "That was really good," she said, delighted.

"It was?"

"Yeah. I really liked it. What's the director's name again?"

"Rohmer."

"Yes, very good. I'd like to see more. I'm impressed."

Stavros thought this very strange. It was as if the hand-on-knee, bared-fangs reaction had never happened. Was that a good sign, or a bad one?

"So what's for supper?" she said.

He was astounded. "Supper?"

"Aren't you hungry?"

Stavros considered this. "Yes ... I am."

They went downstairs to Casablanca, and feasted extravagantly—wine, appetizers, entrées, desserts. A candle burned between them as they talked. Allegra wanted to know about life in Maine. Stavros told her about swimming in rivers as a kid and how he rode his bike everywhere in his small town and built a treehouse in the woods. He made his childhood sound idyllic—happy and carefree, like something out of *Tom Sawyer*, even though it wasn't. He asked about her life in Yonkers. Her parents, she said, stressed education but also fun. Summers were spent at the family cottage in Breezy Point, where high school and college vacations she worked at a clam shack. In winter, the family went skiing for a week in Vermont. As a little girl she was obsessed with lucha libre and had dreams of becoming a professional wrestler. At age twelve she won a Rubik's Cube contest and was on the eleven o'clock news ...

The longer they spoke the more the world disappeared, until finally it was just them two young people, each wholly focused on the other. A universe unto themselves. Eventually the candle expired, leaving a faint whiff of smoke. The lights in the dining room had come on and the restaurant staff were cleaning up. It was time to go. Stavros drove his date home, and from that night on there was only her, Allegra.

* * *

Eyelids fluttering, Stavros woke—and sensed something was off. He was seeing colors, reds and blues ... Then he realized he was wearing the 3D glasses. The house lights were on and the enormous film screen was blank. Two seats over sat Brendan, slumped and gloomy-faced.

"Hey," Stavros said, removing the specs, "what's going on?"

"Nothing."

"Did you like the movie?" Stavros had dozed off half an hour in.

"It was OK."

Stavros turned in his seat. The place was empty except for two ushers collecting trash. "Where's Sally?"

"In the lobby."

"Why didn't you wake me?"

"Dad, something happened … Aimee Gibblin's in the hospital. She tried to kill herself."

Stavros stiffened, and it felt as though many eyes were now staring at him. Hundreds of eyes. Thousands of eyes. Millions of eyes.

"We just found out," Brendan said. "Sally's talking to people now."

"Do you … know why she did it?" Stavros said, his voice faltering.

Anger flared across the boy's face. "*Why do you think?*" he said. He stood and marched up the aisle. Stavros grabbed his coat and followed.

The lobby was packed for the late shows. Against the wall on the far side of the space, away from the busy concession counter and the winding queues, stood Sally. In coat and cap, her face red from crying, she was on her phone. She looked at Stavros, briefly held his gaze, then turned away.

Stavros kept back while Brendan hovered beside her. When Sally got off the phone, her face flushed and tears fell. Brendan vacillated, looking as though he didn't know what to do. He reached for her hand, as if to console her, then abruptly stepped closer and embraced her. Sally returned the embrace.

Watching this, Stavros felt crushed, and culpable. A lifelong acquaintance of Sally's, a neighbor, a friend, had tried to take her own life, and he was more or less implicated. The kids were talking, but indistinctly; Stavros heard Sally say, "cut herself" and "blood."

Brendan turned to his father and said they wanted to go home.

Stavros stepped forward and told Sally he was sorry. He asked if there was anything he could do for her. She wiped at her eyes and said no. Brendan guided her to the door.

* * *

In the car no one spoke. At Sally's, Stavros double-parked on the street and flicked on the emergency lights.

"What are you doing?" Brendan said.

"I'm going inside, just for a minute."

"Dad, don't."

"Brendan, please."

The three of them got out of the car and headed for the house. Patti French appeared at the door. Her solemn expression said that she'd heard the news. Sally went onto the porch and into her mother's arms. Brendan and Stavros watched from the sidewalk. Holding her child, Patti mouthed the words "Thank you" and waved to Stavros and Brendan, indicating they should leave.

"Let's go," Stavros said.

The boy didn't move.

Stavros returned to the car, alone. Ten minutes later Brendan got in the backseat. Stavros turned to face his son. "Brendan, I'm sorry … I feel terrible."

"Maybe you should."

Stavros turned back to the wheel, flicked off the emergency lights, and drove to Champney Street. As soon as the car stopped, Brendan hopped out. Stavros killed the ignition and followed.

"What are you doing?" the boy said.

"I should talk to your mother."

Entering the house, Brendan didn't remove his sneakers or coat. He passed through the foyer and living room and went up to his room. Stavros stopped at the foot of the stairs, watched his son disappear. Allegra entered from the TV room, followed by Dylan, who promptly made a sour face.

"What's going on?" Allegra asked.

Stavros explained, and as he did he expected trouble. He expected her to shame him. To remind him yet again of how she had protested against his partnering with Keller all those years ago; of how she had warned him that his dealings with criminals would affect their son. He expected heated words and condemning glares. But Allegra only said, "I'm sorry, Stavros."

He was shocked. There was sympathy in her eyes, not judgment or rebuke. Stavros was moved. Relieved. And something in him seemed to give. The defensiveness that had been building, like a large protective wall, crumbled, and it left him feeling vulnerable and raw. And then the words came, spilling from his mouth: "I feel terrible … I wanted nothing to do with that case … It didn't feel right … Maybe I should have done more, but what? … What could I have done? … And how could I have known this would happen?"

"You couldn't have."

Stavros stared at her. She really was taking his side, showing compassion. And how grateful he was! Gazing at his ex-wife Stavros realized that he wanted to touch her. Hold her.

But that wasn't going to happen. As if intuiting Stavros's desire, Dylan discreetly stepped forward and placed a hand on Allegra's back. She glanced at him and made a slight, intimate smile. A lover's smile.

Stavros said, "I should be going." But he didn't move. "Also … I ruined his date. His first one."

"I'll talk to him, Stavros. He's a smart boy. He'll be able to untangle this."

Overwhelmed by it all, Stavros didn't know what to do. He turned his attention to Dylan, and for some moments the two men looked at each other. Neither spoke.

Stavros then refocused on Allegra. Her green eyes were fixed on him, and Stavros tried to smile. It wasn't easy. He opened his mouth, but not knowing whether to say thank you or good-bye, he said nothing, and without a word he turned for the door.

TWENTY-ONE

On Sunday morning, two days after Aimee Gibblin's attempted suicide, Stavros woke in a blur of pain. He was hungover—woozy, head-smashed, about-to-hurl hungover—but had no recollection of having gone to bed. He remembered making supper the evening before, but after that, nothing. Nothing at all.

When he'd gotten home on Friday night Stavros had turned on the local news. Gibblin was the lead story. Reporting from outside Mt. Adams Hospital, a reporter stated that "Aimee Gibblin, the former unnamed accuser in the Newt Bellingham date-rape trial," was in critical condition and "fighting for her life."

The next morning Stavros learned that the girl's condition was unchanged. According to the *Boston Telegraph*'s website, Gibblin had cut a wrist while in the bathtub of her family's Cambridge residence. Gibblin's mother had returned home from dinner out with a friend and found her daughter barely conscious. Cambridge Police and an ambulance arrived within ten minutes. In her distress, Gibblin's younger sister—who had been home the whole time, watching television—had texted the news to friends, who in turn had posted it to social media.

As for motive, the *Telegraph* noted that Gibblin had been "vilified online over many months"—shamed, slandered, ridiculed, and threatened with physical harm, including rape and murder. The abuse began before the trial, when her identity was leaked through various websites, but had grown worse afterward with the dismissal of charges. With her name now public knowledge, the attacks expanded from malicious posts, tweets, videos, and comments by anonymous trolls to include hate mail delivered to her home and, in several instances, strangers accosting her in person on the street. "The bullying and the outright hatred she's been subjected to is beyond comprehension," said a family friend. "No one should have to go through that, especially someone as sensitive as Aimee."

Reading this from his laptop at the kitchen table, Stavros was shattered. He kept imagining the girl's suffering, the girl's despair. Her fear, her loneliness, her hopelessness. And he kept picturing her in the bath. The girl cutting her wrist. The water becoming red. The gradual ebbing of life. And then, the mother coming upon the scene. The mother's terror. The mother's grief. It was too much for Stavros. From his chair he fell to his knees on the old linoleum floor, brought his hands together, and said: "O Jesus, I beg you. I beg you. Please let her live. Please let Aimee live ..."

* * *

Throughout that morning his phone rang, showing numbers he did not recognize. Stavros ignored them all. Then a call came from Keller, and it rankled Stavros. He turned off the phone and went for the scotch.

At first, though, he hesitated. Holding the bottle, about to fill the glass, he sensed he was heading for trouble. Oblivion was calling. It was near. And how wonderful it would be—the full-body warmth, the restful release. But part of him knew this was wrong. Part of him knew this wasn't the man he wanted to be. "Lord help me," he said.

Struggling, he compromised, and poured out just a splash. One finger. Yes, he would control himself. Just one small drink to steady his nerves. But with that first taste—hot, burning, narcotically soothing—he knew it was over. He downed the rest of it and poured out another.

* * *

Around one p.m., after he'd put away half a bottle of Glengowrie, a knock came at the front door. It was a reporter. A young woman with an eager air. "Mr. Papadakis, I'm Valerie Voss, from the *Bugle*. I was wondering if you'd like to—"

"How did you get my address?"

She was holding out a recording device. "What are your thoughts on Aimee Gibblin's attempted suicide? How do you feel about that?"

"I have nothing to say. Please go away."

"What about the girl's family? Do you have any words for them?"

"*Get the hell off my lawn!* You hear me? Or I'll call the cops."

"Have you been drinking, Mr. Papadakis?"

He slammed the door, closed the shades in the two front rooms, and went back into the kitchen for more booze. He finished off the Glengowrie and opened a second bottle. Then, around six, he cooked up a steak.

And that was the last he remembered of Saturday.

* * *

After he vomited—hot projectile vomits, four, five, six of them, splashing violently into the toilet as he groaned on bended knees—Stavros rinsed his mouth and took five aspirin. He went back to bed, slept for three hours, ate some toast, then clicked on the news: Aimee Gibblin remained in critical condition. Next, he turned on his phone. Sixteen messages—all press inquiries, except two. In the first, Keller said, "Buddy, what's going on? I've tried you several times." Stavros deleted the message. In the second, Lindsay Vanderberg said, "Stavros it's me. I heard about the girl and I'm concerned about you. Call me ... I'd like to know how you're doing."

Though his brain still felt as though it had been torn into a thousand pieces, Stavros experienced something like happiness, something like hope. He dialed Lindsay back. They'd not spoken since she'd gone to Aspen, and presumably into the waiting arms of Randall the entertainment lawyer.

She picked up on the second ring. "Hi Stavros."

"How are you Lindsay?"

"It's nice to hear your voice."

"Same here. Are you back in Boston?"

"I've been back. For almost a month."

There was silence. Stavros was tempted to say, "Why didn't you call?" But he knew she likely would say, "Why didn't *you* call?" So he said, "Did you have a good time?"

"It's was OK. I think I'm getting a little old for that scene."

"Oh."

"And what about you? I'm sorry about the girl."

"Yeah … me too."

More silence.

"Do you want to talk about it? We could get together."

He said, "I'd like that."

"How's tomorrow, are you free? I'm seeing Maggie tonight."

Stavros said he was free, and they made a plan.

"I'll see you tomorrow," she said.

"OK, Lindsay. Thank you. I'll see you then."

* * *

Later, with the worst of his hangover behind him, Stavros called Keller.

"Buddy, where've you been? I've been calling you for two days."

"I know. I'm sorry."

"Let me guess. You've been upset about the girl."

"Yes."

"And you've been drinking."

"A little."

"Stavros, I'm worried about you. Let's get together. Let's talk about this."

Stavros wavered.

"It'll do you some good," Keller said.

"What are you thinking?"

"Why don't you come into town? I've been to Cambridge."

Stavros smiled. "OK."

"Meet me at the hotel. Come up to my rooms first. I've got some news on Kenny Sunshine."

"What is it?"

"I'll tell you when I see you. We'll have a drink up here, then we'll go get some food. Everything will be fine."

* * *

Keller's suite was on the seventh floor of the Royal Continental. It was a large, clean space with postcard views of the Public Garden.

Seated on the sofa, nursing a glass of water, Stavros told Keller about his last two days, including the blackout and the barf session.

From the armchair Keller said, "I don't think I've puked from booze since college. And in those days it was a pretty regular thing. Keg parties every weekend. All sorts of debauchery. People think the sixties were crazy; the real action was in the seventies." A merry sparkle came into his eyes, and he took a good pull from his scotch.

"So what was this about Kenny Sunshine?" Stavros said.

"Well, there's good news and bad news. The good news is they picked him up. Dickie sent an anonymous email. The names of the schools, the dealers, everything. And long story short, they got him, and they got him good. Audio, video, friendly witnesses, etcetera. All the kids are turning on him. So there's nothing to worry about. He's going away."

"When was this?"

"Thursday."

"OK. Good. And the bad news?"

"The bad news is that Kenny called the office, right after they booked him. He asked for you," Keller said, breaking into a broad grin.

"And?"

"Sal took the call. He told Kenny you'd retired … and that *he'd* represent him." Keller shook with laughter.

"Sal's representing Kenny Sunshine."

"That's right."

Stavros frowned, chagrined by the news, and irked that Keller thought it so hilarious.

"This is funny, Stavros."

"Wyatt, this is my son."

"I understand. But what can we do?"

"Sal doesn't know we tipped the cops?"

"Hell no."

"Maybe Dickie told him."

"I already talked to Dickie. Weeks ago. This is just between the three of us."

"So you're just going to let this slide? You're going to let Sal represent him?"

"Stavros, what do you want me to do? Tell Sal that Brendan's involved? He'd piece it together. He's not an idiot."

"So what if he figures it out? You just tell him not to say anything."

"No. I'm not bringing him in on this. It could be bad for us, and for him too. Stavros, we turned in a client for Chrissakes."

Stavros went silent.

"Buddy, there's nothing we can do. And so far Sal's got squat. I honestly don't see Kenny getting out of this. They've got too much on him. I know it might sting a little right now, but in the end you'll get what you want."

Stavros sipped his water, which he now wished was scotch ... or maybe wine. The thought of scotch, quite frankly, was nauseating.

"I know it sucks, Stavros, but it's for the best. For the good of the firm."

At this, Stavros smirked. *For the good of the firm*: it was the phrase he and Keller had always used whenever some ethically or legally suspect maneuver was afoot. Not, "It's good for me" or "It's good for us"; but, "It's good for the firm." A semantical sleight of hand that seemed to lessen personal culpability, or even erase it outright. That said, Stavros knew Keller was right. Telling Kenny Sunshine they weren't interested in his business was problematic for any number of reasons. It wouldn't do.

"What are you thinking?" Keller said.

"I'm thinking I'd like some wine."

* * *

As Stavros poured himself a glass of merlot at the minibar, Keller's phone rang. Keller checked the caller, then muted the ringer. "I've been talking to the press nonstop these last two days. They all want to know if I feel responsible for what happened to the girl."

"What do you say?" Stavros said, returning to the sofa.

"What do you think I say? Of course I'm not responsible."

Stavros lowered his eyes.

"Stavros, it's not our fault. And it's certainly not *your* fault. You know that, right?"

"I don't know, Wyatt."

"Buddy, this was a troubled kid. A kid with a history of mental issues, a history of substance abuse. She had problems. Problems at home and problems at school. And one night, and not for the first time, she went to a party that she never should have gone to, a high school girl in a college party. She was drinking and she did drugs. She was very intoxicated. And then she went off to the park with Newt Bellingham and they had sex. Was it consensual? I think it was. But the Gibblin family felt otherwise, and suddenly Newt Bellingham is charged with rape. So he comes to us and we do our job. We do what we're paid to do. The reporters ask me, 'Do you feel responsible for what she's done?' Of course not! I feel bad that a young woman wanted to kill herself. I feel bad for her family. But her false accusation could have destroyed our client's life. And in fact, it probably has. This case will follow that kid for the rest of his days, no question, even though he did not rape that girl. If anyone's to blame, it's Donelly. He pushed for the trial, and we all know why … And as for that online stuff, the threats, the harassment, that has nothing to do with us. It's not our fault if the country's gone crazy."

"But we destroyed her, Wyatt, on the stand. It wasn't necessary."

"Stavros, how many witnesses over the years did you work over? For Chrissake it was one of your specialties. Remember Bunny Grifasi, screaming that she was going to kill you? And that shrink, Edward … what's-his-name, having a full-blown panic attack after you tore him apart? They had to call in the paramedics. And what about the guy who wet his pants? You eviscerated him, Stavros, actually caused him to lose control of his bladder, and we laughed about it for weeks."

"That's because he was a crook, Wyatt. He was trying to frame our guy."

"*Exactly*. You were defending your client. You were doing your job. Which is what Sal was doing with Gibblin. And remember, you weren't there. The reports in the press were overblown. It wasn't half as bad as people were led to believe."

Stavros said nothing.

"What if it had been Brendan, Stavros? What if Brendan had been accused of this rather than that snotty shit Bellingham? Would we even be having this conversation?"

"No. But that's different. It's always different with family."

"Is it?"

"What does Sal say?"

"The same. He feels bad about what she did. But does he feel responsible? No. Not at all. Stavros, this is what we signed up for. To defend people. And given the facts of the case, we had to go after her. She accused our client, and it was her word against his. The prosecution forced our hand and we did what we had to do. And I'd do it all over again, the same way."

Frustrated, Stavros said, "You're right. Everything you say is true … But we're still implicated, Wyatt. If that girl dies …"

"Buddy, you're assuming she did this because of the trial. How do we even know that? She was troubled and doing self-destructive things long before this case."

"Are you telling me that if the trial had never taken place, that she still would've slit her wrist on Friday night?"

"We don't know."

"Come on, you don't believe that!"

"Stavros, look. If you want to feel guilty about this, that's one thing. But don't start spreading it around. Don't start pulling other people into this neurotic new world of yours."

"OK. Fair enough. My 'neurotic world.' But it's not just this case, is it?"

"*What?*"

"It's not just this case," Stavros repeated, ignoring the inner voice that was warning him to stop, *screaming* at him to stop. "We've done some bad things, Wyatt. Both of us. We've done bad things and we've helped some very bad guys, guys who should've been locked up. Guys who instead are out there committing more crimes, and hurting innocent people. *We* did that. You and me. And we both know why."

Keller was dumbstruck, floored, looking as though his one ally, his one friend, had just stuck a knife in his back. All his energy seemed to vanish, all his fight.

Immediately Stavros regretted his words. "Wyatt, I'm sorry ... I shouldn't have said that."

With a faint, mirthless smile Keller set down his glass, then rose to his feet. Stavros didn't move. He was terrified of what might come next. Would Keller ask him to leave? Never talk to him again? Why had Stavros said it? What was he thinking?

But nothing happened. There was no bitter retort, no demand that Stavros go. Instead Keller said, "What do you say we get some food? Are you hungry?"

"Wyatt, I am sorry."

"I know, Stavros. Everything's fine. I'm going to wash up."

* * *

After Keller left the room, Stavros went to the bar and refilled his glass. He was furious with himself for what he had said. For selfish reasons, to assuage his own conscience, he had wounded his closest friend. It was an appalling betrayal, unforgivable; something he would never forget.

Glass in hand he stepped to the picture window facing the Public Garden. Darkness was setting on the city. In the park, the antique gas lights glowed. Stavros took in the trees, the old beeches and elms and weeping willows. The statue of George Washington on his horse. People in coats crossing the Duck Pond Bridge. Ten, fifteen minutes passed.

Keller reappeared. He had changed his shirt, and now wore a tweed jacket with a red pocket square. Entering the room he smiled cordially at Stavros. It was the smile Keller used on clients and juries, and it gave Stavros a chill.

"Are we ready?" Keller said.

"Where do you want to go?"

"Let's just go downstairs."

"Is that wise?" Stavros said, thinking of the press and also of the crazies.

"We'll be fine."

"But I thought you were having problems? People coming in off the street?"

"That's stopped. The security's been beefed up. They hired a couple plainclothes guys."

"But considering all that's happened ..."

"Stavros, I've got nothing to hide. We'll be fine."

Stavros wasn't so sure. Quite frankly, it seemed like a dumb idea. But of course Stavros also knew that this was just the sort of situation Keller lived for: embroiled in controversy, the focus of public attention, taking on all-comers. And so, consciously or not, Keller most likely was *hoping* to run into the press. He was probably craving it.

"OK," Stavros said, "let's do that."

Keller's expression then shifted, became softer, unguarded. "And about what you said earlier. I know you too well, Stavros. I know you'll dwell on it and beat yourself up. But the fact is, you didn't say anything untrue. You didn't say anything that I myself haven't thought about in the past, especially over the last few years. Do you understand? I've done some things that I'm not proud of. Things I would change if I could. So what you said, you were right. And now I want you to just forget it, OK? Just let it go."

Stavros was stunned. He nodded. "OK."

"Good … And I also want to say … You're a good man, Stavros." Keller placed a hand on Stavros's shoulder, and gave him a firm, affectionate squeeze. "I'm glad we're friends."

Stavros felt a stinging in his eyes and he looked away, embarrassed.

"Hey, come on," Keller said, laughing gently and patting Stavros on the arm. "Come on."

"I'm sorry."

Keller said, "Let's go eat."

* * *

They rode the elevator to the lobby. Apart from the clerk at the front desk and a liveried doorman taking a break from the cold, there was no one around; no protesters, no press, no paparazzi. The airy space, with its sparkling chandelier and gleaming marble floor, was silent, tranquil, serenely secure.

In the restaurant they were shown to a waiting table. As always Keller took the seat facing the entrance, like a mob boss in a film noir. In Stavros's line of sight was the bar. It was mostly empty, but not unusual for a Sunday night. The bartender, whom Stavros knew, was talking to a woman with maroon hair sitting with her back to the room.

A waitress came over and Keller greeted her by name. She gave Stavros a menu, took their drinks order, then left.

Leaning back in his chair Keller said, "So how's retirement Stavros? Are you still enjoying it?"

"I am. It was the right move."

"And what are your plans going forward?"

"Well, I've decided I'm going to do some traveling."

"Really?" Keller said, becoming interested.

"Yeah. I want to go to Greece. I've been reading a lot about it—in my 'monastery' books," Stavros said with a smile. "I'd like to see Athens and some of the islands. My mother's people are from Aegina. It's supposed to be very beautiful."

"When are you going?"

"In June, after school gets out. I'm thinking of flying into Rome, which I've never seen. I'll spend some time there, then take a train south. Maybe see Pompeii, Naples, Sicily. Then take a boat to Greece."

"Sounds great. Who are you going with?"

"Just me. I wanted to take Brendan, but his summer's already booked. Soccer camp, physics camp—which apparently is a real thing—and a couple weeks on the Vineyard with his mother."

"I'll go," Keller said.

"What?"

"I'll go with you. To Europe."

"You're joking."

"No. I could use a break. It's been years since I had a good vacation. And Rome, Naples, Greece—it sounds perfect."

"That'd be fantastic, Wyatt," Stavros said, thrilled.

"We'll sail the 'wine-dark sea,' Stavros, and no doubt drink some wine too. Let me know the dates as soon as you can and I'll have Katie clear my calendar."

Stavros said he would do that, and the waitress returned with their drinks.

Keller held up his glass. Smiling warmly he said, "Cheers, buddy."

Stavros, smiling too, said, "Cheers, Wyatt."

Just then, behind Keller, there was a flash of movement. From the bar twenty feet away a young woman with maroon hair was coming toward them. Despite the hair, which formerly had been blue, Stavros recognized her. It was the protester who had accosted Keller at the Steak

Club in January, and then again at the Bellingham press conference in February. She was pointing a gun, holding it with two hands.

Stavros burst from his chair, banging against the table and overturning glasses and silverware as he rushed passed Keller and went straight for the girl. Her eyes locked on his and there was a pop, and another pop, and Stavros felt a massive pain in his chest. People were screaming, ducking for cover. Stavros was no longer moving. He wasn't able to. His knees buckled and he went down.

More shots rang out. More screams. Stavros tried to look behind him, to locate Keller, but he couldn't do it. Sprawled on the floor, bleeding through his shirt, Stavros couldn't move. He tried to speak but the words wouldn't come. His awareness was dimming, fading. He thought of Brendan, his son, and his eyes watered. Then he thought of Allegra, his love, and he remembered her when they were young: their bodies at rest, entwined, together. Stavros held onto this vision, growing weaker and weaker until the last of his strength drained away and his earthly life came to its end.

About the Author

Michael Lacoy lives in New Hampshire. This is his first novel.

7676224R00154

Made in the USA
Middletown, DE
02 August 2019